PRAISE FOR P[...]

'The footballer's language knocked [...] cal crudity and wildness; yet under its foul-mouthed, laughing bravado lie deep wounds, a humble and endearing loneliness that moved me.' **Helen Garner, author of _The Season_**

'Brandon Jack has written the great gonzo Aussie Rules novel. _Pissants_ will make you gasp and laugh in the space of the same sentence, and then break your heart when you least expect it. This is literary fiction that takes no prisoners, guided by an unflinching mission to depict modern life outside polite society.' **Lech Blaine, author of _Australian Gospel_**

'Masterful storytelling. Ruthlessly funny. As I read I became more and more frustrated because I was loving it whilst realising it was better than anything I could write. No notes.' **Tony Armstrong**

'Jack is a genius, and this book stayed with me much longer than any of the AFL footballers I've dated.' **Jenna Owen, comedian and writer, co-creator of _Optics_**

'_Pissants_ isn't a story about footy. It's a story about blokes trying to survive each other, and the deeply broken culture that raised them. Brandon captures the light and darkness of the footy world perfectly. It's brutal, brilliant, and it left me rattled in the best possible way.' **@the28yearoldmale**

'Ridiculously inventive and wickedly sharp. _Pissants_ is unlike anything you've read before.' **Vic Zerbst, comedian and writer, co-creator of _Optics_**

'While redefining the Australian literary boundaries of bacchanalia, in _Pissants_ Brandon Jack—startlingly, shockingly and often hilariously—turns the footy sausage inside-out to expose the blood, guts, desperation and human frailty at its core. It ain't pretty. But it sure is a powerfully evocative, elegant, and very daring novel.' **Paul Daley, _Guardian_ writer and author of _Jesustown_**

'Brandon Jack's _Pissants_ puts the F in AFL. With the throb of _Wake in Fright_ and the chaos of the game itself, we are shoved into the locker room by a writer who has clearly smeared Dencorub on another man's thighs. Scientific, ballsy, and strangely moving—this is a one-off of a book that's as terrifying as it is nostalgic.' **Brendan Cowell, author of _Plum_**

'A diary of unflinching debauchery, lust, love and fragility. Life really is just packets and heartbreak.' **@browncardigan**

'Everyone claims to take you behind the scenes with their podcasts and documentaries these days, but none of that comes close to what *Pissants* does. It reads like someone beautifully detailed all those days and nights on the piss that you can't remember. Yes, there are Pissants at every club . . . pray you don't run into them. But use this book as a guide for how to handle them if you do.' **Anonymous former AFL player**

'Be warned: you may never look at your favourite footballers or football club quite the same way again. *Pissants* does for Australian Rules football what *Puberty Blues* did for teenagerhood—shocking readers with its raw exposé of the sordid debauchery that goes on away from prying eyes. It might also be considered the perfect, if alarming, companion to Helen Garner's *The Season* . . . The writing is razor-sharp and full of wit, the voices unfailingly authentic even as the events depicted appall. You'll laugh and recoil at once—a fine achievement for any writer.' **Tim Baker, author of *Patting the Shark***

'*Pissants* ushers you into the locker room, where the degenerate underside of Australian Rules football is stranger than fiction. It takes guts to tell the truth about a game that makes heroes out of sinners. *Pissants* does exactly that.' **Lucinda Price, aka Froomes, author of *All I Wanted Was to be Hot***

'Brandon Jack's writing is raw, evocative and often confronting. Yet behind the bravado there lies an honest fragility and an acute sense of observation that will hook the toughest of hearts.' **Felice Arena, author of *Specky Magee***

'A love letter to the Australian footy club. A tribute to all of the natural leaders, mindless followers, characters and morons that make that world so fucking fun it hurts. You can smell the Deep Heat and spilt lager wafting off the page.' **Clancy Overell, Editor of The Betoota Advocate**

'Like *Specky Magee* for adults . . . if Specky did his shoulder and developed a codeine addiction.' **Jacob Gaynor, GWS GIANTS social media admin**

PISSANTS

BRANDON JACK

S

Summit
Books
Australia

S
Summit
Books

PISSANTS
First published in Australia in 2025 by Summit Books Australia,
an imprint of Simon & Schuster (Australia) Pty Limited
Level 4, 32 York St, Sydney NSW 2000

Summit Books and colophon are trademarks of Simon & Schuster, LLC

10 9 8 7 6 5 4 3 2 1

Sydney New York Amsterdam/Antwerp London Toronto New Delhi
Visit our website at www.simonandschuster.com.au

© Brandon Jack 2025

This book is a work of fiction, meaning none of the people, events or places
written about are real. Any likeness to real people is unintentional and likely
due to the homogenous nature of Australian Rules Football clubs and the
limited scope of nicknames and personalities that exist within them.

Also, no animals were harmed in the making of this book. That includes:
miniature and regular-sized dachshunds, sea turtles, echidnas and
Atlantic salmon.

NATIONAL
LIBRARY
OF AUSTRALIA

A catalogue record for this
book is available from the
National Library of Australia

ISBN: 9781761633072

Cover design: Peter Long
Typeset by Midland Typesetters, Australia
Printed and bound in Australia by Griffin Press

MIX
Paper | Supporting
responsible forestry
FSC
www.fsc.org   FSC® C018684

The paper this book is printed on is certified against the
Forest Stewardship Council® Standards. Griffin Press holds
chain of custody certification SCS-COC-001185. FSC®
promotes environmentally responsible, socially beneficial
and economically viable management of the world's forests.

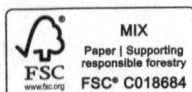

For Hendy Ave.

Now when he saw the crowds, he went up on a mountainside and sat down. His disciples came to him, and he began to teach them, saying: 'Blessed are the poor in spirit, for theirs is the kingdom of heaven. Blessed are those who mourn, for they will be comforted. Blessed are the meek, for they will inherit the earth . . .'

Matthew 5:1–5

The meek may inherit the earth—
but they will never win games of football.

Mick Malthouse, AFL Head Coach

RUN AND CARRY

POLICE ACADEMY

Fangs

I can't see Mud's eyes through the mask, but I reckon he's shitting it. My visor is fogging up to the extent that I feel like George Clooney in that movie, the one about space. Cool Guy George playing Cool Guy George, only thing is he's floating in the vast nothingness of the universe. Really pushing the capabilities of your repertoire there, Georgey Boy.

Alright, I'm doing a final check to make sure I've got everything I need. Baton. Taser. Gun. The safety briefing, courtesy of a meathead who you just know drives around in the squad car hoping someone takes a swing at him so he can swing back. He said go for the baton first. That's your close-range weapon. Use it as a bit of a headfuck to the perp. Then the taser. And only pull the gun as a last resort. I've never held a gun before. Heard too many stories about kids blowing their dads' heads off at shooting ranges. Guns give me the creeps.

This week has been framed as one of those team-building exercises. Something like a defib trying to resuscitate the rotting corpse of the footy club. Jesus, last night I almost fell asleep while the superintendent was talking about *integrity* for an hour. He got stuck in a loop, one of the worst I've seen. Full fucking cooker. I still don't know what the cunt was on about and I don't care for whatever it was. *Integrity, Integrity, Integrity.* That's all I remember.

Officer: Alright, gents, the light's going to go red and then you're in. Are you ready?

Me (muffled): Yes.

Mud (shitting it): Yes.

No, we aren't fucking ready. No fucking way. The ten practice shots on the range and the tedious training video haven't prepared any of us for the apparent life-and-death severity of the situation we're about to encounter. There are people dedicating their whole lives to determining the worth of another breathing soul and we're coming in red hot with little idea of the sanctity of life. Yes, I'd kill baby Hitler. That's a no-brainer. But there's a fair bit of a gap between Hitler and the bloke who delivers your HelloFresh box every Tuesday.

Mud's still adjusting his mask when the lights turn red. I'm getting pushed in from behind. Jesus. I can't fucking see a thing. Mud's gone hard right, just started running like a mad cunt. Ok, I'll be more stealthy: hug the corners, do shit they do on CSI.

I turn the corner and assess the situation, like we'd been briefed. There's a bird down the end, sitting on the floor. I walk over with caution. She might be having me on.

When she sees me she starts screaming.

Woman: MY BOY! MY BOY! THEY'VE GOT MY BOY, HELP!

I crouch down and try to quieten her. Jesus Christ, don't get us both fucked over.

Woman: They've got my boy . . . they took him . . . he's . . . please, help! My boy!

The whole thing's scripted, I know that. I'm sure the academy has some sort of junior theatre operation where they source the talent. Shame that no one's forking out $18 for a ticket. Plus popcorn. Plus a drink. Highway robbery. Clooney at least puts arses on seats.

Woman: Please, you've got to get my boy back . . . you have to help me get Todd back!

Little Toddy boy. Of course it's some name like fucking Toddy.

Me: Ok ma'am, I'll get your boy back.

I almost believe the shit I'm spewing out. I've gone full method. The uniform. The gun. The heat of it all has got me thinking that I've gone my whole life wanting to be a cop. Police officers came to my school in Year 6 and told us all about the good work they do. I turned to my best mate and said, *I'm going to do that one day.* I was a real straight edge through high school, not wanting to get a mark against my name. Did the full Scouts and Duke of Edinburgh thing: archery and kayaking, the whole nine yards. Did my assessments. Topped my class. Graduated with a rod up my arse and now I'm here going full Die Hard to protect the public. I'll be on the news for this. I'll get a fucking book deal out of it.

Me: Ma'am I need you to go out that door down there. There's no one else there; you'll be safe. I promise.

She scurries down the hall and out of sight. Now for little Toddy.

I check my holster because the situation warrants a bit of action. Fuck the baton, no chance I'm touching that.

I walk around the corner and see a doorway on the right that's not being guarded. I haven't heard any gunshots yet.

Which means trigger-happy Mud hasn't encountered any resistance.

I creep down the hallway. Jesus, I'm fucking nervous. This whole situation has tricked my brain into thinking it's real. It's the reverse of a PTSD situation. Those fucking soldiers who can't look at the boxes of cereal without seeing a dead child's eyes looking back at them.

I'm closing in on the doorway and I can see movement inside. I slide against the wall and try to get my gun out. It's stuck in the holster. How the fuck does this thing work again? Lift the flap, push down. Childproof release mechanism. Fuck this. I need the fucking gun.

I walk into the room slowly and see Mud in the corner on his knees. Gun to his head. Of course.

Bad guy: hmphh hmphhh hmpphhh refmp.

I can't make out any of the words he's saying because of the mask covering his face.

Me: I can't fucking hear you man!

Bad guy: HMPHH HMPHHH HMPPHHH REFMP!

I shake my head to indicate I still can't hear. But words don't really matter here. The gun he's got pressed against the side of Mud's head tells me everything I need to know. If Mud wasn't shitting it before, then I bet he is now. Serves him right for fucking off on his own from the start.

Me: Look, I'm sure we can figure this out.

The image of George Bush comes into my head, saying, *We do not negotiate with terrorists.* Is this bloke a terrorist?

He pulls up his mask so his mouth is free. Above his now revealed top lip: a wispy bullshit moustache.

Bad guy: Put your gun on the ground!
Me: Ok.

I fiddle around with the holster and then I look up at him.

Me: It's ah . . . it's stuck . . . I'm sorry.

I reckon there's a momentary lapse in character as he almost laughs at me.

Bad guy: Lift the flap.

Me: I tried that man.

The cunt probably thinks I'm trying to pull a slick move on him. Like I'm playing dumb and then when he drops his guard for a second I'll pop him in the chest. Sadly not.

Bad guy: Push down on the button and lift the flap.

Me: I tried that man! It's fucking child-locked or something.

When I say that I remember the screaming bird and her boy Toddy.

Me: Wait, where's little Toddy?

The bloke smirks and then I hear footsteps. Footsteps too heavy to belong to an imaginary shithead kid dumb enough to get kidnapped.

Woman: Put your gun on the floor!

Fucking hell. She's better than Clooney. She's Streep.

Me: I'm trying but the fucker's . . . the thing's stuck!

She looks over at the bloke with the gun to Mud's head and he shrugs. This is hopeless. I have a flashback to me standing at the urinal with my pants around my ankles, shirt pulled up and held under my chin. The other kids are all laughing at me. Fuck off.

Woman: Well . . . Put your hands behind your head then!

I do it without hesitation and she walks over and tries to get my gun out of the holster. I seize my opportunity and put her in a headlock and she drops the gun. I've got her good, and the bloke across the room doesn't take a shot because he's too worried about hitting her. Fucking prick.

I've got her in front of me. Fifty kilograms worth of human shield. Fuck integrity. I've got leverage.

Me: Alright, everyone's going to play it cool, ok?

I keep hold of her and bend down to get her gun. I can see drops of dried paint all over the floor. This scenario must play out all the time. Someone eventually fires first—it's bound to happen. The sight of the paint makes me realise how fucking stupid this is. How it isn't real.

I'm invincible now. Do your worst.

I pick up the gun and Mud starts glaring at me. He knows I'm going to do it.

Bad guy: You shoot me and your mate's dead!

Mud's eyes are laser beams. He thinks it's real. It's not real, Mud. None of this is real. We're going to walk out of here after and have a laugh. None of it matters. Nothing fucking matters.

I take the shot anyway and hit the bloke square in the chest. There's a secondary noise as his gun paints the side of Mud's mask. I picture Mud's brains spraying the wall. I think he's really got into character because there's a fair chance he's actually shit himself. Skidmarks at least.

A quick assessment of the situation shows not much has been gained here. Team building: none, teammate dead on the floor, shit in his pants and brains on the wall. Resilience and composure under pressure: none, see notes on team building. If there's something else to be learned here, I'm not seeing it. Maybe on the field when the ball's in the air, this will all come back to me and prompt a new neurological pathway, but for now, it's just a mess. The lights in the room go from red to green. The bloke on the floor stands up and takes his mask off. I lower my gun. Mud gets up and takes his mask off too. His face is red and puffed up something fierce. Has he been crying? Jesus. I let go of the woman and she steps away and takes her mask off as well.

Bad guy: So, what went wrong?

Me (is he fucking serious): My gun wouldn't come out.

Bad guy: Wrong. You didn't work as a *team*. You split up as soon as you were in there. How's that going to work for you on the field?

I feel like saying there are no fucking guns on the field and there's quite a bit of difference between a bouncing ball and a gun to the head. But I just smile and nod and accept their version of events.

Bad guy: Righto, head upstairs, boys. Leave your guns in the hall and you can watch the next group.

Mud's got a bit of paint in his hair and leads the way. At the top of the stairs we see the coaching group and a couple of the boys. They're all pissing themselves. Except for the Big Fella. He's got his serious face on. He's probably going to use this against me in some meeting down the line. I can hear it now: *Fangs, you're just not there*. Fuck him. I start thinking about who's going next and then I hear a yell from the hall. Unmistakable: this cunt's the loudest bloke in the world. His volume switch has fried. Stick.

Mud and I are looking down as the scene resets. The bird goes to her spot in the corner where she duped me and I can now see how Mud got caught as the bloke hides next to the doorway of the room we were just in.

The light goes red and the next thing I see is Stick fucking steaming down the hall with his gun already out. He single-handedly makes the case for gun safety. Americans reckon they've got a few mental health problems? Spend five minutes with Stick and you learn we've got more screws loose here.

Stick goes left and sees the bird down the hall. He doesn't speak, he just pops her twice. I can see the other bloke spring into action. Stick turns and sees Big Sexy behind him. He runs past him, blind-turns the corner then starts shooting the bloke, who's firing back as well. Stick's got the gun angled on its side and is shooting continuously while absorbing the stream of pellets coming his way. He's making an absolute meal of it. He's been hit five times already, but that doesn't stop him from firing back. The other bloke's been killed multiple times, too, but they're both still firing. Big Sexy is just standing there, caught in the crossfire, not sure what to do.

The lights go green and Stick's still firing.

Bad guy: Stop! Stop! Stop!

Stick doesn't stop.

NICKNAMES

Yt.

Ed., they call Stick 'Stick' because he's taken more silver-bullet suppositories in his life than any composition of flesh and bone ought to tolerate. Ergo his body is made up of something other than the usual composites. Ergo 'Ballistic'. Ergo 'Stick'. Though I'm also led to believe that 'Ballistic' is in reference to him being what many consider to be a complete psychopath.

Gatesy is 'Gatesy' because he came down with a severe case of glandular fever one off season after going to a Full Moon Party in Thailand. So bad was the initial bout that his spleen almost ruptured during the time trial on his first day back. He was coming down the home straight when the club physios saw him faint. Apparently the club doctor said he was lucky not to die from internal bleeding, which the playing group has since called 'ham'. Anyway, the first three

A note on club vernacular common to the group:

Mare = Nightmare, e.g. 'I had a mare of a game on the weekend'.

Jeffrey Horn, *Jeffrey* or *Horn* = Something that is uncool or unpopular.

11

Chad Kroegers or *Chads* = Cheap petrol station sunglasses.
Deckchair = Someone who doesn't add much value socially.
Sh- (prefix) = A shit version of that thing, e.g. Shit dog = *Shog*.
Shit haircut = *Shaircut*.
Similarly, the mixing of any two words together means a combination
of those words, e.g. Spa + Banter = *Spanter*.
Also prominent in the changerooms is the use of general footy slang
whereby names take the place of words with which they rhyme or
are homophones for, e.g. *Jake King* = All In, *Linden Dunn* = Done.
Ed., I have learnt that it is best to just nod when these are heard and to
figure out the context later as opposed to stopping the conversation out
of confusion. The club is somewhat organismic, and the players are white
blood cells that will destroy foreign bodies.

days of his recovery were unremarkable, then day four and
five came and the sweats hit and he couldn't tell if he was too
hot or too cold. Thermoregulation notwithstanding, he was
confined to his bedroom, barely eating or drinking, but still
excreting liquids at semi-regular intervals. The lethargy was so
strong one day that he could not get himself out of bed and
walk the few metres required to make it to the bathroom, so
instead he relieved himself in the next best thing: an empty
Gatorade bottle beside the bed. Gatesy eventually recovered
and made his way back out onto the training track. Usual life
resumed. Then, it was a few months after, that he went out
one night and came home worse for wear. In the morning,
hungover and dehydrated, he fumbled around for something
to drink and felt the familiar shape of a bottle in his hand.
That's orange Gatorade, he thought, squinting with sleep in
his eyes before taking a sip. The bitter taste came first. Then
his eyes adjusted to the light. Thereafter, 'Gatorade' became
'Gator' became 'Gates' became 'Gatesy'.

They call Potato 'Potato' because he's Irish. If one takes
into account the torrid history of the Irish Potato Famine,
then the nickname is extremely cruel. However, I'm not

going to pretend that all of the players are cognisant of the tragic history of the nineteenth-century potato blight that precipitated the crisis leading to over one million poor souls succumbing to famine and disease and instigating extensive migrational and demographic paradigm shifts. Nor how this calamity illuminated inequities in British colonial policies, catalysing national-ist sentiments and galvanising fervour for autonomy. No. Such knowledge would not be assumed. Rather, from what I understand, it was between that and 'Guinness', and it is well known within the Four Walls that Potato hates Guinness.

Squidman is 'Squidman' because before his first session with the group he was invited to provide a lesser-known fact about himself. One can imagine this to be a daunting experience: fifty pairs of eyes staring back, some of them the eyes of men you've seen nearly put other players to death on the field. That may explain Squidman's unfortu-nate gaffe when he offered to the group that he was from the

Ed., while in this case it has led to a nickname, it is misleading to think that the event of a player consuming urine is a rare enough occurrence for it to be the sole reason for a nickname. I can cite at least four more cases where I have seen/heard of players consuming urinary fluids. 1) Stick has on several occasions performed an act called a bubbler, whereby an individual angles their urinary instrument in such a way as that the stream of urine it expels shoots towards their own mouth, whereby they may drink it, like one would at a bubbler. 2) On a camping trip over the off season, Squidman, Fangs, Shaggers and Mud played a game called 'Fingers' in which the loser (Mud) had to drink a shot of the winner's (Shaggers') urine. 3) During the team's weekly 'fines' session, the Wheel of Death features a tiny sliver (less that 1/96th of the overall wheel) entitled 'Piss Boy'. The player who lands on that sliver is to enact an act perpetrated by Piss Boy at Mad Monday two years ago. The sliver has been landed on more than once. For context, and also for instances 4 and 5, see 'Piss Boy' below.

same town as Nicole Kidman. When Squidman went to say Nicole Kidman, he said Nicole Squidman. Ergo 'Squidman'.

Eggsy is 'Bubbles' because at his first Silly Sunday he tried to scull a beer and spat it all out, saying that the bubbles hurt his tongue. Eggsy/Bubbles also gets 'Pre', which is short for Steve Prefontaine, an American middle-distance runner back in the seventies and eighties. Reportedly the Development Group was given a task by Frank (since departed DC [Development Coach]) who had a background in school teaching. The task was to create a presentation on an athlete of choice. As you would assume, most of the players selected Michael Jordan and Tom Brady, but Bubbles, being the rather peculiar figure that he is, selected Steve Prefontaine like it was the most obvious choice in the world. Apparently, the presentation ended abruptly with Bubbles playing a YouTube video of Prefontaine coming fourth in the 5000-metre race at the 1972 Munich Olympics. Bubbles sat down without saying a word. One of the other players said, 'Then what happened?' and Bubbles, while sitting with his legs crossed, said, 'Oh, he died in a car crash.' Note: 'Eggsy' is, in itself, a nickname. The reasoning being that his brain is a bit scrambled. The two nicknames are used in tandem, with no preference from the players for one over the other.

They call Piss Boy 'Piss Boy' because he drank piss (i.e. human urine) at Mad Monday last year. He didn't know it was piss (i.e. human urine) he was drinking, otherwise I doubt he would've drunk it. Piss Boy thought it was just regular piss (i.e. alcohol). The nickname has stuck because Piss Boy kicked up a real stink about it (the drinking of human urine) afterwards, demanding to know whose piss (i.e. human urine) it was (Pricey's). From time to time, teammates will do imitations of Piss Boy, scrunching their faces and lowering their bottom lips, exclaiming, 'That's not what teammates do,' and, 'We're supposed to be united.' To make things square Pricey drank a schooner of Piss Boy's piss (i.e. human urine) later in the night. However, that did not result in Pricey being called Piss Boy.

Windmill is 'Windmill' because after a few drinks he is known to take his pants off and whirl his penis around like a windmill. What started as a joke has become a regular fixture at all team social gatherings where alcohol is involved. Windmill, a rather quiet character while sober, accepts his called-upon duty with stoic resignation.

Dingo is 'Dingo' because he has terrible breath. A long-running joke is to put a toothbrush and one of those travel-sized tubes of toothpaste into his locker—which the players all take from their hotels after away trips. From time to time Dingo can also get 'Onion' because, and this feels rather mean, he's not the prettiest bloke and he's got a face that makes you want to cry.

Sugar is 'Sugar' because the most interesting fact he has to offer is about the inventor of the sugar stick, who killed himself after realising that people were using his invention the wrong way. The common sugar stick, found at cafés, is meant to be ripped at the centre and then angled around the cup as it sits on the saucer. Instead, what the vast majority of people tend to do is rip one end of the packet and pour the contents out of that now exposed end. This, though interesting to know, is not how or why Benjamin Eisenstadt, the inventor of the sugar stick, died. Rather it was because of complications from bypass surgery.

Shaggers is 'Shaggers' (short for 'Shagger's calf') because after arriving at the club he was sent to the gym for months on end to do lower body weights. One day, after completing a set of calf raises, he felt a twinge in his left calf. An older player asked what was wrong, to which Shaggers replied, 'Fucked my calf.' The older player responded by saying, 'shagger's calf,' a slight twist on the usual 'shagger's back', a phrase that implied a player with a sore back had been over-active in the bedroom. Shortly after, a photo of Shaggers wearing a Tubigrip bandage around his injured calf was taken. The photo must have taken Shaggers by surprise as his face is contorted in a show of complete bewilderment which, when zoomed in upon, makes the players laugh no matter how many times it is viewed (which, in their WhatsApp chat, is often).

Fangs is 'Fangs' because when he first got to the club he had an additional two top teeth coming out of his gums. Reportedly, he didn't go on the footy trip in his first year because he wanted to save up for dental work, which he had done. However, the nickname has stuck. Pringles is 'Pringles' because he is well endowed, and by all reports has a penis with the proportions of a Pringles can. Dennis is 'Dennis' because he's got an alter ego that emerges when he's drinking that is a complete menace. Big Sexy is 'Big Sexy' because he is neither big, nor sexy. Mud is 'Mud' because on his first end of pre-season drinking cruise, he took ketamine and claimed that he couldn't move and that it felt like he was 'stuck in the mud', though when he said it, it sounded more like 'scmuck inz ve muv' with spit and dribble coming out of his mouth. Hally is 'Hally' because he's the one guy you wouldn't want to get stuck in the hallway with: he's got the worst chat at the club. 'Pricey' is Pricey because whenever he goes shopping he will always pick something up, look at the price tag and go, 'Geez, bit pricey.' Georgey-Boy occasionally gets 'Young Trout', because that is what his dad has always called him and in one of his first games for the club his teammates spotted his dad in the crowd with a sign reading: 'GO YOUNG TROUT!' Budget is 'Budget' because when he first got to the club a group of players called him up for a fake interview and he said that the club got him at a bargain so late in the Draft. Bargain then morphed into Budget for reasons unknown. Fumbles is 'Fumbles' because he's always fumbling the footy. Fuzzy Duck is 'Fuzzy Duck', 'Fuzzy' or 'Duzzy' because he once tried to explain a drinking game called Fuzzy Duck and made a meal of it (of which there is video evidence). To this day he is called upon to explain the rules of the game whenever it is played. Sixty is 'Sixty' because his car is always out the front of the club at 7:30 on Sunday nights, when the only other people at the club are the cleaners. Without fail, Sixty is there, as regular as scheduled programming of the news and current affairs program *Sixty Minutes*. Rimma is 'Rimma' because there's a rumour that he goes away to Bali every year with his best friend and on that trip the pair engage in sexual acts with one another commonly referred to as rim jobs.

Ed., though some of the above may be considered dis-tasteful by the uninitiated, there are two nicknames that err on the side of problematic more than any others. These I will refer to as Nicknames That Cannot Be Ignored.

Nickname #1 of the two Nicknames That Cannot Be Ignored: 'Shootsy'. Shootsy—quietly spoken, eighteen years of age (though looks fifteen), not in possession of a driver's licence and as such will wait out the front of the club after training for his mother to pick him up—is a 'Terry', and

Terry = Terry Top Up. It refers to young players who are undrafted and respond positively to the olive branch extended by the club and the promise that if they play well enough in the reserve grade team for a year, and attend all the training sessions, then they may find themselves on the list at the end of the year. It is worth saying that this is never the case.

> The general view of the Terries is that they are glorified witches' hats who come to training only as additional numbers to fill the roles (e.g. Chasing Ass) that the listed players do not want to do for extended periods. While meeting with the List Manager, I rattled off a list of names and asked what his thoughts were on those players. Response: 'Who are they?'

Terries don't usually receive nicknames. W/r/t Shootsy, the nickname originated on May 25, 2022, during a main training session for the ▓▓▓▓▓▓ Football Club. The training sheet for the day involved sixty minutes of skills, comprising two transition drills, a full ground-kick drill and twenty minutes of match simulation at the end. From my understanding, it was a warm day with minimal breeze. This is what I was able to infer from the audio recordings provided to me by the media department, which were captured using mics fixed to the guernseys of two key players as part of a popular form of content creation within football clubs.

> Not entirely true. Another Terry, Joey, is 'Joey no shoulders' because there is already a Joey within the Four Walls and the primary difference between the two is the width of their shoulders. Also, Donuts is 'Donuts' because he played a game for the reserves last year and didn't register a single stat; the tallys next to his name were a series of big fat zeros that looked like donuts. It's the same deal with staff members, who by and large don't have nicknames, with the exceptions being the physio for the twos, 'Matty Two', because there is already another Matty who is a physio, the masseuse, who goes by 'Steakhands' and the reserves conditioning coach 'Scuba Steve', which when uttered is really stretched out to become *Scuuuuuba Steeeeve*.

At 10m 21s into Player 1's mic recording, the following conversation can be heard, though it is unclear who exactly is speaking and there are muffled elements.

Player 1: Fucked about that shooting, hey.
Player 2: Mate, cooked. Fuck that.

Player 1: I don't get why they have guns.
Player 2: It'd be fucking scary living over there.
Player 1: [Inaudible]
Player 2: [Laughter]

For context, May 25, 2022 was the day after the mass school shooting at Robb Elementary School in Uvalde, Texas. Nineteen school children and two teachers were killed after an eighteen-year-old gunman barricaded himself inside two adjoining classrooms and opened fire for forty minutes with two AR-15-style rifles he had purchased days before the shooting. Miah Cerrillo, an eleven-year-old survivor, smeared herself with her friend's blood to play dead. Eva Mireles, one of the teachers, shielded her students from the gunman with her body and was killed.

No such details were mentioned in the player recordings. However, around 15m 38s in, the conversation returns to the subject:

Player 1: Hey, reckon that Reynolds looks like the shooter?
Player 2: Does a bit. Got a real Shootsy look about him.
Player 1: Gee, Shootsy, you got here fast today.
Shootsy: What?

Nickname #2 of the Two Nicknames That Cannot Be Ignored: 'COD'. The nickname COD, from the outset, seems rather inconspicuous, and perhaps this is why it affects one more greatly upon hearing the story. The uninitiated believe it to be the result of the player's fondness for the video game *Call of Duty*. But a deeper meaning was intended by those who gave COD (a former player) his nickname. It came about on his first night out as an eighteen-year-old at his local nightclub.

Reportedly, he wasn't that drunk, but he later specified in a statement that he was drunk enough to be dancing, which is something he would not normally do sober, when a young woman approached him. She (the eighteen-year-old) was from the area too. The pair then left the dancefloor after approximately twenty minutes to get a drink, which was paid for by COD. They spent the rest of the night talking; in the background of some photos from the night posted to the nightclub's Facebook page, you can see them sitting opposite one another, laughing. At around 0130h, and after several (six to eight by COD's count) more drinks, the pair left together in an Uber and stayed at COD's brother's house, which was vacant for the weekend. They smoked several cigarettes and were intimate on the couch. They then engaged in sexual intercourse—which, according to COD and the report of several medical professionals, was 'consensual' showing no signs of force or trauma. About ten minutes after they had begun having sex, the police were called. In a hysterical tone, COD reported that the girl had gone blue in the face and was not breathing. She was declared as 'non-living' by the paramedics upon arrival. Several days later, coroners would declare 'Fatality Arising from Latex Allergy-Induced Anaphylaxis' which is to say that the woman went into anaphylactic shock after a latex condom was placed in her mouth. The nature of the incident was such that whenever it was written about, it was simply referred to as 'a terrible tragedy' and as you can imagine, its specific details would never be discussed outside of what could be interpreted as urban myth and rumour. The playing group, however, seems to have drawn their own conclusions on the matter, determining an alternative explanation for the deceased's death, resulting in the player being called COD, or 'Cock of Death'.

Ed., there is a darkness to the nickname only emphasised by knowing the full facts. Thankfully, in my tenure here thus far, COD has rarely been said aloud, in part due to the player no longer occupying the Four Walls. The primary reminder that interrupts the often long and blissful stretches of absence is from the whiteboard in the gym, where the name COD appears in the top five for the all-time Relative Strength % 1RM Bench Press Test. From time to time, however, the name does still appear in canonical stories which are retold, but rarely as the harsh-sounding 'COD'. Instead, more commonly used are the variations, 'Coddy', 'Codsy' and 'Coo', that overcome the palatal issues of the tongue pressing against the roof of one's mouth and hamper the speed at which a teammate's name can be said on the field.

Ed., I hope this is of interest to you. Massage it as you see fit. More to come.

Sincerely,

Yt.

This information was gained while yours truly was, of all places, sitting on the toilet in the changerooms. A group of players was in the spa when a younger player asked where the nickname COD came from after hearing him mentioned in a story. This was the impetus for yt. to start exploring the story and led to the sleuthing behaviour that has pieced the information together. There isn't much available online about the death itself, nor any articles that link the player to the incident, who, while not running from the nickname, has never provided an explanation for it. While interviewed on the popular program *After the Bounce*, the following exchange occurred during the quickfire get to know you segment: Q: 'Any Nicknames?' A: 'I get COD.' Q: 'Any story behind it? A: 'Ah, not really.' Q: 'Alright, I won't dig into that one. Moving on.' And in the *Match Day Record*, his player profile stated 'Nickname: COD'. So little is out there that the only article that shows any sense of after-effect from the night featured in the town's local paper (*The Foxedale Tribune*), where the young woman's older brother was reported to have been arrested for grievous bodily harm six months after her death, with a 'close friend of the family' saying that the behaviour was 'out of character' and that he'd been 'struggling since a tragic family incident'. The brother was reprimanded and sentenced to time in gaol, with the judge displaying sympathy for his loss in the sentencing.

A JOB ON ████

Stick

That'd be too fuckin' right, eh? Clipboard virgin singling me out. Not Mud, not Squidman—who's happened to play the fuckin' game of his life tonight and about time too, I might add. Surely there's grounds for concern over performance enhancers there? But nah, he's singled me out. You bastard. You *fucking* bastard. Well, I'll save us the time. There's no Lance Armstrong bullshit going on here. And if you think I'm a big enough twat to take coke before a game, then you're fucking kidding yourself. That's not Sticky Stick's go.

Fuck, I'm sore. Credit to them, they were hard cunts. Bloody hard cunts. There's nothing better than playing hard cunts because you get as good as you give. That Sinclair bloke's a fucking nutcase. Also, a right fucking loser. That's one thing I know after spending the week trawling through his YouTube channel for intel to throw at him during the game. He's a genuine loser. I'd have respect for the cunt if he wasn't such a loser.

Alright, here we go. I'll give this bloke donuts. He's a leech. Worse than parking inspectors, this lot, because they actually

22

follow you around till you give them what they want, and what they want is about 50 mls of dehydrated, post-game piss syphoned out of your cock. Closet sickos, the lot of them. Probably get off on putting those surgical gloves on. *Snap. Snap. Snap. Snap. This little fucking piggie went all the way to the prostate.* I bet they go home and tell their kids how the piss smelled and then go into the spare room out the back filled with vials of their own piss which they test every morning— or the residual leftover of all the samples they've collected. Dexter Morgan, eat your fucking heart out. The fine men and women of ASADA or WADA or whichever cockless anti-doping agency is after my piss tonight can get fucked.

I reckon I've had this bloke before. Fifty-year-old Pakistani guy, grey moustache and square-framed glasses. Not just glasses—they're like bulletproof windows, those things: thick as fuck. The parasite's name: *Simon.* Well, Simon, you're in for a bit of a night because I don't feel like pissing. If you'd grabbed me as soon as we came off then you'd have got a nice fresh batch. But I'm empty now. Less than zero and it'll take me a while to replenish the tanks. Sure, I can try to push it out like a tube of toothpaste, but you'll get the dregs. Then we'll have to wait around and start all over again.

Maybe I should be flattered they're testing me. But what's this, fourth time this year now? They're definitely target testing. They probably have sleepers in every nightclub, keeping track of bathroom movements. Time between use. Nose touches. Eyeball width and pupil dilation. Full fucking match centre statistical analysis courtesy of the Mega Wall. Well, you've got the wrong guy, I tell you. My vice is on your approved list, so fuck off.

I'm sculling this water down. He can see me. I want to get out of here. I want to lose this fucking tagger. Jesus, he's on me more than anyone who bloody played out there tonight. Maybe we should give this fucker a trial? He wouldn't be any worse than some of the spooks we've taken punts on.

Cunt's got the eagle eyes on. Has to keep me in eyeshot. Otherwise they're worried I'll strap a condom filled with someone else's piss to the inside of my thigh. Sadly, we're not that technical around here. And no glory holes in the cubicles either to pass samples through; we need a full-time piss slave living inside the walls churning it out whenever we need it. Not a bad job for someone whose only skill is producing clean piss.

The sooner this is over and done with, the sooner I can meet the boys. Feels like a we're Stewy fucking Dew for it. Don't want to go back to HQ after what happened last weekend. They'll have us on the red list. The bouncers were right fucking pricks though. I could've taken one of them, no doubt. But three of the fuckers? Weight of numbers. Different ball game. Not like Fangs would've been much help. He was too busy talking to that bird he'd lined up on the apps. The tactician getting to work. Shits himself when he has to talk to birds without a few drinks under his belt though. Steve Jobs and Zuckerberg did that guy a favour; without those apps he'd still be a virgin I reckon. But at least he was there. Fucking Squidman MIA again. Smoke bomb.

Sorry buddy, this piss ain't coming. I've got a proper case of stage fright now too. What's that trick that Georgey-Boy uses? The times tables. Three times six. Eighteen. Seven times four. Twenty-eight. Four times fuck this. Who fucking cares? Even Simon is aware of the trepidation taking hold of the neural pathways between my brain and cock. He's turned the tap on.

'Look, it's not going to happen, mate.'

He really is clutching that clipboard tight, isn't he?

Clipboard Boy. *Clippy*. Hey, follow me, Clippy Boy, I may as well get changed out of my playing kit. We're in for a long night, you and I. Better call the hugs and kisses now and let her know. There will be no Sunday roast and hanky panky for you tonight. You're tied at the hip to me. My Siamese twin for the night.

Looks like I'm not the only lonely soul still hanging around. Old Sixty Minutes looks a right mess. Down a rabbit hole, hunched over his phone. He will, no doubt, be doing an intense session of groundies in the dungeon after everyone leaves. Never seen a harder worker than the prick. It's a shame the demons in his head prevent it from translating to on field success. Perhaps he should do the old Moist Mike trick and get Botox injections in his hands to stop the sweat. Never did help Mikey though. Now he's busy sticking another form of needle in, juicing up. One or two cycles never hurt anyone. But shhhh I won't say that out loud around you, Clippy. As far as you know, the only thing going into my body is a generic brand multivitamin, a permissible limit of silver bullets—exemptions granted on the basis of a pre-existing quote unquote addiction—and a variety of piss on the weekends, which you are currently holding me back from.

Come with me Clippy Boy, I'm feeling dry and barren down there and until I need to piss, we may need something to keep us occupied. There is a theatre around the corner and you do look like the movie-going type.

With those goggles on, Clippy Boy, you'd be sitting as far back as possible. The reflection from the screen onto your lenses may even cause a bit of a solar flare. I will keep in your sights at all times and out of sheer courtesy I will pay for your ticket, but do not expect any snacks from me. This is not Sarah Lindhoff and a screening of *She's Out of My League*.

There is no smoochy-smooch coming your way, Clippy. Unless you follow Sarah's lead and leap across and put your lips on mine. But I know that isn't what you're interested in. You are after one thing and one thing alone and it is currently pooling in my bladder.

Ah, as much as I despise you, there is a beauty to this relationship, Clippy. In that not a word can be spoken between us and you must follow me around like I am the Mother Goose. Come on then, Clippy Boy, up the stairs, we're going to the movies because an extra large drink and a bullshit action drama is just the thing that will squeeze the golden liquid you covet out of the hole on the end of my cock . . . Hang on a second. No fucking way, that's the fucker there! That's the cunt who bent me over and gave me a real reaming tonight. Mr ████! Where's he driving off to? Fucking nice car he's got, by the way. Course it is. Cunt's on what, 900 a year? One point something? Plus the boot sponsorships and all the free shirts and jocks and food products. The rich get richer, eh? And they put me on him tonight? Fuck me dead. Never stood a chance. You know what? Fuck it. I had a job today and I'm gonna finish that job. I'm going to at least get one thing right. Clippy, come with me, there's been a change of plans. Not like the cunt's got any say in the matter. He's got two rules: 1. Don't let me out of his sight. 2. Collect my piss. The latter cannot occur without the former. So, you're on my watch, Clippy. Come on and buckle up.

Ah, where are you going, Mr ████? Where could you possibly be driving to after such a game. A church? Thanking god for the divine abilities he has bestowed unto thee? There is no other explanation for how the ball continued to bounce your way tonight. If it's true that good things happen to good people, then you, Mr ███, you must be a pure fucking saint. Mother Teresa-type operator. Whereas I, well, I must be a complete Josef Fritzl.

Yes, I have you firmly in my sights, Mr ███. *The lion hunts its prey in the wilderness.* The roles have been reversed: you are now the antelope and I am the apex predator, accompanied by my dear friend Clippy. Shhhhh, Clippy Boy, we must not spook ze prey. We must stalk until we have it within striking distance. And then I will wrap my teeth around the jugular and—*Oh, you're fucking kidding me.* Fucking piggies pulling me over. Of all times. The Red and Blue Lights of Death.

Hello, officer. No, I did not know I was speeding. It is very unlike me to drive in a manner that causes danger to anyone else. Oh, yes. I was at the game tonight. Yes, that ███ did have a fucking great game, you fucking prick. Fuck off. You can fuck right off. No officer, I have not had any drinks tonight. Though I can point you in the direction of 40,000 individuals who may be convinced otherwise, due to my performance earlier this evening. Yes officer, I can count to ten for you. One. Two. Three. Four. Shall I stop there? Thank you, officer. No, I am not aware I was driving in a menacing manner. I will try to keep an eye on that. Thank you, officer. Thank you . . . Prick.

Alright, Clippy Boy, we are back on the trail. The scent may be gone, but let's not abandon hope.

Where would the fucker have gone? Where would I go if I were rich, had just played the game of my life and had the world at my feet? Well, me, I would be out at one of the venues which let us in. There's no doubt about that. But Mr ███, Mr Golden Child, from what I understand from my research during the week, is a consummate professional a.k.a. a bit of a deckchair, so there's fuck all chance he's staring down the sink somewhere. Also, he was driving. So one is inclined to believe that if he is out then he is at a fine restaurant perhaps. A nice five-course meal, appetisers and all, to accompany a five-star performance. Now, where would he go then? Clippy Boy? Keep your eyes peeled, we are on the hunt. The hunt for Red October. The Hunt for Mr ██. The hunt for . . . YES! There it is. The ball has finally bounced my way. I am no Fritzl after all! Yes, there Clippy Boy, his car parked nicely out the front of Dolce Fuoco. Of course, a nice bit of Italian for Mr ██. Washed down with a glass of red perhaps. Clippy Boy, hold on tight, we're going in. But shhhh, we must approach with caution. There, have a look, you can see our prey through the window. Just the sight of him turns my blood into a gaseous substance. Clippy Boy, forget the silent approach! I'm going in. Ah, hello, Mr ██. Why the look of horror? I'd say I should look familiar to you, but there was a distance between us on the field tonight, eh. Well, let's fix that, shall we. Mind if I pull up a seat here? Course you don't. First time you've seen me all night, isn't it Mr ██. That's ok. I'm here now. I'm here to do my job. Dinner looks divine. What have you got there? Mind if I take a bite? Course you don't. And the lovely lady you're with, well done, Mr ██. Though I'm sure it isn't hard for you, is it? Poster boy. This does feel rather cosy, doesn't it? I can feel the rage soothing. Ah, the weight has been lifted off and there's a warmth inside me. I can feel it all over. This is better than any silver bullet experience. It's really . . . in fact, there's a bit too much ease!

'Clippy Boy! The cup! Where's the cup?!'

Yep, it's happening now. No fucking time. Defcon One. The flood gates are about to open. There's no time, Clippy Boy, where the fuck is Clippy Boy?! Plan B. Mr ██, give me that wine glass. Don't look at me like that, prick. Take your millions

28

of dollars and your property portfolio and your lovely date for the night and fuck off. I've got a job to do—two jobs—and I'm fulfilling my duties simultaneously.

Ah, sweet release. There you go, Clippy Boy. After some minor transference issues between vessels, consider your job done too.

A DOUBLE DATE

Fangs

Here's a few things I find extremely funny at this very moment. The first is that this is the bar where Quincey got done for coke last year. It was a real horror show. Long story short, Quincey rocked up late to pres and we made him play catch up. Fed him shots and made him scull all the drinks he'd brought with him and by the time we left he was absolutely Troy Cooked. Him and a few boys went in on a bag that night. Mind you, Quincey was a fiend before he came to the club. That's why he got traded to us in the first place. Damaged Goods. Anyway, the way Quincey tells it is that an undercover had their eyes on him when he came out of the bathroom, then they ushered him out into the back alley where he got pinned up against the wall and searched. He was in a knee brace at the time, so truth be told, he wasn't meant to be out drinking at all let alone sticking a key up his nostril. Quincey said he would've run for it too if he wasn't incapacitated. A few of us had to remind him that of all the blokes at the club, Quincey, formerly Queeny on account of his turning circle being akin to that of the *Queen Mary*, wouldn't have been one to get away.

30

PISSANTS

We all got a text about it Sunday night and the next morning
we had a meeting that we will likely quote till we're all pushing
daisies. The Big Fella even did an impression of Quincey at
one point, saying, 'I'M QUINCEY, I'M TEN FOOT TALL,
SURROUNDED BY GOOD-LOOKING PEOPLE, I'VE
GOT THE GEAR ON AND I DON'T GIVE A FUCK!!!'

There was restrained laughter from all parts of the room.
Especially when the Big Fella repeated it again, this time
adding, 'HE DOESN'T GIVE A FUCK ABOUT YOU! OR
YOU! OR YOU!' and it was like he was firing off bullets at
every bloke he pointed at. That and the spit coming from his
mouth. It really was something else.

When it went down, Quincey still had a year left on his
contract. So, he's currently in a sort of football purgatory
where he knows he won't ever get a game here, but he's got
no trade value to any other club. He says that the Big Fella
hasn't said a single word to him since the day it came out. The
only time they cross paths is when Quincey runs past his office
to check his pigeonhole. God bless Quincey, though. He had
diamond hands when the club asked who he was with on the
night. He didn't rat any of us out. Saved us all the strife, but
cost himself a career as a result. The CEO came out the next
day and interviewed everyone twenty-one and under asking
what they knew.

Me: Never touched the stuff before. Swear it.

The irony of the whole thing is that Quincey now gets a free
bump off anyone when he's out as a way of us saying thanks.

The second source of entertainment for me is the rapidly
expanding circles of sweat spreading across the armpits of
Squidman's shirt. The reason being that he's seated opposite
Ruby, a prominent social media influencer whose ascension
came off the back of a brief stint on a shitty reality show,

31

a very choreographed and staged romance with somebody on that show, and an increasingly popular OnlyFans account which is reported by various reputable and esteemed digital news outlets to make her more than $100,000 a month. That's important context, because Squidman had previously subscribed to Ruby's OnlyFans account and received a message upon sign-up. He is too sober to know how to bring it up right now, but you can tell by the expanding sweat circles that he is worried Ruby might remember the message. I am convinced, however, that it would be Ruby's management running the account, rather than Ruby herself, sending dubious messages to all the desperate losers and horny fuckers with more money than sense (Squidman leans more towards the latter) in order to drag them in.

I am grateful for Squidman's situation. A double date is far more palatable if someone else is also uncomfortable. I can't say I really do dates. Let alone double dates. Let alone double dates with a girl who has a boyfriend (Rachael, who is the fourth member of our party). The usual order of proceedings is an interaction on socials, a drunken back and forth, a loose plan to catch up later and then more drinks until we stumble home to someone's house. Also, I tend not to leave my 5 km area. My libido isn't so high that the promise of sexual gratification will dictate my life. That's where me and the likes of a Dennis differ. He's addicted to sex, or at least the pursuit thereof. Will happily throw you under the bus if anyone gives him the eye. The situation is only intensified by what I call the Dennis-Chase-Down Paradigm; which is the more followers a bird has, the more he goes after them. He would be filthy if he knew that Ruby, with her 540,000 followers, mostly blokes who wank off to her, I assume, was sitting across from Squidman and not him.

I focus back on the brains-trust conversation.

Ruby: He said he wasn't done sleeping with other people. Can you believe that?

Rachael: What a fucking idiot!

Rachael is the orchestrator of tonight's events. She sent me a text less than an hour ago asking if me and a friend were free for a drink on account of Ruby's recent breakup. Rachael reckons she's a right genius. She studies law and is in a long-term relationship with an Olympic rower or one of those bullshit sports everyone pretends to care about every four years. Though she's had half a glass of wine and has already moved herself onto my lap. We flirt occasionally on social media, no doubt because she's a fan of the club. I can tell when she and the old boy have had a Matt Rowell because she posts a video of her dancing out at the club and then messages me saying *come out*. Tonight she got in early.

Squidman (arms tucked in, conscious of his sweat stains): Yeah, what an idiot.

The girls don't acknowledge what Squidman says, turn to one another and suggest another drink.

Me (as they leave, under my breath): Nah, we're all good. Thanks for asking. Chat later.

Squidman: Maybe she's a plank of wood in bed. A real starfish.

Me: What?

Squidman: That's why the guy left her, maybe she's a dud. Gives me little hope if a guy gets sick of sleeping with a girl who looks like that.

Me: You're not taking into account one crucial factor though.

Squidman: What's that?

Me: The ex is a real Jeffrey.

Jeffrey. Jeff Horne. A person lacking in the usual social awareness that prohibits cringe worthy behaviour. I open my phone and show Squidman a video of Ruby's ex running with one of those camel water backpacks on. He's wearing Oakleigh running glasses and the caption is some bullshit about Being Your Hardest Self.

Squidman: Fucking Jeffrey.

Ruby (returning with drink in hand): Should we dance? I haven't danced in forever. I really want to dance.

Rachael (very drunk): Woooo, let's dance, bitch.

We stand, drinkless, and follow them out onto the dancefloor. It is a funny thing to watch Squidman dance. At times, it seems he doesn't understand how long his limbs are. But at others, he moves in perfect synchronicity, able to clear the dancefloor with his arms and create a small circle of space for his group. Tonight, his go-to moves consist of an array of hip shakes, shoulder shrugs and elbow flays. His feet shuffle slightly in time with the music; this, he has told me multiple times, is the most important part of dancing. So long as you move in time with the music, that is all that matters. And watching him now, and the way that Ruby has moved herself towards him, I cannot help but think Squidman might be on to something.

When it comes to competing with Squidman for birds, you've got little chance. His height makes him the immediate talking point of every room he enters. That and his boy-next-door demeanour, topped with unkempt sandy blond hair. Prick looks like every nineties heartthrob rolled into one. So, it might seem a poor choice to invite him, but of the options available, he was the safest bet. I couldn't have tolerated Stick screaming in Ruby's face calling her a virgin after a couple of drinks. Or Mud, sitting there, playing with the bolts under the table, going full Humphrey Bear like he always does in front of birds.

I need another drink to match Squidman's intensity. I gesture towards my tall friend and he nods his head. I then do the same to the girls and they scream out, *Yeah*, which I feel they would say regardless of the question asked. *Is this place shit? Yeah!!!! Do you think Santa Claus is a twat? Yeah!!!! Do you think that 9/11 was an inside job? Yeah!!!!*

My journey to the bar takes me past an array of interesting characters. Blazers appear to be in vogue, or maybe a real estate agency is having a work function here. Lip fillers. Botox. Fake tits. Guys with ribbed foreheads and plucked eyebrows. It's hardly the most disturbing facet of the night as the DJ simultaneously manages to fuck up both a Smiths song and a deep house trance track by mashing them together. Out of the corner of my eye I see a bird who looks familiar. I try to place her and feel her look back at me. Fuck, where is she from? It takes a minute but then I remember. End of last year. We went back to hers and she asked me to wait on the bed while she got something. She pulled down a box from the top of her wardrobe and then tipped it up on the bed. I shit you not, six vibrators fell out.

Girl who owns six vibrators: We're using these.

Me (unsure if she meant one or all of them): Sorry, not for me.

Girl: Well, you can leave then.

Me: Ok.

Interactions like that should stay in the past. Unfortunately, the demons drift along with the current of time. The fuckers. I'm about three deep in the line, which has ambled along, when I feel a tap on my shoulder. The long arms of Squidman. Behind him I see that the dancefloor has cleared out. Then, standing in the centre of what is now an empty space, I see Rachael with a pool of vomit at her feet. Ruby is holding a hand over her mouth and nose and trying to pat her friend on the back with the other. But the disgust on her face seems to override her actions as a caring companion.

I walk over to the girls and the confronting odour of vomit and coconut, which I assume was in Rachael's cocktail. There is a surprising amount of vomit on the floor. The human body truly is amazing sometimes.

Me: Is there anything I can do?

Rachael (with watery eyes): G-G-Get my phone out of my bag.

Me (noticing that she has vomit on her hands): Ok, sure.

Ruby (muffled by her own hands): You're ok, darling. (However, this could also have been: 'You're no Robert Starling' or 'Cherokee passing'.)

Going through Rachael's Louis Vuitton bag a small flicker of light catches my eye. What do we have here? The lights overhead reflect off a little button bag which looks half-full. Perhaps I was wrong. Double dates are not so bad after all. Double the odds. Double the chance someone will surprise you.

My eyes shoot to Squidman hoping that our time as house-mates has rewarded us with some ability for ESP.

Me: Squidman, we're on here. The girls were preparing for more than just a couple of drinks.

Squidman: Travis Cloke?

Me: Half a bag.

Squidman: Should we?

Me: When the fuck do you ever ask that? It's a Sunday night. And at worst, yeah, 'Cloggers Cocaine Controversy', that's a headline people would care about.

As I look at him, I can't determine if this exchange has taken place, or if it's just my brain telling itself what it wants to hear. Regardless, I slip the bag into my back pocket and hand Rachael's phone to her. She still has flecks of vomit on her face, her hands, her everything.

Rachael: I'm getting an Uber home.

Ruby: I'll come with you, baby.

Squidman (throwing what you might call a Hail Mary): Are you sure?

Ruby (snuffing it at the goal line): Yeah, I'm sure.

Me (doing some simple math in my head): Ok, well, that's a real shame. Do you want us to wait with you?

Rachael: It's ok, we're—(covering her mouth and staggering off)

Alone on the dancefloor, I open my palm and show Squidman the bag. I take much delight in the unveiling. My fingers blooming like the petals of one of those flowers the people will queue for hours to see. Imagine the makeup of that crowd if the contents within were what I have in my possession, instead of a sewerage smell.

Squidman: Ooo, hello.

Just the reaction I was hoping for.

Me: After you, my good man.

We head into the bathroom and stick a twenty up our noses. There's another thing I'm finding funny now and I begin to laugh. This could be the exact same cubicle Quincey was in the night he got caught. This is more of a tribute than a memorial. Best we finish it off and flush the evidence less some undercover Steve Buscemi-lookalike fuck tries to drag us down. That, or we start limbering up for a footrace. The cautionary tale of Quincey serves us well: Ten foot tall and roaring. Surrounded by good-looking people. He's got the gear on. *He doesn't give a fuck about you! Or you! Or you!*

AMSTERDAM

Elliott
DAY 22

If you ask yourself the questions, you'll give yourself the answers. The person asking the question is the one answering, and whether they realise it or not, they'll manipulate the situation to tell themselves what they need—or want—to hear. We serve as our own protectors.

That's what I'm thinking sitting on my bed in Amsterdam, writing, with some shitty comedy show on in the background. Pete, whose idea it was that I start writing again because it's something I enjoy, is on his bed beside me, shirt off, scrolling through his phone, eating a chocolate bar from reception. Occasionally he laughs at something or moves, reminding me that I'm not the only one in the room.

This morning I rode through the empty streets on a rented bike. The canals extend like fingers and the town itself is like one giant hand. I rode to where Pete and I had walked the night before. The windows along the alleyway which had been filled by naked women dancing, beckoning people in, were

38

now covered by curtains. Then it had been packed with groups of men looking in at the women, the smell of weed hovering above. We walked slowly to soak it in. I saw several men come back from the rooms into the street. A professional-looking man with a leather satchel, grey coat, glasses, emerged with a subtle smile on his face, hands in pockets, moving quickly back out into the noise. For the few seconds while the door was ajar, I peered inside the room. It looked clinical, like a prison cell. Cold and sterile.

I couldn't find any open cafés, so I rode back to the hotel, passing the Rijksmuseum, losing count of how many rusted, abandoned bikes were chained to poles.

When I got to the hotel, I still wanted to be alone, so I sat on a bench by the canal, watching the water with my head-phones resting in my lap. It was a very still morning; the boats in front of me did not move at all. I looked at the buildings on the other side which were all similar, same height, same windows. I have heard myself saying that I could live here, but there feels little truth to that outside the fact that I think the buildings are nice and that right now, I want to be some-where new.

As I sat in the quiet, the sound of a bike bumping down the road behind me caught my attention. After it passed me I heard it stop abruptly. The sound of the kickstand clicking into place with force was followed by unevenly paced foot-steps coming closer and closer. It was a young woman, about my age, wearing all black, knee-high boots, fishnet stockings, a mesh top. It looked like she was on her way home after a night out.

I figured she was going to sit on the spare bench beside me, but then I felt her next to me.

'Can I sit here?' she asked.

I nodded. 'Sure.'

We sat facing the water, a moment of silence between us, unsure what the dynamic was, whether the bench was something that connected us or which gave us both the space to exist in our own worlds.

'This is my favourite part of Amsterdam,' she said.

I turned to face her. She had a nose piercing and paint on her pale face, red and blue crosses under each eye. A strong smell of alcohol emanated as she spoke and a string of safety pins held her skirt together above her thigh.

'Are you from here?' I asked.

'Yes, I grew up here.' She paused, and it was like she had to catch the words before speaking. 'Where are you from?'

'Australia.'

She didn't respond. She moved her jaw slightly, swaying gently.

'It's remarkable that we have this.' She pointed to the sun rising behind the buildings on the other side of the canal. She looked back at me. 'Aren't you cold?'

I was wearing a blue Tokyo T-shirt that I had bought from an underground op-shop in Shoreditch and a pair of shorts. I could see goosebumps on my crossed arms. She had hers folded too and her legs crossed and her jiggling foot hit mine a few times.

I shook my head. I have only worn T-shirts this entire trip because I want people to see my new tattoos. For the last two years I have always worn long-sleeved button-ups over the top of short-sleeved shirts. I was insecure about my arms. I still am, I haven't been to a gym in a couple of years now, but the tattoos at least make me think I look interesting.

'The sun is beautiful, isn't it?' I said.

She smiled and kicked her feet out in front of her. I didn't think she'd heard me. She seemed only fifty per cent there.

'It's weird how no one here wakes up early to come and look at it. You're all so lazy.'

She laughed. 'So, are you just sitting out here taking it in?'

I thought for a moment that I would tell her everything. About how this trip has done nothing for me so far. That I just want to go home. How I cried after checking Instagram last night. How I wanted to punch Pete at Soho House in London because he was flirting with Daisy when her boyfriend was there. But instead I just said that I'd been having a bad morning.

'Oh, what's wrong?'

'It's a long story.'

She didn't ask anything else. I caught another whiff of the alcohol on her breath, as she turned towards me. She seemed scattered and tried to tell me a story about how she listened to Fat Freddy's Drop while running but couldn't remember their name for a while.

As she went around in circles, I intervened. 'Is it expensive to live here?'

'It's getting worse,' she said. 'A lot of people move here and make it harder for the locals to afford anywhere.'

She tried to find the Dutch word for people with money who come and live here.

'Tourists?' I said.

'No, not tourists; we have another word for it.'

'Parasites?'

She laughed again. 'Not as harsh as that!'

I was waiting for the pauses in the conversation to force them full. Eliza always said I went inside myself.

'So what do you do?' I said.

'I study medicine.'

'How long in?'

'Three years,' she licked her lips, which were dry, and played with the pins on her skirt.

'But I don't know if it's what I want to do. I don't just want to be another number. I want to be someone who cares about their patients. I don't have a great relationship with my own doctors. But I've met some great people while studying, some great friends.'

'That's good.'

'Yeah, but I think I want to study psychology now.'

'Psychology is interesting.'

'Yeah, you can really change the world with it.'

A few bike riders passed behind. Slowly the town was coming to life.

'This is my favourite spot in all of Amsterdam to sit, you know?'

'Really?'

'I used to sit on this bench with my best friend. I loved him, as a friend—it was never romantic. But yeah.'

The way she paused and hesitated was familiar to me, as though she was trying to convince herself of what she had just said.

'He moved to Berlin,' she said, 'and now he isn't really grounded in Amsterdam.'

I didn't ask what that meant, but assumed it meant that he had changed. That he could no longer feel settled in the place he had grown up.

The boats in the canal started to bob in front of us slightly. You would only notice if you were looking closely.

'What should I do in Amsterdam today?'

I suddenly felt bored by my own voice. Like I had asked something that I didn't care about, just for the sake of asking.

'Have you been to the museums?'

'Yes.'

'Are you more into paintings or photography?'

'I don't have a preference.'

She said the name of an exhibition, but I didn't hear her properly. I had already forgotten her name and figured I would ask for it again at the end of our conversation. I remember thinking briefly that she might be an escort, that at the end of the conversation she was going to ask if I wanted to go somewhere with her and then tell me a fee: fifty euro for fifteen minutes, something like that. We talked about jazz, and how she was good at theory and sang and played the violin. She said that when she rode her bike home the other night that she had to scat to herself while cycling so she didn't fall asleep.

We both laughed at that and I thought to do a scat impression, but didn't.

Eventually she got up to leave and she said that she was going to a festival tomorrow. When I said, 'Festival on a Monday?' she said, 'No—Sunday.'

'Today is Sunday,' I said, and we both laughed.

We hugged and I thought to ask for her number when she was getting on her bike but didn't.

HENRY THE SAUSAGE

Fangs

We have this conversation once a week. For specificity's sake, it happens every Monday when we eat Thai, which we do after we've watched Gatesy's sister's latest YouTube vlog, dissected at length what we did and did not like, screamed out our recommendations for the following week, and before we go into the club for Shower Time.

Waitress: Are you ready to order?

Stick: Yeah, can I get one chicken Pad See Ew.

Shaggers: Two please.

Mud: Three.

Me: Four.

Squidman (looking at the menu even though he knows what he wants): Five, but can I get my one without capsicum, thanks.

And that's all it takes.

Stick: Just eat the *fucking* capsicum, it won't kill you. Seven billion people and you're the only cunt who's allergic to capsicums, I reckon.

Seriously, that's all it takes.

Stick: Fuck's sake, just order something else that doesn't already have capsicum in it.

Squidman: No.

Stick: What do you mean *no*?

Squidman: I mean I can't eat capsicum.

Stick: Can't or won't? You got a stress rash before a game because you were rattled. It's got nothing to do with capsicums or string beans or artificial fucking food colourings.

Squidman's trying out a new diet. Every two weeks, he reintroduces a new food. He started off only eating rice and green beans and has worked his way up to Modern Neanderthal, where he can eat everything except capsicums apparently. It started after he rashed up before a game last year—the reason for which has never been unanimously agreed upon—and his progress is scrupulously logged into a special food diary prescribed to him by the club dietician. I don't know if I'd take any dietary advice from Squidman, considering last year he ate an entire roast chicken every night after dinner to put on weight. As in he would eat dinner and then, as a separate meal, a roast chicken. He thought the Big Fella said he needed to bulk up. When he came back from the break, the Big Fella took one look at Squidman and asked what the hell he'd been doing, then organised a sit down chat about how important it is for him to be able to *cover the ground* and that he can't do that when his weight looks like a three digit area code. It was evening walks and modest lunch servings for two months after that for Squidman.

The capsicum conversation usually resolves itself, but it helps if someone railroads it, which, judging by Mud's face, is what he's about to do.

Mud (scrolling on his phone): Man, can we fine Pleb for posting about his new shog so much?

45

Shaggers: He made an Instagram account for it. It's crook.

Stick: If we start fining blokes for doggy accounts then you've got expenses coming your way.

Shaggers: Fuck off.

Stick: Ooo don't be so *surly* Shaggers. You're always so *surly*.

Me: What would you fine him?

Mud: I don't know.

Stick (after almost finishing his Coke Zero in one go): How about he has to fuck the little doggy.

Shaggers: Jesus Christ.

Stick: What he fucking loves it so much?

Shaggers: Why don't you go fuck your PS5 then?

Stick: Why don't you go fuck your—

Squidman: What if we kidnap it?

Mud: Kidnap the shog?

Squidman: Yeah.

Me: And do what with it?

Squidman (really thinking about it): Send him like ransom photos of it or something. It'd be funny.

Mud: That would be pretty funny.

Stick: Yeah, and then we fuck it.

Shaggers: Shut up cunt.

Me: Where's Pleb live now? Doesn't his place have a balcony?

Squidman: Yeah, that's where the little doggy sleeps, I'm pretty sure.

Fair dues to Squidman. From time to time he has these moments of ingenuity. It's like his brain was programmed for the refined environment of a football changeroom. It's no stretch to say that he's a savant at photo edits—his vault is the deepest I've seen. There is not a player who's been on the list over the past four years of whom he doesn't have an array of face-morphed headshots. It's a shame that his intellect doesn't transfer over into more useful areas of life.

Dinner is consumed without much conversation, Mud is bullied into paying, and our loosely laid plan begins to unfold. Stick drives us all in his metallic green Commodore, jelly bean air freshener dangling from the rear-view mirror—a confusing choice of accessory that goes against every other piece of intel I've acquired on him.

Mud (wedged in the middle seat): Did you boys hear about Steely's meeting today? Apparently, Dossa called him in for his review, but instead of the review he pulled up YouTube and they watched a clip from *The Lion King*.

Shaggers: He's lost it.

Mud: Yeah, the clip was like Timone and Pumba or something, telling Simba not to worry about the past and hitting him on the head and shit. It's because Steely had a mare on the weekend but it's also fucking racist.

Shaggers: Cause Steely's black?

Mud: Yeah.

Shaggers: You're a fucking idiot.

Mud: How? He didn't show it to me or you, cunt. Seems pretty sus the only cunt he's showing it to is the cunt from Africa.

Shaggers: Steely isn't African.

Mud: Yeah, he is.

Shaggers: No, he's not, cunt.

Me: Yeah, no he's not. He's Tiwi.

Shaggers: You thinking he's African, that's a serious breach.

Mud (full sooky socks): Well, the way I see it is we're all fucking African anyway. We all came from there. So, you're the racist cunts.

There's an opportunity here to further push Mud towards full tilt by pointing out that it's not Timone and Pumba who hit Simba on the head, but Rafiki, the monkey. But, if pushed, he'll become dead weight and will suck us all down with him like the black hole that he can be. The cunt's got some form of bipolar and when he's down, you know about it. Rollercoaster Mud. Admit one.

Stick pulls up out the front of Pleb's apartment complex.

Stick: Out you get Squid.

Squidman: Me?

Stick: Your idea—you go get the little doggy and bring it back.

Shaggers: Yeah, seems fair.

Mud: Yep.

This is definitely Stick's retribution for the capsicum angst. *V for Vendetta* is the cunt's middle name.

With little pushback, Squidman exits the vehicle and we watch him scamper across the road and then climb up Pleb's balcony. It strikes me that for a tall bloke, he is surprisingly nimble. Not quite a gazelle, but in comparison to the likes of Mud, who runs with peg legs, he's a smooth operator.

After successfully making it over the railing, Squidman disappears from sight as he crouches down. A few more seconds pass. Doubt creeps in. Is it possible Squidman has been attacked by Henry? Trust him to have a tombstone that reads 'Ankle bite infection courtesy of sausage dog' for his cause of death. As the engraving is about to begin, Squidman reappears. Not only reappears, but triumphantly steps into view, raising his arms in the air and presenting the shog that is Henry towards us like a trophy.

The odd tangential emotion to ecstasy that has gripped the car rises then quickly subsides as two things then occur which signal the unravelling of this kidnap plan. First: the lights go on in the hallway and we see Pleb and his fiancé Kylie walk in through the front door of their apartment. Second: a direct result of the first, a look of panic comes over Squidman as he holds the dog in his hands. It's clear he can't quite figure how to get down. The obvious solution here would be to leave the dog and jump. But, for whatever reason, that thought does not enter Squidman's brain. Either that, or he is hell-bent on his commitment to this gag—which I do admire.

The contingency plan, which doesn't exist, is now me running over to provide both moral and physical support to Squidman, who appears paralysed on the balcony several feet above.

Me (aggressive whispering): Just drop him down gently, I'll catch him.

Squidman (aggressive whispering): It'll fucking break his neck.

Me (aggressive whispering): He's a fucking sausage dog. He doesn't have a neck.

Squidman (aggressive whispering): His fucking spine. He's all spine!

Me (aggressive whispering): For fuck's sake, Squidman, when did you become such an animal rights activist? Just drop him! I'll catch him.

Squidman (aggressive whispering): Alright, I'm going to drop him on three.

Me (aggressive whispering): Yes, just hurry the fuck up.

Squidman (aggressive whispering): Alright. One. Two. Three.

A clean drop. A clean catch. Squidman jumps down just after and we head back to the car. I got you little Henry, you're safe now. Come and meet the rest of your new pals, and yes, it is with great pleasure that I declare you are an honorary pissant for the night . . .

As we congregate in the centre of the changerooms, I think it's the sight of five fully grown professional footballers standing over a tiny sausage dog wearing a sign saying *Save me Daddy*, that makes the stupidity of the situation hit home.

Stick (doing a weird voice): Daddy, daddy, look at me, I'm a good little doggy!

Mud (doing the same voice): Yeah, a good little doggy!

Squidman (trying to break through his own laughter and do the voice too): Good doggy! Good doggy!

Squidman crouches down and takes a couple of photos. He starts giggling to himself and then puts his phone in his locker. He is the creative director of this endeavour. He spent the entire car trip to the club searching for online ransom note generators, clearly specifying to the rest of the car that he wanted that 'cut out magazine letter font thing'. Ok, Squidman. Run and Carry with the idea. Don't let me, or any other cunt with a firmer grip on reality, get in your way.

The room starts filling with steam, indicating that our showers are ready. Henry, you're on your own for a while. Be a good boy and hold down the fort while we wash away our demons with near-boiling water.

Squidman (sitting on a Bosu ball in the corner of the showers): Horror names?

Mud (sitting on an upturned bucket, eyes closed as water runs over his face): Go.

Squidman: Craig.

Mud: Fuck, Craig's elite.

Shaggers: Craig's top two.

Mud: Yeah, for you.

Squidman: Barry.

Mud: Kiron.

Shaggers: Nah, no one is called Kiron. They have to be real names to qualify.

Squidman: Shiron.

Stick (wearing his speedos): Jethro.

Shaggers: Brenton.

Mud: Fuck me, Brenton. That's cruel. Top ten.

Me: Brenton Speed.

Shaggers: Brenton Sanderson.

Squidman: Nathan.

Shaggers: Nathan!

Me: Nathan Hauritz.

We get out of the showers and go do a couple rounds in the spa. It's in a putrid state, but the Out of Order sign doesn't deter any of us. There's a build-up of hair—pubic and leg—all over the walls. It's hard to decipher which is which. Mould on the roof too. But it doesn't really bother us because spanter cleanses the soul like nothing else. A bad game? Spanter. Parking ticket? Spanter. When the bubbles stop we dive into the ice bath to get the blood flowing then run back into the showers, which have been kept running this whole time in order to preserve the Ideal Temperature. After a final rinse, we walk back into the changeroom. It's Shaggers who speaks first.

Shaggers: Hey, where's Henry?

Stick (doing the voice again): *Henry's a good little boy!*

Mud (also doing the voice again): *He's a good little doggy!*

Shaggers: Yeah, but where is he?

Stick: He's just sleeping over there.

I hear Shaggers' footsteps as he walks over to inspect the dog.

Shaggers: Henry?

Oh fuck, what was with that inflection? *Henry*. Fucking *Hen-ry*.

Shaggers: Ah, guys. Little Henry's not moving.

Stick: Yeah, he's just sleeping. Been a big day for him.

Stick again (after walking, crouching down and giving the dog a little shake to wake him up): Oh fuck.

Shaggers (putting his hands in front of the dog's nose to see if it's breathing; turning, panicked, to the rest of us): Fuck, do you give dogs CPR?

Mud: Surely it's not *not* breathing.

Mud walks over. There are now three big naked bodies huddled around the little dog.

Mud (after checking the dog's vitals): Oh fuck. This cunt's dead.

Squidman (towel around waist, joining the rest of us): What's going on?

Mud: The little doggy is dead.

Squidman: Oh fuck.

Me: Squid, you didn't send the photos yet did you?

I thought that nothing could accentuate the lunacy of this situation any more than five fully grown footy players standing over a little sausage dog. But how wrong I was. Turns out it feels infinitely more stupid if the little dog is fucking dead.

Stick: What the fuck did you do to it, Squidman?

Squidman: Me? If anyone's likely to kill a dog around here it'd be you.

Shaggers: Yeah, that's true.

Me: Yeah.

Stick: Oh, you can all fuck right off.

Mud: Do we call a vet or something?

Stick: And let them tell Pleb we stole his dog?

Squidman: And murdered it.

Stick: We didn't fucking murder it.

Shaggers: Well, we kind of did.

Stick (vein popping out of his neck): Alright, well let's fucking do something about it. We're going full Milat, get rid of the corpse. Put this shitshow to bed.

Stick takes a towel out of the bin in the corner of the room and wraps Henry in it. He's Liam Neeson and little Henry is the daughter who keeps getting kidnapped while on exchange. I think. I don't know what to think right now. The dog's fucking dead.

The rest of us fall into line and get dressed then follow him up the stairs and cram into the car-turned-hearse. Squidman is the unfortunate soul who must cradle the wrapped body of Henry between his knees in the back seat.

Shaggers: How far are we going to drive?

Stick: I don't know. Just far enough.

Mud: We should just throw him in the ocean.

Stick: What and then let him wash up in two days' time? Didn't you hear about the bird's foot that washed up the other week?

Mud: Yeah, but surely a dog, like, decomposes and shit faster.

Squidman: Or maybe the sharks will eat him.

Mud: Nah, sharks don't eat dogs, man.

Shaggers (running his fingers down his face): Yes, they do.

Mud: No, they don't. They don't eat dogs. I saw it on an episode of *MythBusters* as a kid. They don't fucking eat them.

Shaggers: Sharks eat fucking dogs.

Mud: No, they don't!

Shaggers: Yes, they fucking do. You're a fucking idiot!

Me: No they d—

The stimulating back-and-forth is halted as Stick abruptly stops the Morgue on Wheels. Without saying a word, he gets out of the car, opens the back door and grabs the tightly wrapped corpse of Henry. He beelines it towards a bin on the other side of the road. He opens it, takes out the top bag of rubbish, puts the dog in and covers it with the bag he's just pulled out. Christ, it's concerning how at ease he looks. We're all just watching on, mouths open, Humphrey Bear passengers.

Stick (back in the driver's seat, as though that was a very normal thing that just happened): Alright. It's done. You're all very fucking welcome.

There's silence. Is everyone thinking the same thing here? How that didn't look like the first time Stick has done that.

Shaggers (scared he might detonate a bomb): Stick, did you take its collar off?

Stick: What?

Shaggers: The collar with Pleb's number on it. Did you take it off?

Stick: I don't know. Yeah sure, why?

Shaggers: I don't know, say someone comes out, goes through the bin, calls Pleb. I don't know.

Stick: I'm not getting out of this car again.

Shaggers: Well, who's going to do it?

I play out some scenarios in my head. Incompetency all around. Shaggers probably could do it, but he's too much of a stubborn cunt. Squidman is traumatised by the whole ordeal and Mud, well . . . I just wouldn't trust him to do it properly. Taking Stick's lead, I get out of the car without saying anything and make my way towards the burial urn. I open the bin and am immediately hit by the stench. I feel like I'm gagging. I'm going to throw up. Oh god, don't throw up on the dog corpse, that'll just make things worse.

My hands plunge into the abyss and feel through the waste. I don't want to know what I'm grabbing at. That I'm hoping it's some part of my teammate's dead dog says enough. Happy place. Happy place. Get to your happy place. It takes a minute but I get a hold of the tail and gently pull him up towards me. I don't reckon there's much give in dogs, especially not miniature dachshunds, and I don't quite care to find out what one's tensile strength might be. My mind goes back to my childhood, to our little Maltese terrier named Trixie. Fuck, she was good—and then we had that little prick Keenan Fritsch over for a week. He tormented the shit out of her, dragged her by the back legs across the carpet. We couldn't have anyone over after that without locking her in a room, because she'd go for them. She was traumatised, but at least she died a more dignified death than this. Blew up like a balloon one day and we took her to the vet and Dad was stroking her paws while the syringe went in. Solemn silence for a while after that. Dad put her in a towel and buried her next to the house. Little red collar on a white cross that he made too. That's the way to go. Not like this. You deserved better, Henry.

I start tinkering with the collar and it's a fiddly fucking thing. The grime isn't helping. I get a look in the dog's eyes. Rolled back whites. He's still sort of warm. It's like he's having a nap. Got his little tongue out too. If you were out in the wild, you'd have no hope, little buddy. Imagine a pack of wild sausage dogs roaming the forest floor. Instead, they're nice little handbags for people who want some social validation; another Instagram account, photos of fuck-all bullshit. Does my head in. I take it back, Henry. I'm almost glad you're dead, so you don't have to deal with the forced photo shoots, the sombreros and Santa hats, tea towel ghost outfits. You're free now, little buddy. I almost envy you.

As I grip the collar, a set of headlights illuminates me as a car pulls into the driveway next door. Fuck. Let's get out of here. A woman gets out of the car.

Woman: Hey there.

Me (fuck fuck fuck): Hey.

Woman: Do I know you from somewhere?

Me: Ah, probably not, I don't know. I'm not from—

Woman: I do! You came to my school the other week to talk to our students. You're a footy player.

Me (fucking hell): Oh, yeah, that might've been me.

It undoubtedly *was* me, and that school was ill-equipped to handle two of the lesser-known players of the ████████ Football Club. The Principal, some quasi-incarnation of Mr G and the manager from Flight of the Conchords, had me holed up explaining the full extent of his Under-16s football career. 'The Train' he called himself, even being so kind as to show me the large green and white steam engine that he'd had inked on his lower back to mark the name. An unwanted memory in this moment and all others.

A door slams and then another figure joins the woman, kissing her on the cheek.

Man: Hi, honey.

Woman: Dave, this is one of the footy players who came to our school the other week and talked to the students.

Man: Oh wow, like professional players?

Me: Yeah, yeah.

Man: Like ah, like Patty Cripps, Crippa?

I can feel the juices of the bin dripping down my fingertips which are clutching the collar. Drip. Drip. Drip. My mind is doing what it can to make me suffer, calculating the percentage breakdown of the vile liquid. I can only imagine what the guys in the car are making of this.

Me (10% undrunk coffee, 30% dead-dog excrement . . .):
Yeah . . . Yeah, like Crippa.

Christ. Sorry, little Henry. Truly, truly sorry. Your collar clutched between my fingers. Your body wedged beneath plastic bags of food scraps and brightly coloured plastic packaging. Maybe there is such a thing as a soul and yours is floating up and away. Say hi to little Trixie up there for me. Tell her things are going well down here . . .

OUTSIDE SHOULDERS

THE PISSANTS OPEN

FACEBOOK

Private event

Group created by: Sir Michael Fangbender

Going	Maybe	Not Going
20	**1**	**0**

Event details

Def 1: According to Kurt Vonnegut, a pissant is a guy who thinks he's the smartest prick in the room and can't keep his mouth shut. A guy who argues with everything and reckons he knows best. I was going to quote him on this, but I hear the cunt's estate is pretty litigious and I'll be arsed if they get a cent out of me.

Def 2: A tiny black ant, sometimes called a 'sugar ant'. It is called this because this type of ant is a favourite target in urinals. (Urban Dictionary)

Def 3: An insignificant or contemptible person or thing. (Websters)

Pissants,

It is that time of year where we must ask ourselves how we wish to be remembered in the annals of history. Every morning, when you look in the mirror, what is it that you see? Do you wish to be defined by the words of others? Or do you wish to stand up and reclaim what was taken from you . . .

Gentlemen, it's that time of year again. Time to sort out the pretenders from the contenders. Time to don the glove and compete in the illustrious PISSANTS OPEN.

RULES:

The rules for the fourth annual Pissant's Open are as follows:
1. All entrants must wear appropriate golf attire. This includes:
    a. Long pants and belt.
        i) Shorts are not permitted on the course.
        ii) Neither are short-longs
        iii) Neither are long-shorts.
        iv) Club slacks are not acceptable (if anyone even has any).
    b. A collared polo shirt.
    c. Golf shoes or New Balance 624s.
    d. Golf glove.
        i) Must be worn at ALL times.

    e. Optional, but encouraged:
       i) A pair of Chad Kroeger's—the speedier the better, bonus points for flames.

2. Tee off time is 10:00 am sharp. Not 10:01. Not 10:02. 10:00. Late arrivals will be penalised before entering the course. Penalty will be decided on the day, but is likely to be shot of black sambuca. Unless you're Hally, in which case it'll be a shot of absinthe. If no absinthe is available, then the cheapest house vodka will suffice.

3. Only beer or cider to be consumed, unless otherwise specified. Skin fold concerns are not an acceptable justification for consuming seltzers.

4. Freezemaster is in play. The first Freezemaster will be the first person to finish a drink. Freezemaster can only be used once every thirty minutes. See <u>Appendix A</u> for the rules of Freezemaster.

5. The first to consume three drinks gets to make a rule.

6. The first to consume five drinks gets to make a rule.

7. The first to consume ten drinks gets to make a rule.

8. For Shit, Outlawed Rules see <u>Appendix C</u>.

9. The scoring system works as follows:
    a. We will be spending 30 minutes at each pub. The designated timekeeper will say when the clock has started and will give a two-minute warning when time is up.
    b. Each pub is designated a par score.
    c. Par score is the number of schooners you must drink to score par at that pub.
    d. For a drink to count, it must be completely finished at the end of the 30 minutes.
    e. For every drink over that par, you receive an additional point under par. E.g. if a pub is a par three and you drink

five drinks, then you are two under for that hole. If you drink six drinks, you are three under and so on. It's not rocket science.

    f. If you do not make par—that is, if we are at par three and you only finish one drink, you are two over for that hole. Again . . . it's not rocket science.

    g. The winner at the end of 18 holes is the person with the lowest overall score (i.e. the most consumed drinks).

10. Closest to the pin will be played on the 7th hole. Rules for closest to the pin will be shared on the day.

11. Longest drive will be played on the 12th hole. Longest drive is judged by the length of piss streams in the back alley. You are allowed line up your shot for ten seconds, any longer than that (aka stage fright) is a disqualification.

12. BUBBLES' RULE: You are not permitted to take your drink with you to the bathroom. The first instance will result in a warning. The second instance will result in elimination.

13. The following are also grounds for <u>immediate</u> disqualification:

    a. Vomiting

    b. Getting kicked out of a pub

    c. Sitting in the corner playing BMX bike rider games on your phone . . .

14. Scorecards and pencils will be provided upon entry.

Appendix A: The Rules of Freezemaster

When the person designated as the 'Freezemaster' stands still with both of their hands placed atop their head, everyone else is to freeze wherever they are. The last person to freeze is the loser and must scull their drink and assume the responsibilities of the Freezemaster for the next round. This is UNLESS we enter a Mexican standoff situation. See <u>Appendix B</u> for the rules of a Mexican standoff situation.

It is the role of the Freezemaster to ensure that they are in the field of vision of the playing party so that the game catches on, i.e. they, the Freezemaster, can stand anywhere (corner of a room, behind the DJ, centre of the dancefloor) so long as they can be seen. If for whatever reason the Freezemaster does not catch on, the current Freezemaster must scull their drink and hand duties over to someone of their choosing. NB: Drinks consumed as punishment for losing Freezemaster do not count towards your overall score.

Appendix B: The rules of a Mexican Standoff

Should a situation occur in which everyone is frozen and there is no demand for the last person who freezes to drink, then it is deemed a Mexican Standoff and the first person to move loses and must scull their drink. However, if there is no movement for some time, then the Freezemaster may call a name at random and that person will be deemed the loser of the round and have to scull their drink. This is unless the group deems that to be a Virgin act, in which case, the Freezemaster must scull their drink.

Appendix C: The list of Shit, Outlawed Rules

The list of Shit, Outlawed Rules include, but are not limited to:

- 'No talking'
- 'No pointing'
- 'Everyone has to walk backwards'
- 'Buffalo'

FORM GUIDE:

Big Sexy $50—If there was a link between piss-sinking and low centre of gravity, then Big Sexy would be in pole position for the Open . . . shame there's not. Making his debut appearance, will Big Sexy leave a memorable impression like he did in the disabled bathrooms with that bird? Or will he be home before dark feeding the rabbits of his host family in his backyard? A long shot smoky in the field, worth throwing a couple of bucks on, but nothing more.

Sixty Minutes $60—*Tick tick tick tick tick tick* . . . Good evening, and welcome to sixty minutes. Tonight's story, a young man who may abscond at some point to go and get his extra groundballs in at the club looks to leave his mark at the Pissants Open. Sixty has quickly become known as the Hardest Working Player at the Club™, but how does that translate to having a few drinks? Will he be seeing double in the dungeon, or will he put on a display for the ages? Stay tuned to find out.

Walshy $12—Without doubt the most exciting new prospect this year. Arriving on his first day at the club in a moon boot which he hadn't told anyone about, and also hiding a DUI from club officials, we think that Walshy is a seriously rogue operator. Be sure to keep him away from any tattoo parlours adjacent to the course, he may add another horror sticker to his collection. Perhaps a kettle or something even more random to go with the fridge. But truth be told, we love that about him . . . Will Walshy be the first of a new generation to rise up and take the baton? Or will his inexperience get the better of him? Either way, fireworks are expected.

Fuzzy Duck $7.20—*So basically, I say fuzzy duck and then the next person says fuzzy duck and then you say duzzy and it changes direction and then we gotta say ducky fuzz.* Doesn't matter how many times he explains it, we've still got no fucking idea what he's on about. Fuzzy Duck, with his right peg that just won't stay in place when he runs, is one of the favourites of the field. A big fan of Captain Morgan, with a habit of shotgunning cans in a manner that makes his dentist's eyes light up with dollar signs. Fuzzy Duck has endeared himself to crowds with his antics in recent years, but the real question is, *Duzzy* have what it takes to win the open?

Hally $5—The most seasoned player on this card by a long way. Known for saving his best piss-up performances for footy trip, screaming *Ten before one, or one before ten,* will Hally be able to muster form this early in the season? We're told that he is still yet to recover from shell shock in the showers after being confronted by the Big Fella post-game while having a rinse. Will the proverbial whipping boy break free of the shackles, or will Hally cop another spray after the Open is done and dusted?

Squidman $14—A crowd favourite of the Open. We've all seen the infamous food diary . . . but let's hope he's been busy researching the nutritional value of tap beer. Does it contain phosphates? B12? Ammonium iodine? Vitamin D? We'll know after the first drink if he's going to stay around or if he starts blowing up in hives. Maybe bring an EpiPen to be safe and someone keep the doc on speed dial. Squidman is good over-head and will compete hard. One to keep an eye on.

Budget $220—Two things we know about Budget, first is that he rates himself, second is that he's not a fan of drinking, which may or may not be linked to him being a tight arse. There are some serious rumours floating around that he has been in the

DMs of someone's sister. Not naming names. But someone keep Gatesy away from Budget if it looks like he's snapchatting. A long shot, but if he can keep it together, by some miracle, he could pose a threat.

Gatesy $8.12—The Prince of the North is one of the most reliable piss-drinkers in the field . . . that is, when he's not pissing in the corner of the room while his missus is trying to sleep. There are question marks over how he will go drinking from an every persons' pub. Maybe his year of slumming it in a share house took the edge off, but reports are that last time he was at a pub, he asked the bartender where the waiter and yacht were. Will he be around towards the end of the night, or will he end up like the Black Hawk Downs he kicks at training?

Windmill $5.30—What do we know about the Windmill, aside from every square inch of his cock as it circles around in the air? Well, we know that he defends to the death, and he's got a sphincter that is always clenched from being one on one in the square . . . The real question with the Windmill isn't whether or not he will make it to the end, but at what stage he will succumb to the demands of the public and give us a show.

Quincey NO ODDS—Ah, Quincey. We do love you. But we know there are many things stopping you from being a threat at the Open. More of a 'make a wish kid' style appearance, Quincey will likely be sitting in the corner, having a quiet beer or two reminiscing about days gone by when he could have a bit of fun, before it all went to shit. Don't get caught talking to him about the Night in Question, it may drag you down and ruin any chances you have of taking out the Open for yourself. Treat him as a natural hazard on the course. Avoid if possible.

Fumbles $12—These odds may surprise betters, but there is a good reason Fumbles is being billed as a genuine dark horse of the field. Punters who've done their research will realise that he does, in fact, live above a pub and there are strong rumours that he has been doing some off-field extras during the week. Will he be clean when it counts, or will the pressure be too much for him and cause him to fumble his chances of victory? Go easy on the grippo, please, Fumbles.

Fangs $8—[Written by Squidman] One of the more consistent piss drinkers at the club, and the organiser of the event, will likely find himself in the midst of the action as he takes on the role of commentator for the day. (Oh, haven't you heard? He did a creative writing subject at uni once . . .) For Fangs, there are two questions that the day may answer: Do extra teeth help you drink faster? And can he go one better than last year and take home the coveted blazer?

Jenko $80—We're quite unsure of this one. He's from a place called Deniliquin, where it seems like there would be fuck all else to do except for drink. But we are yet to see any sign that this is the case from him. He may just be trying to put his best foot forward, but if that's the case, he isn't doing it very well for the Open. Known to need a toilet pit stop during running efforts, will the group be willing to wait for him between holes, or will he be left behind? Time will tell.

Mud $21—Not many have had an introduction to the club that involved getting kicked in the face by the skipper, then inch worming along the floor like a slug covered in piss. Will be interesting to see if he can find a polo shirt that's GUCCI. May have to forsake his usual hype beast persona to fit in, but it's all G baby, you know how he does it. We're all excited to see how he goes in his second Open.

Pricey $4.40—If White Line Fever were a person, it'd be big Pricey. Thankfully for us, there's no painted lines on the course, so our heads are all safe from Pricey's swinging fists. After podium finishes the last two years Pricey looks primed and ready to take the Open by storm. May be affected by the loss of his mate Georgey-Boy who's got the call up to be the Emergency for the ones this week. But that might also drive him harder to do it for his mate. Nothing Pricey about those odds betters, get on him, hard.

Shaggers $6.40—Shaggers loves a schoo schoo, but we know that every now and then he gets the call from Gee asking him to come home. Does Shaggers have the hall pass this weekend? If so, he may give the Open a real crack. Went 16/16 in pre-season sessions for throwing up. We're hoping he's got it all out of his system, which might mean there's extra space for a few mothers' milks. Could give things a real shake in the back 9 if he keeps the leaders in sight.

Steely $16—Some say that he is still running around ████ Park after falling off the back of a 10-minute fartlek . . . but if he has found his way back, we know that Steely will bring his best to the table (assuming we can keep him away from the Wild Turkey). *Wot u doin* will always shoot his shot, and for those who need refreshing, the first and only rule of drinking with Steely is *Don't ever talk to me about fucking pussy, cunt.*

Dennis $1.95—The defending champion and hot favourite. Dennis has shown time and time again that he is one of best two-way piss-sinkers in the competition. He has climbed the highest peak and, as we saw in Thailand two years ago, not even being hooked up to an IV drip in hospital can stop him from making an appearance at a piss-up. He's hard. He's relentless. He finds piss as easy as he finds the footy. If he gets that glazed look in his eyes, and Dennis comes out, it's Game Over.

Bubbles $501—The only bloke who has ever complained that the bubbles of a Passionfruit UDL hurt his tongue when he drinks it. Let's not beat around the bush, Bubbles is not a seasoned drinker. Will be bringing up the field from the rear. Don't waste your money on this bet.

Piss Boy $128—The only competitor in the field to have had his own surname trampstamped above his ass, will Piss Boy finally cut loose on the Open? Word is that if he takes home the kitty he will be spending it on a new bed base, seeing as he's a few slats short after the Silly Sunday bonfire last year. Just keep him away from a schooner full of piss because that might hold the event up for 45 minutes while he complains. Shut up and drink up, PISS BOY!

Stick $32—Sticky stick can drinky drink. We all know that. But he can also cause a scene and get himself kicked out of a venue faster than anyone else on the course. There's also some serious question marks about whether or not his body will hold up this year, though no doubt he'll have a supply of pharmaceuticals at the ready to get himself across the finish line. Will he stick around till the end? Or will it be an early night and a packet of Endones for our vocal friend?

Potato $56—This might be the first time Potato has seen any of the sights and sounds outside of the footy club. Can someone make sure he knows how to get to the first hole, he does only know the one road after all. 'No, I don't fooken drink!' Well Potato, you won't get very far at the Open with that attitude. But fingers crossed his competitive streak comes out and applies itself to something other than a training drill or bike session. The international contingency has never made an impact at the Open, here's open the luck of the Irish changes things. Welcome, Potato!

*** VALUE BET SPECIALS ***

Piss Boy rocks up wearing all black kit—$2.50

Piss Boy drinks piss again—$50

Someone does a bubbler—$7

Someone gets kicked out of a venue—$1.01

Over 2.5 games of Fuzzy Duck played—$14

Someone needs to get stitches—$22

Additional market for location of stitches:
   Head—$3
   Hand—$6
   Foot—$12

*** VALUE BET SPECIALS ***

Injured Senior player turns up trying to get leadership votes—$10

Someone rocks up wearing Tubigrip—$9

Fumbles does 5 clean schooner ground balls in a row—$501

Dennis forgets he's allergic to tequila and rashes up —$64

Shaggers throws up on the front 9—$3

Shaggers throws up on the back 9—$2.40

We see a Terry—$15

RUNNING COMMENTARY:

Hole 1—The Union

Welcome to the Open, ladies and gentlemen and people of all sexes and genders. I am your host for today, Sir Michael Fangbender, and I will be giving you hole by hole recaps on the proceedings.

Hole 1 of this year's Open plays with a gentle dogleg. There's a slight breeze coming from behind. Most of the players have played it safe and used a four iron off the tee, laying up for par (2 drinks). Several have gone a more aggressive line, a la Bubba Watson or Tiger Woods prior to the whole car-crash-broken-leg-fourteen-affairs-fucking-hookers-at-truck-stops situation.

Windmill, Gatesy, Pricey and as expected Dennis all going with the latter approach, getting birdies (3 drinks).

Initial fines distributed too: Walshy and Sixty for wearing club polos. Thank you to their respective housemates for orchestrating.

Hole 2—The Royal

Well, as expected, the early-hole jitters look to be getting a hold of some of this year's new blood. Notably, Sixty, who had his knife and fork out while sculling his punishment drink. If we look at it on the slow-motion replay, we can see most of the drink spilling on the front of his shirt rather than in his mouth. Fair chance he's home by the fourth hole.

True to form, Dennis is in the lead right now at two under. Keeping pace with him, Stick, who is already starting to slur a little. The course adjudicators have reminded him that this is an 18-hole course, to which he replied: 'Shut up, Virgin.'

FIRST RULE OF THE DAY (created by Dennis): You have to tuck your ears into your hat like Hally did on Fan Day for the entirety of the next hole.

Hole 3—The Imperial
Welcome back to the Pissants Open and thank you for tuning in again, loyal followers. In order to spice things up, we have introduced a buddy system for this hole. Zip ties are in effect, and everyone now has a partner who they have to follow.

Already we've seen the dire implications of this. Sixty, still feeling the effects of that first beer, took a trip to the bathroom with Walshy in tow. Reports are filtering in that Sixty couldn't hold in his spew and was bent over the bowl with Walshy patting his back the whole time.

Dennis is three under after three holes. He's looking very comfortable in his back stroke. Pricey also yet to break a sweat. The surprise of the day is that Big Sexy is keeping up with the front group. We've called ahead to the next pub to make sure they've got some waters ready for him, because we cannot see him keeping up this pace. Bubbles nowhere to be seen.

SECOND RULE OF THE DAY (created by Dennis): Everyone has to put their pants around their ankles and pull their shirt up under their chin when they piss.

Hole 4—Rimma's Parents' House
In an unexpected turn of events, hole 4 has been replaced [Green Under Repair—several big birthday parties going on, was taking too long to get a drink]. Instead, we have been invited into Rimma's family's home, which happens to be across the road from the pub.

As a result, we have a few challenges that will reward in extra shots off:

I.   One shot off for anyone who is able to secure Rimma's dad's credit card.

II. One shot off for anyone who gets Rimma's mum to do a shot of something (anything . . . please be sensible).

III. Two shots off for anyone who finds one of Rimma's old guernseys and gets a photo in it.

IV. Three shots off if you find the helmet Rimma wore after he broke his jaw and wear it out to the next pub.

V.   Four shots off for anyone who takes the parents' dog on a walk around the block.

Hole 5—The Frog and Squeak

We revert to the course as originally outlined. Congratulations to Windmill for getting Rimma's mum to do a shot of black sambuca and congratulations to Pricey for finding the helmet and wearing it out to the Frog and Squeak. If anyone asks, please just act like Pricey has a learning impairment and that should alleviate all further questions.

The results of the Longest Drive competition are as follows:

Winner—Gatesy, by a concerningly large margin. It makes you wonder if that Gatorade bottle he pissed in was enough to contain his fluids that fateful night.

Runner up—Squidman, who had been holding onto his piss since before proceedings took place in an attempt to improve the length of his flow. Sadly, not enough to win it this year Squid.

Dishonourable mentions—Big Sexy, Stick, Sixty for getting stage fright.

Hole 6—The Horse and Cart

DING DING DING, ladies and gentlemen, we have our first exit for the night! Budget is OUT! This was completely unexpected from the field. We've got an interview with field correspondent Sam Canavan at the scene:

Yes, hello Fangbender, I'm here outside of the Horse and Cart where bouncers are currently escorting Budget from the premises. There are reports that this debutant took a number of coloured shots off a tray that was sitting at the bar while waiting to order his next drink. Early word is pointing towards financially stringent motivations for the act. Yes, yes . . . more in now . . . we are getting word that he stole and consumed five of the shots before the bar staff alerted the bouncers, who Piss Boy is now arguing with out the front. Phrases heard include: 'Meat head failed rugby players' and 'I didn't do fucking nothing!' which is an obvious double negative but which we are not going to pry into right at this moment. More to come, back to you in the studio Fangbender.

Thanks Sam. We are all still coming to terms with what we have witnessed here, but I would like to take this moment to thank everyone for the joyous send-off they gave Budget as he left the pub. In light of these events a new market has just opened up:

We see Budget at the next pub—$4.50
Budget asks some of the boys to split his Uber home—$1.01

Hole 7—PJ Gallagher's

OBSTACLES ON THE COURSE—There is a wild hens' night at the pub. Please keep Big Sexy away from them . . . they're only human. It seems that the group hails from some part of Ireland and speak with a very thick accent. If you need translations, please use Potato as your go-between.

Also, a warning has been issued. Bubbles has been sighted walking with his drink to the bathroom. If this occurs once more, it is grounds for immediate elimination.

First Freezemaster of the day has claimed its victim, Sixty Minutes, who was returning from the bathroom while the game was in play. That's just Smart Footy by Squidman, the instigator, who saw the opportunity for an easy get, and took it. Sixty is now Freezemaster and the 30-minute clock has been set.

CLOSEST TO THE PIN—The rules for closest to the pin this year are quite simple. You will notice that this bar has a mechanical bull . . . closest to the pin will be awarded to whoever can get closest to a 10-second ride on the bull.

RESULTS—Congratulations to Windmill who has taken out the closest to the pin with a very impressive time of 9.95 seconds. Spectators were then treated to a patented Windmill move in celebration and the playing group was escorted out of the venue.

Hole 8—The Toolshed

Gents, a word of caution about this bar courtesy of Rimma: Do not accept drinks from strangers. This predatory behaviour should not be confused with generosity. Play it safe, stick to the middle of the fairway. Avoid any unsolicited advice on your stroke from the vicinity of the men's room, e.g. 'Keep your head down and spread your legs.' There may be some firm shafts in there, but play soft and look after your hole.

Hole 9—Bridge Crossing Hotel

PAYOUTS!!!!

WHOEVER HAD MONEY ON SOMEONE (WALSHY) TO DO A BUBBLER, CONGRATULATIONS! ALSO, WHOEVER HAD MONEY ON PISS BOY TO DRINK PISS . . . CONGRATULATIONS! Yes, it seems that Piss Boy still doesn't know the difference between a Schooner of Piss (bodily fluid) and a Schooner of Piss (alcohol). What he ingested was severely dehydrated, it would've sat somewhere around 1.25 on the piss dehydration scale (when asked to confirm, Piss Boy sooked up and said, 'Fuck off'), so to whomever was the pissee, a few Hydralytes are in order.

At the turn of nine, here is the score update:

Windmill 6 under

Gatesy 6 under

Dennis 5 under

Pricey 5 under

Fangs 4 under

Mud 4 under

Hally 4 under

Walshy *3 under (*Bubbler Piss doesn't count)

Big Sexy 3 under

No one else worth mentioning.

Hole 10—The Rat Famish

To start the back nine we've decided to give Fumbles a chance at proving how clean he can be by taking five schooner groundies in a row. He started off strong, showing good technique, getting his fingers down into the carpet and cradling the schooner. The second groundie was just as clean, good technique, strong base, ran through it cleanly. The third involved a slight bobble, but the crowd decided it was still clean. The fourth was back to his best. Ran through the schooner with confidence and didn't look like fumbling. The fifth effort was where the pressure became too much. Tensing up, he has made a meal of it and grabbed the glass so hard that it has shattered in his hands. An impromptu medical assessment has determined that yes, this will need stitches, and a call to the club doc has been made. The broken glass has also meant we have been kicked out of this venue before the half an hour was up. All players receive par score for the hole.

Hole 11—The Four

Sixty has disappeared off the face of the earth. We suspect that after seeing Fumbles get in that extra touch session he felt like he had to go and get his own extras in early. Someone go and check the club, he's probably 100 groundies deep at the moment.

For those of us staying on the course, Dennis has made a big surge, taking advantage of the Any Drinks Allowed rule for this venue, and is loading up on double shot vodka sodas. Pricey is neck and neck with him. Windmill looks likely too. Highlight of the hole: Freezemaster being utilised (Sixty's absence passed it to Walshy) and the loser being the bloke who looks like Georgey-Boy and thinks that we're all getting around him. A slow 'Virgin' chant in the direction of the fake Georgey took over the entire pub.

Hole 12—The Duke

I ACTUALLY CANNOT BELIEVE WHAT WALSHY HAS JUST DONE . . . There is a 21st going on here and somehow he convinced the father of the bloke to let him give a speech.

Walshy took the microphone and recited, word for word, a piece of commentary from his goal after the siren to win the Talent League Grand Final. Not only that, the entire Pissants Open Field rode the wave of excitement and crashed the stage, throwing themselves and their schooners over Walshy after his final cry of 'IT'S A GOAL! IT'S A BALL BUSTING GOAL!' Better yet, the father of the kid whose birthday it is joined in the celebrations, copping one in the face as he did.

Hole 13

Hi, unsure if anyone will see this, but your friend left his phone open on the table before leaving the venue. We will keep it behind the bar if you want to come back and get it. Thanks, the Duke Staff.

Hole 14—Duke 2.0

Courtesy of the punishment drinks I have just been made to consume, I can no longer be fucked with this. Scores TBC.

Hole 15—Sharkfins

Thanks, Basil. I just want to give you a bit of an insight into the Saturday afternoon team. We're a bunch of unique individuals—Malthouse, Harley, Zempilas, McLachlan and myself. We're gonna engage with our minds and our hearts. We're gonna exchange ideas, thoughts and even our energy. And to speak from your heart you need to have courage. You need to be honest and authentic. We're not always going get it right. And sometimes, you're not going to agree with us. But that's okay, because just like you, we care. Just like you, we're passionate about the game. So if you want to come along for the ride, join us on Saturday arvos, because we just love the footy.

Hole 16—Doc's house

Doc's house is the hole now and we're all drinking so come fuck up with the doc and winner is first one to get here now we're playing play! Come play! Playyyy!!!!!! BELL AVENUE GET HERE BRING DRINKS TO drinks and don't be a little pussy cunt. Sick of littttle virginssss not having a cracckkkk. Sixty doing extra virgins at the club!

SCORE UPDATE COURTESY OF DOC

Gentlemen, in my various conversations I have been able to ascertain the following information:

Pricey 12 under

Dennis 11 under

Hally 10 under

Fangs 10 under

Windmill 10 under

Gatesy 10 under

Walshy 9 under

In my expert medical opinion, none of you are fit to continue drinking at another venue. So, in accordance with the rules I have just read above, it is my honour to announce Pricey as the Pissants Open winner. Congratulations, Pricey.

THE MIRROR COMES AROUND

Coach Mac

. . . the mirror comes around . . . this guy next to me is saying something . . . shit . . . what's that? Oh yeah, I love the communal aspect of coke too . . . Yeah, yeah . . . Yeah . . . it really does bring people together, doesn't it? Christ, his jaw is swinging and his pupils are the size of craters . . . Head shaped like a box too . . . Shit it's dark in here . . . and who the fuck are these people . . . fuck . . . where was I . . . doesn't matter, it's my turn now *** *** *** fuck, that's pretty decent shit . . . yeah, that is decent rack, here you can go next . . . yeah, go for it . . . what's mine is yours . . . have we met before? No, no sorry . . . I don't think we have . . . no, I don't really know anyone here . . . I actually . . . I don't know how I got here . . . funny that . . . Ah, have I heard of a place called Kittens before? Can't say I have . . . oh, really? And it's just down the road? Well . . . I'm ok for now . . . but maybe a bit later I'll come . . . thanks for asking though . . . ok . . . see ya later . . . Who the fuck was that guy? . . . Oh, sorry, did I say that out loud . . . no, my mistake . . . I just . . . who was that guy? . . . ah huh . . . ah huh . . . Douggie . . . cool, and

82

how does he fit in here? . . . He's Ray's Dealer . . . and Ray is . . . oh right . . . I met Ray before . . . yeah, yeah, yeah he's the guy who cycles . . . works for his dad in that warehouse . . . yeah, seemed like an alright guy . . . cool, so he pays Douggie 450 a week and he just rocks up wherever he is and gives him rack . . . That's a pretty good deal . . . no, I don't have Snapchat . . . I know what it is though . . . didn't know people used it for coke though . . . that's pretty crazy . . . younger generations, eh . . . What's that? Oh fuck, really . . . he didn't mention that . . . ah huh . . . ah huh . . . fuck, there's a bit of coke in my nostril that I can taste . . . get it without them noticing . . . act interested . . . ah huh . . . ah huh . . . wow, so he's on the sex offenders list for that? Shit, that's bad luck . . . how was he to know that the kids on the webcam were that old . . . and everyone at their school was watching it, and he's just the one who happened to film it? . . . Shit, if she was a year older he would've been ok? And what if . . . sorry, this might be a stupid question . . . what if Douggie was a year younger? Shit he would've been fine too . . . ah huh . . . ah huh . . . Hey, I'll be back in a second, I'm just going to get some more drinks, do you want any . . . you sure? Ok, no worries . . . I'll be . . . I'll be back in a second . . . actually, before I go . . . just one more little line if that's ok . . . sure, thanks . . . *** *** *** Yeah, fuck that is pretty good stuff . . . where . . . where did you get it from? . . . I might have to get some because the stuff I've got lately is shithouse . . . baby powder . . . it's bad . . . ok, cool, well if we need a bit more later on then I'll come for sure . . . yeah . . . yeah . . . ok, I'll be back in a sec . . . Man, that was good coke . . . pull yourself together a bit Mac . . . don't go over the edge yet . . . you're still in control . . . Just have a couple of drinks to level you out a bit . . . bring you up, bring you down . . . ok, what's in the fridge here . . . Woah, what the fuck is that dog . . . that's not even a dog . . . that looks like one of those things from Star Wars . . . Hey, have you guys seen this dog . . . look at it . . . it's like . . . like one of those Star Wars things . . . Fuck . . . they think I'm a right prick don't they . . . that guy in the cowboy hat was looking at me like I had no right to be here . . . Well, maybe I don't . . . but I am here . . . so we may as well all get along . . . hmmm . . . why does this cunt only have American beers in the fridge . . . what the fuck . . . what else has he got . . . ah, bottle of vodka in the freezer . . . that could do . . . and a bunch of orange wines . . . every fucker is into that these days . . . I'll just take the vodka . . . that'll get me nice and settled . . . then I can have another line . . . then I should be right . . . Oh, hey, can see you're having a little trouble rolling that note there . . . just ah, give me the little ring thing off that can over there would you . . . yeah, rip it off . . . ok, here's a little junky trick for you . . . Fuck, did I just say junky trick . . . you really shouldn't say junky trick Mac . . . fuck . . . Ah, so yeah, there you go, it'll stay together now . . . oh, that's really nice of you . . . are you sure? Well, it would be rude of me not to then, wouldn't it *** *** *** Yeah, shit that's good gear too . . . fuck, what's with everyone here having good gear? It's crazy . . . I really need to hang out with you guys more often don't I . . . me? I'm a mechanic . . . yeah, fix cars . . . yeah . . . done it for a while . . . anyway, what do you do? . . . ah huh . . . ah huh . . . oh wow, the kids must love that . . . that's a real respectable job . . . I'm sure they love seeing you come in with your clown make up on . . . can you juggle? Sorry, that's a stupid thing to ask isn't it . . . Hey can you give me a second, I've just got to go to the bathroom quickly . . . shit, shit, shit . . . Can you juggle . . . what kind of fucking question is that . . . you idiot . . . and a mechanic? Christ, they could've asked any sort of follow up and you'd be cooked . . . that's not the line . . . speaking of lines . . . fuck, where's that guy from before . . . I need to hit up his dealer . . . that was good shit . . . pure shit . . . Ah, the drip's waning . . . I need a bit more now . . . Hey, hey, have you seen that guy with the . . . the ah . . . fuck what was he wearing . . . doesn't matter . . . actually, hey, where are you guys going . . . oh really? Mind if I jump in . . . I'm keen on grabbing some myself as a matter of fact . . . yeah, you're welcome to go in on mine if you want some more . . . but I'm getting some regardless . . . yep . . . oh shit, Uber's here now? Well, what are we doing . . . let's hit the road . . . I'll squeeze in the back . . . not a problem . . . Hey that party was fun wasn't it . . . did you guys know the host? . . . Nah, I actually, I didn't know anyone there . . . I'm just a stray that got brought in . . . but everyone was super lovely . . . oh, hey, sorry if this is a bit much, but do you mind if I get a little bump of that now . . . fuck, that's so kind of you, I'll give you some of mine when we get to the place . . . which is . . . where are we going again? Ah, doesn't matter *** *** *** Yeah, that's good shit. Good. Shit . . . Makes my teeth feel like they're about to explode . . . that's the sign it's good stuff . . . Oh, what's that . . . we're here? Shit that was quick . . . Alright, cool . . . calm . . . pull it together for a bit here . . . get your gear . . . then fuck off . . . then get away from these people . . . fuck, here comes my brain again . . . where have you been you prick . . . ok . . . shit . . . what the fuck is this scene . . . a fucking garage . . . weights set in the corner . . . three young dudes . . . really young dudes . . . shirts off . . . they're the dealers? Fuck me . . . Hey, I'm after just one . . . Oh, is that your dog? Yeah that's a nice dog . . . Fuck me the cunt's chained up like a dragon . . . One is how much? Shit . . . that's expensive . . . so how much for two? Ah, ok . . . just the one . . . yeah . . . Ummm, no sorry your friend doesn't look familiar to me, sorry . . . should he? . . . What the fuck, he's just spun his beer into a little whirlpool thing and sculled it then licked the bottle . . . Ah, yeah, that was cool . . . oh, you have how many followers? . . . Oh, on TikTok . . . yeah, I'm not on there . . . too old . . . that's why I wouldn't recognise you . . . that's impressive though . . . so, yeah . . . cool . . . just the one thanks . . . beautiful . . . ok . . . hey, do you have a bathroom around here? Thanks, yeah, just going to go for a quick piss . . . Nah, nah, I'm ok . . . I don't need a beer . . . thanks for asking though, that's very kind of you . . . Fuck, where am I . . . let's get home . . . in a bit though, just need to level out . . . ★★★ ★★★ ★★★

WHAT IS SAID VERSUS WHAT IS MEANT

Matchday Appearance: Interview during half-time of Seniors' game
Location: Members' Lounge
Talent: Fangs, Budget

	What is said	**What is meant**
Journalist:	So, mate, what a rollercoaster of a first half that was. What do you make of the game so far?	Ok kid, we've got ten minutes to kill. You're already five minutes late to this thing and looking bored. Let's just be professional about it, ok? You blokes usually give me absolutely nothing, so please, for once can it not be like drawing blood from a stone? The media manager has assured me that you're a bit of a talker.
Player:	Yeah look, it's a good contest out there. The opposition has been in	'Mate'? Christ, did you not read that bit of paper with my name on it? Yes, elephant in the room, I'm five minutes late, but you're

some good form, and we knew what to expect coming in. But it looks like our boys are sticking to the game plan that we came up with during the week. Sure, they got a run on there with a couple of goals in the first, but we wrestled momentum back and that started with our midfield who are really cracking in hard. I think it's going to be an interesting second half. They'll definitely come out firing, so I think whoever weathers the other team's pressure better is going to go a long way towards winning the game.

lucky I'm even here. None of the boys were up for a trade. The only reason I'm here with a morsel of care is so I can get fifty bucks off Shaggers, who has bet me that I can't work the phrase '*Batman: The Dark Knight*' into our little interview. Should be easy enough . . . Alright, fuck, how many people are in here? Fifty? Sixty? Do they even care that we are here? Most of them haven't even turned around yet. God. How embarrassing. I reckon ninety per cent of the people here don't even know our names. Or if they do, they'll do that thing where they stand off for a bit with a scarf or hat and ask for our autograph and then when we are midway through signing they'll say something like *Sorry, I don't mean to be rude or anything, but what's your name* before explaining how they aren't a huge fan but they know their kid will love the signature. Jesus, *Weather the other team's pressure*? Pulled that straight from the Handbook of Bullshit Players Say. What's really going on is that we have better players than them and those better players are playing better football. That's it. Look at our midfield. Look at their midfield. Look at our forward line. Look at theirs. We have better players. That's all that you need to know.

Journalist: Let's hope you're right and the boys do crack in straight away in the second half. So, just on the boys, it looks like a pretty close-knit group out there. What is the feeling like in the locker room at the moment? I'm sorry for these questions. But we can't really go for *War and Peace* in this time slot. If I'm being honest with you, this wasn't my dream at all. I never wanted to be a sports journo. I got into the whole journalism gig because I wanted to bring down governments. Shit, I have a degree in literature and political science, but they needed someone to cover the sports desk and then a month secondment turned into a full-time role. Then, well, I fell in 'love', had a kid and now I have to pay for school fees and guess what? That literature degree doesn't do it, so I've got to come do gigs like this on the side. Do you have any idea how much school fees are?

Player: Yeah, we really are a close-knit group. We spend a lot of time together on and off the track. It's like going to work with forty of your best mates every day. And we're big on being a united team. We value trusting each other and when you go out into the heat of the battle, it's good to look at the bloke next to Yeah, no shit I'm close with my teammates. But what do you mean by *close*? Christ, I've got a photographic memory for every one of my teammate's cocks as a result of the three showers a day we have together. Don't believe me? Well, shit, I didn't think it'd be true either, but here's a little taster. This bloke beside me, Budget? His is pretty thick; dead white with albino pubes. He's one of the few uncircumcised at the club. He had a semi in the showers one time and literally turned to face the wall when the room was full trying to get

89

you and know what you're going to get.

the flow of blood to redirect itself. Everyone knew what was going on. We figure he just really enjoyed the session. That's also how I know the size of it doesn't really change when it gets hard. Windmill's gets wider the further down it goes. It looks like a Hammerhead shark. Deep down I know the cunt takes great pride in it when he's swinging it around in front of people after he's had a few drinks, acting like he could knock you out with it, which he probably could. Pringles' is like Windmill's, only bigger. Which is saying something. It's the biggest cock I've ever seen. Hence the name. Thing resembles a Pringles can. Apparently, he's had birds tell him it's too big. At least that's what Shep used to say anyway, and they had a threesome together one time—Shep and Pringles. I normally wouldn't believe any of the shit that Shep said because he was a chronic liar, but he filmed it and sent it around. Also, it was with a girl who used to work upstairs in the marketing team, and then they put her on reception so we all had to walk past her every morning and act like we hadn't seen her, Shep and Pringles fucking each other's brains out. Pricey's got a cock like a shrivelled anteater snout. It's a different skin tone than the rest of

his body because he's so tanned
and his cock is so pale. He looks
Mediterranean; maybe he's got a
bit of wog in him. Squidman's got
a bit of a fire poker. Whitey and
Richo have the exact same cock,
which is funny because that's the
only resemblance between them.
Whitey being good value on the
piss and Richo being the hard ass
captain who actually can't sink any
piss without screwing up his face.
But god forbid you say anything to
him when he pours half a schooner
down his shirt instead of in his
mouth at Mad Monday for the traditional sculls. He'll go full sooky la
la on you, but being the captain and
all, you can't peep back. Georgey-
Boy has what I'd expect most
people think the average cock looks
like. He's got a thick bush around it
which indicates he hasn't had a root
since he moved here. Gatesy's is a
bit bigger than Georgey-Boy's and
not unlike Pricey's in shape. Thing
is, you'd pick Gatesy to have a big
cock just by looking at him. He's got
big ears and carries himself like he's
got nothing to hide. Bubbles' is tiny.
Almost like a third nut. Same with
Mud, but Mud's has a bit more of
a point to it than Bubbles'—it kind
of looks like he's perpetually just
getting out of the ice bath. Bubbles'
is literally round. Even if he does

wear speedos, which he does on occasion, joining the Mystery Dick Club, you can see his little bob of a cock poking out at attention.

Journalist: Well, that's great to hear. You can really tell watching from the stands that this is a group who care about each other and want to go as far as possible with one another. Now, just on your own season to date, how's your form going? Are you excited to get a game out there soon with the boys?

No, like seriously. Do you have any idea how much it costs raising a kid? We are paying $200 a week for music lessons alone, and I'm sorry, but the kid is no Louis Armstrong. I mean, from time to time it might sound like he's playing jazz, but it sure isn't intentional. I've started staying back at the office later and later each day so I don't get home and hear him practicing a baroque version of the Itsy Bitsy Spider on repeat. And let me tell you, my absence is adding a lot of strain to the marriage right now. Couples therapy . . . that's burning a hole in my pocket too. Sometimes I genuinely wonder if we're capable of monogamous relationships. Seriously, the concept of marriage and love is such a socially constructed idea. But I'd never dare say that aloud. Yeah, therapy says we are supposed to air out our feelings to stop from building resentments. But imagine if I said that one. I'd be out on my arse quick smart. And me, getting back onto the market now? I'd have no chance.

Player: Oh yeah, competition for spots is hot right now. That's the sign of a really healthy list. We have forty odd blokes all fit and healthy and all of them would be trusted to take that field. I know I've got some things in my game to work on and I'm doing everything I can to be in that team and be right so that when my opportunity comes I'll take it. We played earlier today and I was pretty happy with my performance. I think this footy club has a lot to look forward to in the future, the ressies had a great win today. You know, some of the first year players, like Budget who's with me today, are really exciting and we're all pushing each other to get better constantly, and that's a great thing for the club.

Thank you dearly for the reminder that I am of no utility to the team with my position here, talking to you. Am I doing enough to get a game? I don't fucking know. This week the Big Fella has gone with Aidz, who he has some sort of pscyho-social, paternal soft spot for. I don't think I've ever seen the guy play a good game, but he gets babied because he carries with him a sense of confidence more fragile than a piece of tissue paper (note to self: new nickname for Aidz— Tissues). If I had his numbers, I'd be treated like a lepper. But when he has them, it's what's expected of him, so it's all good. Carry on then. Christ, no one in the team respects Aidz. His only mate was Shep and he's fucked off to another club because they threw a bit of coin at him. Sure, sometimes I do feel bad that we don't get around him, but at the end of the day, fuck him he's an absolute deckchair socially. And the prick's getting $600,000 a year and carries on like he wants to get traded whenever the tail end of the season comes around. He sulks in the corner and just wants everyone to say, *No, no we want you, come back.* And the whole club enables him.

Shit, sometimes I think maybe I should go to another club and if I get on my hands and knees

I could get the Aidz treatment. Given the chance, I could create a whole new image for myself. Drop all the baggage I got here and escape the ideas imprinted in the coaches' minds. Walk in and be Mr Hard Cunt and go around acting like I don't give a shit about anyone's feelings. Act like I was some sort of fucking secret ops robot that some nerdy prick like Zuckerberg programmed for one thing and one thing only: to win matches of footy. Now would that fulfil me? Who cares. Beats doing things like this.

Journalist: Well, all of us here wish you the best for the rest of the season. Be great to see you out on that field cracking in like the rest of the boys. Let's all hear it one more time for our special guests today.

Seriously, you think any women will be interested in me with this hairline? Look at the arches. I've been taking Finasteride since I was eighteen and that's done sweet fuck all. If anything, I would've preferred to have gone bald sooner, because then at least I'd have put a bit more effort into my body to compensate for it. But now? Fucking hell. Life for me is just one perpetual back and forth about shaving it all off. From a practical sense, how much time each day will I save not looking at my hair in the mirror wondering if it is time to shave it off? I have not been able to walk past a mirror, or any reflective surface (car windows, the glass doors of the apartment block next door, spoons) without my eyes homing in on the ever-deepening pockets on top of my head. If I do this twenty times a day, each time is an interruption to the flow of work. Each glance a cessation of momentum. In a numeric sense, there'd be two to three seconds at each glance. Sometimes I have spent up to twenty seconds staring at myself in the mirror. So all up, I'd lose about two minutes every day to this exercise. Two minutes per day. That is almost fifteen minutes per week. That is time that could be spent learning a language, practising meditation: any of those pursuits that would make me a more whole and complete version of myself. And that doesn't even include the time spent thinking about it (or the weight of unconscious thoughts too, which seems incalculable). Going completely bald will be as if a weight has been lifted from me. How much of a difference will the space freed in my mind make? But if I do it, then I'll be bald and all bald men look the same. It's fucked how little character is in our faces. There are two categories of bald guys. The tough Hollywood stars like Jason Statham and Woody Harrelson to a lesser degree and then there's the guys with a lot of charisma. The guys who walk into a room and are the centre of attention because they are so fucking hilarious and chivalrous. Do I have the personality to pull that off? I don't have the body for the tough guy approach. Add another one to the list. What's his name. *Pulp Fiction* boxer guy. Can't remember his name. Fuck. He's another one though. He gets women. He totally gets women. But their look is so engrained into the public psyche. It's like some crooked archetype—maybe I could leverage off that. But I haven't worked out in a long time and I really can't be fucked trying to get back into it again. I'd have to buy weights because there's no way I could go to the gym looking like this. I'd be so embarrassed. So maybe I'll do that. I'll buy some weights online and then pump iron at home until I feel like I look good enough to go to the gym and use the big boy weights. I'll watch some YouTube videos and see what the ultimate home workout is. What if I just buy a couple of dumbbells? But then I can't overload when I improve. Ok maybe I'll just stick to body weight stuff. Can you get jacked doing bodyweight exercises? But it's not like I even want to get jacked or anything, I just want to be trim. I don't want to put on any weight because that involves meal prep and protein supplements. I just want to have a decent V-line around my hips and maybe a couple of veins that pop out and maybe a sixpack. In fact, all I want is a sixpack. I'll just do core exercises—you don't need weights for that. I'll start doing one set a day. Maybe two. No sorry, two sessions a day. I can totally do that and get a sixpack. I'd look good with a sixpack and a shaved head.

Actually, what's the point in getting trim? No one can see it anyway if I'm wearing a shirt. If I'm standing at a bar, I'll look the same as all other bald guys from behind. Jesus, if I do end up back out on the market and I get a new girlfriend and we go out she won't be able to come up and hug me from behind because she won't be able to tell if it's me or some other bald guy. Worse yet, what if she goes and hugs someone thinking they are me and it ends up being another bald guy and then they hit it off and he takes her home and fucks her? Fuck.

Player: Thanks for having me. Just ah, one more thing from me, you know, you look a lot like one of the characters from

Done. And not a moment too soon. Budget gets off the hook without having to say a word and that's the easiest fifty bucks I've ever made. Pay up, Shaggers. Truth be told mate, you look nothing like any

Batman: The Dark Knight. Sorry, that's a bit random.

of the characters from that film. Though I'd have to double check with Shaggers seeing as it is his favourite movie. Who knows, you could be a bit of a closet sicko, a bit of a Joker. Never judge a book by its cover. But, you know, with a shaved head, you'd look a bit like Bruce Willis. Maybe that's something for you to consider.

PARIS

Elliott
DAY 24

I am sitting at an intersection in the 6th, drinking an espresso at a red table. This morning I bought a travel pass for five days so I can get around on the trains. The people here don't wake early either; the cafés are still closed at 8 am. There is an overflowing bin across the road and a vandalised letterbox. The guy next to me is wearing a scarf, also red, and reading a book. He finishes his coffee, places two coins on the table, then leaves. I have spent all morning repeating: 'Sorry, my French is not good—do you speak English?'

My first impression of France is that the sky is a different shade of blue here. While waiting at the station in Amsterdam, I got a haircut from a man who told me he had spent five years in Australia where he'd met the love of his life. They would always go to Thailand together, he said. They are no longer a couple, but he is going to visit her in Thailand in six months' time. Pete and I had a Coke and some chips on the train and I gave up the window seat for a woman who needed to use

99

the table for her laptop. She spent ten minutes working on a presentation and then didn't use it again for the rest of the trip. Pete sat opposite me, nervous the whole time that his luggage had been left behind because he kept getting notifications from his air tag. There was a dog in our carriage as well.

When we were packing our bags in Amsterdam I told Pete that I needed to be on my own and would stay in Paris when he left to meet our other friends. I had gone to a café that morning and while I was waiting for my coffee I saw a photo and video of Eliza out at a club on one of her friend's Instagram stories and it made me feel like there were thousands of small needles being pushed into my neck and arms. The thought of her out, happy, of new men approaching her. Of her going home with them. I felt my whole body constrict and I said *fuck* out loud and walked out of the café. I sat down by a canal and messaged my brother, asking if he was free for a call.

When he picked up I started crying again.

'How's it going?' he said, his voice softening, like he knew what I was going to say.

I took time before saying, 'It's not good. It's not working. This isn't working. I still miss her. I still just want her.'

My brother said, 'You've got to get out and meet people. You don't want to regret this trip.'

'I know, but I just don't know how. I don't know how to be happy. I'm scared I'm just waiting to come home so I can message her again.'

He told me how he'd gone travelling after his second breakup and how he felt sad too. It was the first time we'd talked about that breakup. Now he and his wife were awaiting their first child in a month. Or two months. Two months.

The last thing he said to me on the phone, 'It's only been a few weeks. These things take time.'

DAY 25

The water in front of me is between green and brown. Rippled by the wind. Olive chairs and small swallows by my feet. There are no clouds in the sky. Blue. People run here too. People run everywhere. And there are poor people everywhere and a woman was rugged up with her two children on a street corner last night and we walked past a man on the sidewalk who was unconscious in front of an expensive clothing store. Another man checked his pulse. We kept walking. Today I think I will just walk around and not feel that familiar need. Not look at the clock as it counts down or up or whichever way it is clocks count. The wind picks up.

DAY 26

Scenes in front of the Eiffel Tower—a woman with two large balloons, one in the shape of a three, the other a seven. Her husband, or brother maybe, it's hard to tell, takes videos of her doing different poses with the balloons. Then a woman in a black leather outfit and black hat does a Michael Jackson dance. She's wearing sneakers, Nikes, I think. She does the same moves a few times, checks the video then leaves. A group of seven wrap their arms around each other and do a coordinated set of moves. Everyone is dancing and filming themselves. The girl to my left is drinking and says something to me about the people doing the videos. She's American. She leaves and doesn't say goodbye. When I check my phone there's something about a rapper being shot in the head. TMZ has photos of it online. I head home to charge my phone and message a girl called Madeleine who I have matched with on Hinge and says she will show me around town. The shower at the hotel fills with water and I realise once it's up to my shins that I've left the plug in.

DAY 28

Last night was my first night alone. I had a wine in the common room of the hostel and the receptionist asked what I was doing for the night.

'Not much,' I said.

He replied, 'Everyone is going to the rugby, Australia versus France.'

'I didn't even know it was on.'

'Do you like sports? You look like a sports guy.'

I felt like laughing at the question.

'Not really, not so much.'

'Well, you should go anyway, it's a spectacle,' he said.

So I did. I bought a ticket and caught the train to Stade de France where the queue to get in was very long. There were police patrolling the front, almost like a riot squad. I sat next to two young French guys, late teens at most, and when they sung the French national anthem they stuck one hand up in the air and held the other balled up against their chests. The French have an enthusiasm to them, it is worn on their faces and in the way they express some words. I stayed till half time and then left because I didn't want to get caught in the chaos of people funnelling themselves towards the station. While waiting for the train, I bought two chocolate bars for my dinner from a vending machine. I followed myself on maps the entire way back to the station near the hostel.

When I returned to the hostel lobby the receptionist was watching the television screen intently with a few people.

'What are you doing here?' he said.

'I left early to beat the traffic.'

He just looked at me strangely and then returned his attention to the screen.

The score was 26 to 25 France's way with less than a minute to go. I watched the final plays with the group and then I sat in the common room and picked up a French version of *Catcher in the Rye* and then got a glass of wine. I put the book back and thought to enter a conversation about tennis and Novak Djokovic that was going on beside me, but sat reading Anne Frank's diary instead.

Books. You always escape into books. That's another thing that Eliza said. She'd asked me to stop taking them to breakfast so we could just talk.

I'd just finished the first page when a woman at the high table next to me asked if I wanted to join her game of Jenga. Eliza and I had played on New Year's Eve once. The week before we took our first break. Driving home from her parents she asked if we could go to the park and talk. *I don't know what's wrong with me*, I said. And I started crying. I spent the next week running around the park hoping to pass her so she could see I was working on myself. Trying to change.

'Do you know how to play?' the woman asked.

'You just take the blocks out till it collapses, right?'

'Right.'

She was setting up the game and then she stopped and said, 'But you mustn't use two hands! You can only use one.'

'One hand, ok, got it.'

The woman's name was Nora and she was from Holland. She had blonde hair and told me she had two kids. She had just bought her youngest their first bike. Apparently most people in Holland learn how to ride a bike before going to school.

'How many bikes do you own?' I asked.

'Most people have an everyday bike, a work bike, and a bike that they can afford to lose—so if they are going out at night they don't mind leaving it behind.'

I asked if Nora wanted a glass of wine and she hesitated for a second and then said, 'Sure.'

During the game she became quite competitive. She was very fixed on winning and whenever I won she'd demand a rematch. Her friend Ella (not pronounced Ella but she didn't mind how people pronounced it), who was from Israel, came and sat with us. Ella and Nora meet up once a year and have done for fifteen years.

'How did you guys meet?' I asked.

'We were both in a hostel like this, staying in the bunks opposite each other. We both woke up hungover after a night out and since then we've been friends.'

They are here now because there is a tennis tournament on they want to watch.

Before long, a guy from Pakistan, also in town for the tennis, joined us and so did a girl from California. When I said where I was from, he pointed to the girl and said, 'She said you'd be Australian.' While the rest of the table talked and drank, the girl from California and I exchanged glances and I caught her staring at me several times. It got to midnight and one more guy joined, Matthew from Canada. I had a few glasses of wine and was the most fun I had been for some time. We said our goodbyes and then I fell asleep with the light on. When I awoke, it was 8:46 am and the room was very dark.

DAY 29

I sat with the Californian girl and talked over breakfast. She told me she'd found a three-wheeled scooter on the side of the road yesterday and that was how she was getting around.

'Here, look,' she said, showing me a video of her moving very slowly on the scooter.

'It was just lying there,' she said, taking a bite out of her toast.

'So you took it?'

'Uh huh.'

I asked what she did and she said she wanted to be a nurse, but deferred accidentally and had been in Paris for four months working as a nanny. But the work was more intense than she'd agreed to, and the people she was working for cancelled her French lessons. She was going to have to do something about that. Californians talk in a way that makes you feel like they are always bored by you or looking at something behind you or off to the side. Her name was Christina, and she said she'd learned French for four years but couldn't speak it.

DAY 30

I was at a very French and very fancy restaurant. Chequered serviettes and no soft drinks. There was a date taking place in front of me: she was American, talking about how she ran 6 km in twenty-five minutes; he was French and asking lots of questions while playing with a thread on his jeans under the table. She was speaking English slowly and using her hands a lot to gesture. The couple ordered the half chicken, fries for him and salad for her. I started going through my wallet and pulled out a piece of paper with Eliza's signature on it and I felt the fall again. As though the air couldn't hold me and I was sliding down.

DAY 32

I met Madeleine out the front of the Pompidou. She told me she speaks French, English and Spanish; her mother was Argentinian, and her father French Algerian. He was a language professor but used to play music at the Moulin Rouge. The line to the Pompidou was very long. She explained how it was a gift to the nation from the president upon his departure.

'It is something all of our presidents do,' she said.

We sat down for coffee and exchanged stories. She was twenty-six and well travelled. I asked how her brain works when thinking in different languages. She said she didn't consider herself multilingual because she still had to translate words in her head and that her language use was based on who she was with and what she was doing. When discussing politics with her father, she spoke French. With her mother, she spoke Spanish. With me, she sounded quite Australian, but occasionally a word would come out in a very French way—*pardon*, for instance. That was very French.

We sat in an outdoor area of the café, tucked in the far corner on a comfortable velvet lounge. She ordered on my behalf and then when we went to pay she explained that going up to the counter here was usually considered rude.

'It's a very Australian thing to do,' she said.

'Everyone here must think I'm an asshole then.'

She smiled at me and laughed.

'Not everyone,' she said.

We finished our coffees and began walking through the streets.

'I want to take you somewhere that I think you will love,' she said.

It was an artists' residency, six storeys high and open to the public. I found it more interesting than any of the other galleries I'd been to so far on the trip. You could talk to the artists and see the squalor of their working environment. There was paint on the floor and unfinished works and discarded projects all around.

'You can come back and write here,' she said.

'I can pretend I'm one of the artists,' I replied.

'Or maybe one of their pieces,' she said.

'Broken soul, flesh and bones.'

We caught the train towards Montmartre and climbed the stairs to the Sacré-Cœur. There was a man out on the front steps offering trips around Paris and a busker singing Ed Sheeran and Coldplay. Inside the church there were elderly women reverently touching the statue of St Paul and, beneath it all, a gentle hum constantly playing. We walked the streets of Montmartre. I said this was the Paris I had wanted to see. The cobbled streets and the lighting, it's a very beautiful place. Or maybe it's just that I've seen it so many times in movies and on TV that to me, this feels like somewhere more special than it is.

'You are lucky that there aren't many people here now,' she said. 'Sometimes this is the worst part of Paris.'

Madeleine would stop and explain the history to me: Louis XIV, the places where van Gogh painted, Napoleon the Third and how his architect redesigned the city and the differences in temperament of the districts and how everyone thought there was some deep and historical meaning behind the Wall of Love and all of the locks, but it had been a thing on *Sex and the City*, and that's why people did it. I found that funny.

My favourite story came over dinner, after several wines at the Bouillon, where we were sat next to two elderly men. The one beside me was drawing a young man seated at a table across the hall, and he asked if the waiter would go and give the image to the young man, and when he did, I watched as the young man's friends all laughed and commented. The young man then started doing a drawing of his own, of the man beside me, and he gave it to him before leaving.

Madeleine told me the story of how her great-grandfather had been at a bouillon at the end of the war with a young artist who had fought with him. The artist said that he would one day be famous. He ripped the corner from a placemat and drew on it and then gave it to her great-grandfather. I felt I knew where this was going. When her grandfather rode home, he threw away the paper because it was flapping in the wind.

'It was Picasso wasn't it?' I said.

'Yes,' she said. 'It was Picasso. Stop ruining my stories!'

We walked around the 9th and stood outside the Palais Garnier and then we walked to the Café de la Paix. I said that this had to be the best place in the world for watching people, even though there was nobody around. We walked through the Golden Square and saw the Ritz hotel and it was cold and I could see my breath when I breathed out but did not mention it.

DAY 33

I was feeling very sad. I walked the quiet cobbled streets and I could not stop thinking about Eliza. I thought about how she sat down on the couch and cried and said she couldn't even say it. I thought about the noise she'd make before she cried, like she was almost forcing herself to. I thought of the last night we slept side by side and I couldn't remember if we held each other or not. I thought of how we sat on the balcony at her parents and drank tea for hours while it was warm and still and how the ocean was close by and you could hear the waves and how that moment was the last time I had been happy. I was thinking about it all again. I kept walking because I thought if I moved the thoughts might go away, but they did not.

DAY 35

I was sitting on the bed listening to Madeleine tell me a story about an opera singer from Marseilles who ran a drug cartel. Madeleine was wearing a black top and a red bra. The night before we'd had many drinks at a bar and then moved on to another bar, called Bar Australia, where we met a woman called Diva and her partner Tom who had studied together in Paris and fallen in love and lived in a small unit in Montmartre.

Diva was very drunk and was giving us all drags of her cigarette and talking about how her professors at university had smoked pot with her and how they had all tried to sleep with her. Tom was just very quiet while she was telling us this but Diva assured us it all happened before his time.

When you said something to Diva it would take her a moment to reply, like she was waiting for you to say more.

I went inside to order more drinks and got myself a triple shot of vodka because I had sobered up on the walk and wasn't feeling very drunk. When I rejoined the group, Diva was saying, 'Do you guys want to come and shake your ass on the dancefloor? Tom and I are going to go and shake our asses.'

Tom, who was quite young and had red eyes, followed Diva to the dancefloor.

Madeleine and I left while they were inside and walked towards my hotel. We bought a bottle of red wine from a convenience store on the way for nine euros. When we got inside I poured her a glass and I drank from the bottle. I was trying to get myself drunk so that my brain would switch off. I didn't want her to ask me why I was being odd or strange or if I was ok.

After sex we laid in bed.

'You don't sweat much, it's nice,' she said.

We fell asleep alongside each other and I opened the blinds around 10 am. It was a nice day outside. I asked Madeleine to teach me some French phrases. Like how to ask for another coffee, how to say 'after you' (après vous) and things like that.

Then she crossed her legs and started telling me the story of the opera singer.

When I put my shirt on, she asked if this was me telling her to get out.

DAY 36

It was 8:30 pm and I was sitting in my room feeling tired. I had two cups of wine and splashed water on my face, then took the key down to reception. The man at reception told me to look up at the sky; the moon was nice, he said.

I walked the streets looking for something. A conversation I could understand. Someone I could smile at and join in with. I walked several blocks and saw a projector shooting out against a wall and a group of young liberal-looking uni kids milling outside a gallery. I walked to the cinema to see what was on, but it was all in French. I checked my phone while I walked. In a convenience store I bought two Twix bars and the machine started beeping when I walked away and the woman on the other side of the room called out in French and I said sorry, sorry. She motioned to me, and I didn't understand what she was saying, so I went to just walk off. She called out louder and I turned and she gave me the receipt for the Twix.

I walked up a hill, turned left, then went down another hill and saw an empty seat in an outdoor wine bar. I ordered a glass of red. I figured that if I had four wines I could go back and ask about the art gallery. Four drinks would make me someone else. The guy beside me had a camera tripod and was eating alone and I put my book on the table hoping he would ask what I was reading.

The Dutch couple who had just sat next to me were arguing. I couldn't understand them, but the way he moved his hands and the way she held the menu up to her face without saying anything made it clear. Then when they ordered she didn't get anything, and they had 'just water'.

Someone a few tables down said in English, 'You are not going to marry him, are you? He's fine to date, but you are not going to marry him.'

There was a rat on the road and no one cared.

DAY 37

'You are a masochist,' she said.

'I know.'

'Because you sleep when it is so bright.'

'And with the fan on.'

111

'No, the fan does not mean you are a masochist, just the light. It is too bright.'

'I am not going back to sleep.'

'Come closer.'

I stayed facing away.

'You are so strange.'

'I know.'

We spent another night together. This time I was not as drunk and I would have been content going to sleep on my own.

It felt very much like we were getting deeper into a relationship. I was reading a book on the bed and she asked to borrow a T-shirt when she came out of the shower. She had just shaved her legs. We had stopped off before dinner so she could buy essentials for the night: razors, face wash, make-up remover. She carried them around in a paper bag for the rest of the night.

There was a homeless man sitting in front of a convenience store. We walked inside and she bought him a sandwich, a bag of chips and a bottle of milk. She said that was something her father would always do for homeless people, and she felt that she should do it too.

Earlier that day I had walked to meet her as there was a train strike on. I walked across Paris to the Shakespeare and Company bookshop, which is near where she lives with her mother. I was early, so I sat reading upstairs. A man walked in and pressed a few keys on the piano and then asked the guy in the corner if he could move the chair so he could play and the guy, who was reading Harry Potter, said yes. The man then started playing the most beautiful tune. When he finished he said, 'Sorry, I made a few mistakes.'

Madeleine arrived and said we were going somewhere that

was a surprise. When I asked where, she said that she had not been there and I remembered from a conversation the day before that she had not been to the library. When I guessed where we were going, she was slightly deflated.

'That is why you never let people guess,' I said.

The woman at security yawned and let us through and did not seem very interested in her job.

Inside the library there were no seats. It seemed that people had got there very early to set up. We walked laps around the building.

She said, 'You could come here and write.'

We spent an hour in the library, listening to classical music through the headphones in a booth. She picked up a large book on a fashion brand and flicked through while I took my copy of *Green Hills of Africa* out of my bag.

'I'll go find out where the English books are for you,' she said.

I told her not to bother, that I was happy with the book I had.

From the library we walked into centre of Paris and saw policemen with armour and shields and batons and smoke bombs lining the streets in clusters. There was a sense of something in the air—paranoia, tension. The sky overhead was grey and I felt nerves inside me.

We continued in the direction of the noise and saw smoke near the union protest and walked towards it just down the road from the opera building. When we turned the corner to where the rally was, there was a loud noise beside us. Madeleine was a step ahead of me and next to the bin, which erupted in a large red flame. People around us scattered and she almost fell over. She turned and there was a look of fear on her face and she came straight towards me. I grabbed her arm and we ran back down the street. She was slightly in shock, and it was as though she could not hear me when I asked if she was ok. There were several others that had moved to the safety of the street we were on. An American woman had stopped in the middle of the street saying she was going to have a panic attack and that she just wanted to find the bus.

'Which bus?' we asked.

'The big red one, so I can get a refund.'

Madeleine, who's hearing had returned, said, 'That is very American of you.'

We walked back against the flow of the protest and to a café we had thought to try the night before. Over dinner I learnt that she had an opioid addiction years ago. She had got involved in dealing while in Australia, and said that she'd once caught a train to the Gold Coast from Byron to go to a festival and that at the station there were police sniffer dogs on the platform approaching when she had 150 pills on her. Thankfully the police turned around because someone else had caught their attention. She got on the train and her heart was beating out of her chest. She told me she climbed quickly and was making big money—thousands per deal at one stage—but her own addiction was too serious so she had to remove herself from that world.

We then went back to mine and lay on the bed.

While we lay there she felt my thumb and asked, 'What is this?'

'I bite my fingers,' I said.

'You should not.'

'I know, but I do.'

As I was about to go to sleep she started to kiss me but I turned away.

'Is there something wrong?'

She kissed me again and instead of saying anything we had sex and then we talked for a bit with the lights off.

'Do you think I move around so much now because I had stability as a kid or because I didn't?'

'I don't know,' I said.

She said she was sorry for telling me about her opioid addiction and I thought of how she covered herself during sex and wanted the lights off. That's when she called me a masochist.

I spent a long time in the shower and thought that maybe she would leave while I was in there and leave a note on the bed saying thanks or something like that. She didn't, but she did leave shortly after.

I went out to a café and when I got back to the room I saw her toothbrush on the top of the sink. I thought to myself she'd left it as a joke, as the night before she had said I needed a new one.

Since then I have been thinking of how I want to book my next flight to somewhere else, wherever is cheapest, which I am going to do now.

★

There are many empty seats in the airport. People have their feet on their luggage and the guy next to me is scrunching up a wrapper and taking a sip from a Coke Zero, cherry flavoured. Airports are purgatory. You're nowhere waiting to go somewhere and time seems to operate differently, slower, or faster, I can't quite tell. The lighting makes me tired and you can always hear people walking and putting on their jackets. For lunch I ate two large fries from McDonald's. My bag was heavy on my back while waiting and I didn't get a straw for the drink. I don't think there were straws.

MONKEY FUCKS SPIDER

Fangs

Watching Stick play golf is, as Squidman so eloquently puts it, like watching a monkey trying to fuck a spider. Because of his multiple invasive surgeries (2 × shoulder reconstruction, 1 × ACL) and an assortment of soft tissue injuries too long to name which resulted in veal blood being injected into him by some mad German scientist last off season, his body functions more as a disharmonious conglomerate of independent parts than an operating whole.

Watching him swing, I'm pissing myself laughing because it's one of the few things he's fucking atrocious at. Still, it doesn't stop him from abusing the rest of us after every shot we play.

It truly does make me feel bad for the blokes that he plays on each week. Two hours with Stick in your ear will leave you broken. Stick took tissues out with him one game. Shoved them in his jocks. When the bloke he was on had a shot at goal he pulled them out and asked if he was still having a cry. We'd heard from one of his teammates that the guy had let the waterworks happen in the bathroom at their BNF last year for coming second. The crying sledge in itself is pretty shit. It's the typical 'you're shit' 'nah you're fucking shit' crap that any prick can muster. The rattling part of it is the psychological aspect of the guy then wracking his brain as to *how* Stick knew he'd cried and then trying to figure out which one of his teammates ratted him out. It breaks down the bonds of the team. Last year there was a rumour that an oppo player had left his wife for one of his club's physios. Stick lined up on the bloke, and just before the ball went up he whispered in his ear: 'Which one is she?'

It rattled him big time and the bloke couldn't get near it. That's what Stick does better than anyone I've seen. Plants the seed and watches it grow. That's how he plays a game of footy, a two-hour gardening exercise, and if he doesn't see the fruits of his labour by the third then he just starts hacking away at the weeds.

Stick: Ahhhh fuck you, you stupid fucker!

Today he's gardening in a different way.

Squidman: I don't reckon we'll get through a round carrying Stick.

Stick: Game for fucking virgins.

Shaggers: Good game for you then.

Stick: Oi don't be a little cunt.

Golf is, admittedly, a fucking shit sport. We booked in this round last week on a whim. Only sadistic cunts would do this every week. It's torturous, a schmoozers game for rich kids in suits taking out other rich kids in suits for business meetings. Board members with VIP parking spots and psoriasis on their ballsacks. I hate everything about it. Put a coffee mug on the ground in the office, same shit.

We are uninvited guests. Squidman is standing behind Stick looking at the head of his club like he's Sherlock Holmes.

He bought a new set from the pro shop before we teed off. Set of Callaways with blue handles. To go with the clubs Squidman also bought a glove, bag of balls and five of those long Super Tees. I reckon he's halfway through the bag of balls already because he's too lazy to go and find them when they get lost in the trees. He can hit a long ball though.

Stick pulls another ball out of his pocket and puts it on the tee. He does his Charles Barkley swing routine and slices it hard right. Then he goes full Happy Gilmore and starts beating the shit out of the ground with his club. He's giving it a real go. It's the closest he'll get to therapy anytime soon.

Stick: Can someone give me another ball?!

I'm sitting in the cart and throw him a shitty driving range ball, yellow as Keith Richards' teeth. Beggars can't be choosers. He puts the ball on the tee, winds up with his feet still stuck in the mud and launches the thing into the water off to the left. Shortly following the ball is his club, which travels through the air with more direction than Stick has managed to muster all day.

Shaggers: Going for a little swimmy swim, Stick?

Shaggers sets up his ball on the tee then takes a few little practice swings. He's been hitting them fairly straight all day. So, with full confidence, he opens up his stance a little bit. When he unwinds, he cooks it and the ball slices viciously to the right. It disappears from view and into the ether. And then we hear the crash. The unmistakeable sound of a window exploding into a thousand little pieces.

It wouldn't be much of a deal, except Shaggers is all out of balls and his reputation as a tightarse is well known. He's currently banned from several Coles supermarkets for putting through steak as onions. He reckons they took his mug shot and everything. Single light bulb hanging from the roof sort of situation. He rocked up with one ball today and refused to pay for any more at the pro shop. And he knows that Squidman will never let him live it down if he borrows a ball off him after all the grief he gave him for buying them in the first place.

Without saying a word, Shaggers gets in the cart with me and starts driving. We follow the fenceline around to where we think the ball might have hit. It gets me thinking about how living by a golf course is like living under a flight path. The ratio of hack golfers and the consistency of scheduled flights may exist in parallel.

Shaggers is going silent. In his own head. I'd rather he just lose it than this.

The cart stops hard and fast, almost sending me through the windshield, and Shaggers points up to a broken window. The back gate of the house is open and I'm guessing that this isn't the first time a ball has entered their property without forewarning, so seeing a couple of strangers poking around wouldn't lead them to hit the panic button.

The title of my self help book is akin to my current situation: Looking Through The Thick Grass For The Little White Ball But All I'm Finding Are Bits Of Dried Dog Shit.

Me: This cunt needs to buy a shovel or get his dog's insides checked out.

There's no response from Shaggers. Instead I hear a click.

Me: What are you doing, cunt?

He's walked up to the back door and pulled down on the handle. This has gone from a looky-loo to a break and enter.

This is pushing the limits for me, but weighing up my options between petty crime and the grief Shaggers will give me for staying out here on my own, I decide to follow him in. I get a good look at the shattered window as I do.

How Shaggers has managed to put it through there is miraculous. Couldn't do it again if he tried.

Before we take two steps inside the house, we're greeted—well, not really greeted, more so confronted—by the homeowner.

Guy: You've broken my window, you gotta pay for it.

Salt and pepper stubble. Hasn't been to the dentist in a decade or two. Wrapped in a Bintang singlet stained by three, no, four different types of liquid.

Shaggers: Sorry?

Guy (slower, annunciating every syllable): You have brok-en my wind-ow, now you got-ta pay for it.

The guy holds up a white ball as he does. Exhibit A in our current trial. I can see the red come into Shaggers' face. He's not in the mood for pleasantries, especially from this piano-key-mouthed fuck.

Shaggers: Well, what the fuck do you expect living on a golf course?

Guy: You have to pay for it, that's what I expect.

We're two chairs away from a *Jerry Springer* episode. I look around and see a couple that might work. Also, one of those smart fridges which you can upload your shopping list to and which, by the looks of this guy, is his main source of companionship. I'm doing my best not to think about the height of the ice dispenser and how tall old mate can stand on his tippy toes. Christ.

Shaggers: No, that's not happening. I'm sorry about your window, but we're not paying for it.

Shaggers grabs the ball out of the guy's hand and then turns to head back onto the course.

Guy: You pay, or I'll go to the *Daily Mail.*

Jerry. Jerry. Jerry.

Shaggers: What'd you say?

Guy: I said, I'll go to the *Daily Mail* about it. I know who you lot are. Pay for my window or I'll have you in the papers.

Of course we manage to hit the only house with a nuffie big enough to know who Shaggers and I are. And of course he calls the online website 'the papers', despite the fact that there is no print version of the *Daily Mail*.

Nine out of ten times, we'd just walk and call the guy on his bluff. But nine out of ten times Shaggers isn't in the position he's currently in. Coaches have been in his ear for weeks telling him he's 'close' and really pumping up his tyres so that if he does get a game, he's in a more sound mental state than he otherwise would be. This specific chemistry on their part means that as of right now, he's thinking he's close to getting a match and small things start happening when a bloke gets a sniff of a game. He starts getting to training a bit earlier. Starts watching more video vision before meetings. Stops coming out on the weekends to ice up a non-existent injury. Starts putting himself first, essentially. It's borderline delusional behaviour, but Shaggers is in that space now and it's clear he doesn't want any unnecessary detractors, i.e. this prick going to the *Daily Mail* saying, 'Two Professional Footballers Broke Into My House, Shat In My Toilet And Diddled My Kids'. I know the exact photo of Shaggers they'd run with too. Cunt's always got his mouth open in photos, which makes it perfect for any number of photo edits.

Me: Ok, look. I'll just pay for it, buddy. How much for a broken window?

Guy: Well, actually, now I'm thinking that it's not just a broken window. I'm thinking that the ball hit me as well and there's going to be some physiotherapy involved.

Shaggers: You're fucking kidding me.

Guy: All up, I'm thinking about $500.

121

Fuck me. For 500 bucks you'd want to be getting a massage from a Sydney Sweeney lookalike.

I turn to look at Shaggers, who's in the doorway, steaming. As I do, there's a bit of glare that makes me squint. Out the window there's clear sky peering through a very localised, diminished tree line. Odd, that a golf course would be so negligent as to expose a place like this. That's a lawsuit waiting to happen. Especially with a cunt like this. That's who he should be blaming here. Not us. I go to say that, to try and make a bit of peace, but then I see them. Hanging out of this prick's front pocket, a pair of gardening gloves. Thick, heavy-duty fuckers too, which look like they've seen a bit of action. Guess Stick's not alone in his weed whacking today.

I walk over to Shaggers and take the ball from him.

Me: Shaggers, what ball were you hitting?

Shaggers: Srixon 4.

In my palm is a Nike swoosh. Exploit the kids in the workshops, sure. But this? This is a step too far.

Me: This cunt trims his own trees.

Deer in headlights. The closer I look at him, the more I can see that he's got two rings around his eyes. Looks like an owl. Cunt's been using binoculars to watch us from his little hidey hole. Waiting for a stray shot so he can cash in. This is a ruse. A Samsung Smart Fridge fucking ruse.

Guy: No, that's, that's just another ball. You blokes broke my window and . . . and . . .

Maybe he's reliant on blokes being so rattled they won't stop to read the ball he's pulled from the bucket by his little mole hole. But there's a level of mental insurgency that has prepared us for moments like this.

Shaggers: And fucking nothing, cunt. Fix it yourself, you prick.

The final piece of the scheme is clear when we see a stack of business cards on the table. *Rick's Window Repairs.*

Shaggers takes the ball back from my hand and walks out, leaving me alone with Rick and the fridge, which he may or may not be romantically involved with, gently humming in the corner. Many, many questions come through my head, questions that I think will remain unanswered.

WWJD: What Would Jerry Do?

Tonight's guest left his family for another woman . . . and then they wheel out a fucking fridge and the crowd erupts.

I walk back through the long grass and dried dog shit and join Shaggers. He's dropped his new ball on the edge of the fairway, lines up his next shot and sends it flying clear to where the green is.

Shaggers (without looking at me): That's one shot so far.

Me: Sure.

It isn't, but I'm not going to argue about it. Not today.

MD STAKES

Sixty	Jenko

Big Sexy
Potato
Fumbles
Budget
Walshy

No! I keep losing at deals and I don't wanna make a deal anymore!

150cc Mushroom
Cup Wins:
Squidman: 23
Fangs: 20

THE BOTTOM HALF OF FANGS' AND SQUIDMAN'S FRIDGE

Yt.

Ed., on the lower half of Fangs' and Squidman's fridge there is a small box which states: '150cc Mushroom Cup Wins: Squidman: 23, Fangs: 20'. Last week, the score was Fangs 20 and Squidman 15 (information attained while shadowing the Welfare Officer during regular house inspection). The reason for this drastic shift in momentum is easily explained. The final course of the 150cc Mushroom Cup in Mario Kart N64 (MKN64) is Koopa Troopa Beach, a rather straightforward course with one shortcut, which, if taken, can save seven seconds off of each of the three laps. The shortcut occurs in the second half of the lap and involves driving up a ramp that is about the width of two carts before passing through a waterfall and into a cave. Driving through the cave is relatively straightforward and exits the driver on the other side of the central rock formation of the map.

There are relatively (I will explain the use of this word in a moment) minor tactics involved in the jump. One does not want to get too far ahead in relation to their opponents

125

as it will result in poor prizes from the boxes (while a speed boost prize such as a mushroom is desirable for the jump, it is not necessary) and opens the potential for opponents to deploy a red/blue shell timed at the optimal moment, where one is jumping into the secret tunnel, to completely derail the attempt. That is unless, of course, a green or red shell is held behind the player's cart at this point as a defensive mechanism. However, the mechanics of racing are made more difficult while holding down the additional button needed to affect this manner of self-defence.

Ed., Squidman's consistency in hitting the tunnel jump has seen him win more Mushroom Cups of late. Though, to label this as a 'shortcut' feels almost dishonest, given how it compares to other, more demonstrably advantageous skips to the game (which brings me back to the aforementioned 'relatively').

Ed., allow me to introduce you to the world of 'Speed-running', in which individuals try to complete video games as fast as possible (simple premise, yes?). For context, Ed., speedrunning is a rather niche yet loyal community, though it is larger than one originally thinks.

Ed., the Koopa Troopa Beach Cave Jump Shortcut pales in comparison to what is sometimes within this community referred to as the Greatest Speedrunning Feat of All Time, which, incidentally, takes place on MKN64. The feat—the hitting of three consecutive 'Weathertenkos'—was first performed by a streamer named Beck Abney in 2017. Forewarning: I am sure you have never heard of Abney before and a written description of the Greatest Speedrunning Feat of All Time does on its own explain the low following and viewership of Abney. The stream of the Greatest Speedrunning Feat of All Time itself has only had 1,900 views in the six years it's been online, and there is a point in the three-hour-long run (at 2h 05m and 06s) where Abney mentions that there are just ninety-four viewers of his stream. It is unclear if he says this with irony or pride. His voice does have that peculiar quality of self-deprecation combined with what could be interpreted as arrogance.

Lasting for 2h 59m and 41s, the 3/3 Weathertenko Stream is an endless loop of the following series of events (brace yourself, Ed.): Abney, who has what looks to be a set of old cabled iPhone headphones in his ear (left ear only) is situated in the corner of a poorly lit bedroom, awaiting the countdown that starts the time trial on the Choco Mountain Course. After the third beep, he initiates a small reverse burnout, followed by an adjustment of his character's (Toad, one of the three characters you would choose for this shortcut, the others being Yoshi and Peach, based upon their size and speed) cart along the track until he arrives at a particular point just past the start line. When lined up, all of which takes about 2.2 seconds from the start of the race, he drives directly at a wall face, using a mushroom to boost his speed (NB: after the use of which Toad says, in a very high-pitched voice, 'Here we go!') and attempts to hit a frame-perfect jump (affected by the R button) which, if executed at the precise right moment, will push Toad and his cart to the top of the wall face and activate a checkpoint, as the game believes the player is on a different part of the track than they actually are.

The design of MKN64—and most other video games—is based on geometry. Each racecourse on MKN64 is divided into checkmarks, which are invisible straight lines that run across the course. These lines help to track where racers are on the course; if they go out of bounds, the last checkmark they passed will be used to place them back on the course (facilitated by a little ghost called Lakitu). Another key part of this is that the courses themselves are made of geometric shapes, called polygons, and these polygons sit between checkpoints, so hitting certain polygons activates corresponding checkpoints. I know, Ed., it's all a bit technical. The point is that there are many ways that this system has been abused, which is essentially what speedrunning is all about: finding a way to manipulate a game's internal mechanics and architecture in order to weaponise it to achieve the game's overall goal. For instance, on a track called Frappe Snowland, reversing from the start line, passing a checkmark on the bridge and then driving off the course and affecting a jump that lands you on one very specific polygon, allows you to recreate the same sort of lap skip that occurs with the Weathertenko. W/r/t the Choco Mountain Time Trial, and the Weathertenkos, the discovery that the checkpoint activated at the top of the wall face (leading the game to think you are in a tunnel towards the end of the lap) near the start line would cut most of the course, was originally completed in a TAS (Tool Assisted Speedrun—a run performed by computer code rather than a human) by Drew Weatherton, and was then first completed using human anatomy by Abney, who at the time was not a highly ranked speedrunner and secured a one lap world record (his first) by completing the feat. This fact goes some way to explaining Abney's obsession with achieving the 3/3.

This manoeuvre allows the player to roll down the wall face and back over the finish line (i.e. from beyond the finish line to behind it), the game assuming they are at the end of a lap, in essence skipping the entire lap, which would normally take around thirty seconds, in somewhere between five and six seconds. It's worth stating that the most manic part of all of this is the music that plays in the background, which, when listened to for several minutes makes you feel irritated up to the point where it becomes unnoticeable, like white noise. However, the downside to this is that the familiar melody will then haunt you in your sleep or while you are at the grocery store or while you are doing any number of mundane activities that can broken by an utterance of the phrase, 'What am I humming?' and a brief search through the inventory of your brain to pinpoint where that particular melody has come from.

The song itself is something like a reversed *She'll Be Coming 'Round the Mountain When She Comes* that is just a beat behind where it should be.

As statistics and the stream itself show, this success is not the outcome of each attempt. Statically speaking, it is estimated that hitting a Weathertenko occurs about once in every forty attempts and so for Abney to successfully complete the feat he set out to, he would have to complete that set of movements three times in a row, which, if you have your calculator handy, is a probability of around one in 64,000.

So, in actuality, the more likely outcome of a mushroom-fuelled drive towards a wall is failure. Failure means that Abney will either land on top of the hill (causing him to immediately pause and reset that time trial) or hit the wrong spot on the wall and roll back down, at which point you hear Toad's little scream, sort of like a 'neoooooow' or 'waaaahhhhhh' (also leading Abney to press pause and reset the trial) or, most unfortunate of all, he will fall prey to frame rate-related

This presents a good opportunity to mention that while streaming, Abney responded to the question: 'What are your plans for after you get 3/3?' by saying, rather numbly, 'I'm going try to beat the Train on Calamari short cut [Sic] 3/3.' Then, 'Probably go to the Mario raceway and try the 3 lap shortcut.' For six years Abney held the world record for a 150CC all cups (skips) complete game run on MKN64. In 2023, several new shortcuts were found, which opened the door for other runners who were about 1 minute behind his pace at that point in time. Within a few months of these discoveries, Abney, for the first time since gaining it, lost his record. You might think that after that long at the top it would be a relief to step away from the game. To provide a comparison, Abney is the Michael Phelps of his sport, or the Usain Bolt, or Don Bradman. He is as dominant in speedrunning as any athlete has ever been in his or her particular field. Within two weeks of losing his record, Abney regained it. The total number of views for that stream was 1,200.

Here are some other videos I've seen of late that garner more views than Abney's World Record Feat: (1) A series called 'I throw things at my housemate each day until he guesses what they are', in which Housemate 1 throws a random object (e.g. large traffic cone, waffle iron, etc.) at Housemate 2, who is blindfolded and standing in a braced position covering crotch, after which Housemate 2 will attempt to guess said object, which they invariably fail to do. (2) A series of videos called 'How many will it take?' where the host conducts scientific experiments to see how many of a certain object it will take to support his weight. The series includes: 'How many hangers', where the host goes from one (instantly snaps) to two (instantly snaps and flies in a fragmented manner that seems dangerous) to five, ten, twenty-five, etc. etc. and 'How many pieces of spaghetti', which goes from one to two to five and so forth until he reaches 10,000 (or an estimate of 10,000 based on how many straws of spaghetti were in the one packet counted) which are taped together by large pieces of electrical tape at the ends and are able to hold the host's entire weight for about two seconds. (3) 'I eat a picture of Jason Segal every day until he eats a picture of me' (841k views for day one, lowest view count is 2.7k—still almost double that of Abney's world record footage—on day seventy-two). (4) A series called 'POV: I try your combos', where the creator has a fisheye camera taped to his head, the view from which morphs his proportions humorously, and, in a slightly sped-up video (probably done at about 1.2–1.4 × real speed) reads out requests from the comments (e.g. beer beer vodka vodka sprite coke coke vodka coke coke coke pickle juice vodka) while creating the concoction and adding little flourishes to each word (e.g. 'beer' is always pronounced as a low-pitch 'bear', sprite is 'spriiiiiite' with a little tongue roll on the 'pri') before consuming the concoction and showing either his delight or disgust at what he has created. The concoction previously stated garnered 1.1m views.

issues which—barring a lengthy explanation of the game's physical frame rate mechanics and how complete dumb luck can determine whether a certain frame occurs at the precise wrong moment, causing the game to essentially implode in on itself—also results in a reset. So, in reality, what viewers of the stream (again, ninety-four in total) watch for nearly three hours is a little Toad man drive a cart repeatedly into a wall over and over again on a five-second loop with weird polyphonic 64-bit music playing in the background (see def. of insanity often attributed to Einstein). And this was just one of the many daily streams Abney carried out between August 14 and October 29, resulting in the 26,000 attempts he undertook before succeeding.

What adds to the case for the feat itself being so monumental is that for those few who understood how significant it was and tuned in, there was no charismatic persona to offset the monotony of the task at hand. There was no other reason except for the absurdity of the feat itself to keep them invested. Abney's on-camera persona is not really a persona at all. He goes to little effort to draw new viewers in. He makes half-hearted mentions of a Twitter account as his only social media, used only to post links to his streams, and a YouTube channel. There is absolutely no attempt to gain followers. Giving Abney the benefit of the doubt, that he is utterly immersed in the task at hand, he is still, for want of a better word, boring. After hours of viewing, the only real evidence of character that yt. saw was the audible 'tsk' laugh-sound Abney makes after breaking the world record. This 'tsk' is always followed by a sort of side-eye movement to his left, towards a set of three screens, not through self-adulation to see if the camera has caught what has just happened, but rather to gauge the response of those watching. It's there, in those several seconds following a world record or between the end of one lap and the start of another, where Abney's stream (and dare I say, speedrunning) starts to make more sense. In the 3/3 Weathertenko Stream, between the moment he stops an attempt and starts again—about seven seconds in total—Abney's eyes move to one of the three monitors he has set up beside him which feeds him the comments from the chat. These comments are largely nonsensical in-jokes, such as: DangerMoll: 'Eat some pizza with mild chillies on it and start crying to prove it's you, Greg [another member of the chat]', and a gentle ribbing: 1ted59: 'Abney have you ever thought of getting 2/3, then hitting the third one?' These chat messages come in from the same number of people who might occupy a cramped living space in a parent's basement, or use a single bed and floor for seating in a college room. Speedrunners fight tooth and nail to shorten their runs and spend the least amount of time in the game, but the process by which they do so involves hours and hours of gameplay, and an opportunity for others to feel a part of that with them. Perhaps this is more the point than anything else.

I am sure you might be asking why any of this is important to me, Ed.? Why we are talking about a man in his room controlling a virtual Toad figure into a wall again and again for the sake of saving time in a game that was released nearly three decades ago? Well, Ed., you have asked what I feel the essence of the ██████ Football Club is, and I unequivocally believe that any attempt to define or distil the goings on inside these Four Walls would rely heavily upon one word: Efficiency.

Of all the mantras that the HC tries to instil within his players (of which there are many, and yt. has been informed that there seems to be a practice every year whereby new philosophies are introduced and then thrown out prior to the commencement of the Real Season), the one that ascends due to sheer ubiquity alone is this one word: Efficiency.

It is front of mind, back of mind, side of mind. Wrapped around the mind like a pig in a blanket. It *is* the mind. It stares you in the face in big black letters (Arial Bold, size 144 font), with each letter taking up its own A4 piece of paper, held up by what I assume to be Blu Tack on the whiteboard behind the HC's desk.

Yes, it definitely is, after several meetings yt. can see the subtle grey coming through the corner of each letter, with the exception of the 'Y' which has only two blots of Blu Tack in the centre top and centre bottom. No, Ed. the irony is not lost.

Just as speedrunners like Abney search every possible frame for opportunities to shave seconds off their gameplay, the players, staff and coaches of the ██████ Football Club pursue optimisation in their day-to-day activities. Of the various ways in which efficiency is optimised on a daily basis within the Four Walls, here are what I deem the most noteworthy:

The speed at which the Sliding Glass Door opens at the

After noticing that the door at the front of the club moved at a slightly faster rate than the same kind of door on level three—where the marketing team is situated—I enquired with the manager of the building who passed me onto EntranceTech Pty Ltd, the company who manufactured and installed the doors. From their head of design, I was given the following information: 'We had to create a special algorithm for the door to open at the right distance and right speed so as not to cause players to slow themselves on approach. It was about finding a sweet spot because if the door were to open too fast it would rush the players, much as an orange light does at a set of traffic lights. This Sweet Spot has since been patented and several other clubs have reached out and enquired about our services.'

entrance of the club is perfectly timed so that players do not break stride upon approach. The logic seems to be that when players enter the club, they are 'starting off on the right foot', while perhaps also leaving as little mental barrier as possible between the outside world and the Four Walls of the club. The players glide in without realising they have entered and they exit at the end of the day without that split second to pause and reflect that they are clocking off. Perhaps while driving home the player will realise that they are no longer at training, but they won't have that Pavlovian response whereby the club feels like a place of work.

These are the reason that all players have a solid training-bra tan year round. During the summer months, they will often train with their shirts off ('Rigs out') and the GPS unit sits inside a thin rubber latex bra.

GPS units, used to measure a player's movement during training, are put on the back of a training guernsey after the player has put the training top on. This seemed illogical to me at first, as a faster system would be to place all of the units in the players' guernseys prior to them putting them on. However, Rob, Head of Strength and Conditioning, informed me that when the units are put on the guernseys prior to the player putting them on, the neck of the top will catch on the player's head and create a ripple effect where the guernsey becomes caught around the chest of the player and requires assistance to be pulled down. This is in part due to the skin-tight nature of the playing guernseys, which are in themselves an attempt to optimise performance. Rob assures me that the time taken to put a GPS monitor in is less than the time it takes to pull down a player's guernsey.

Veteran masseuse 'Steakhands' has his massage table positioned in the far-right hand corner of the physio room. From this angle, Steakhands is unable to view the 42-inch plasma screen TV that is mounted to the wall. Enquiries reveal that several players had made complaints to the head physio that Steakhands would on occasion reduce his massage pressure for long periods of time. After observing the various instances when this occurred, it was found to be in correlation with Steakhands' use of tables which provided a clear view of the TV. The TV in the physio room is forever stuck on ESPN due to a remote control malfunction and Steakhands, a fervent supporter of the NFL, found himself being transfixed by games and analysis to the point that the massage he was giving became secondary. A quasi-SWOT analysis was completed on whether it would be better to let Steakhands go or to simply move the TV. Given his tenure at the club and the payout required, the latter was chosen. To his credit, Steakhands has what the playing group call 'magic fingers' in those moments when his attention is on the task at hand and not the offensive line issues of the Minnesota Vikings. Note: the masseurs all tend to employ the same rubbing motion on the lower backs of players, which starts along the spine and then extends outwards from there like the branches of a tree. Rubbing is always done upwards first (i.e. towards the head of the player) and then down (i.e. towards the feet of the player). They will all do approximately eight minutes of manipulation with their hands before moving on to the greater pressure of their elbows.

Trainers hold water bottles at a position just above their waist and on an angle that yt. estimates to be somewhere between 70 and 80 degrees, making it optimally positioned for the arc of movement inherent in a player grabbing the bottle in one fluid motion while running past and then raising their hands from waist to mouth.

Now, Ed., there has been much opined about the intellect—or lack of it—of football players, which to my mind is an unfortunate stereotype. Yes, there are countless examples of dribble blurted out in interviews and none of them seem to be in danger of being awarded a MacArthur Fellowship anytime soon. However, what these players display more often than not is a level of understanding towards efficiency and decision-making on a subconscious level that could be deemed as trigonometrically inspired. The clearest example of this: the player parking area is part of a shared lot several hundred metres away from the entrance of the club. Players are permitted to park on level three in two sets of reserved spaces which function on a first-in-best-dressed basis. Ed., over the course of a week of observing the players' parking habits, I determined that, more often than not, they chose the optimal spot to make the most efficient use of their time, as opposed to the closest spot to the exit, or the first spot that they see. To calculate the Optimal Spot, one must factor in: Average Driving Speed, Driving Distance, Average Walking Speed (Flat), Walking Distance from Park, the Speed of the Elevator (which fluctuates at peak hours) and Average Speed of Walking (Stair). The result gives a series of parks that are preferential to others by the barest of margins, but nonetheless, contribute to optimal time. These spots, as it turns out, require players to drive further than the first spot they see, and park closer to the stairs, which, while being three flights, are significantly faster than the elevator.

I do believe one should view not only the buildings but also the players' psyches as an extension of the Four Walls. This unwavering drive to the Nirvana of efficiency is intrinsically tied to the players' actions (whether conscious or not), ergo lives, ergo identities. Just as the speedrunners obsessively search for the most efficient way of navigating their games of choice, playing within the confines of the ones and zeros to break new ground, so too do the players and staff of the ▮▮▮▮▮▮▮ Football Club.

DEFEND TO
THE DEATH

SILVER BULLETS AT THE COCKTAIL FUNCTION

Fangs

My thumb, forefinger and middle finger push the capsule up into the abyss of my arsehole like one of those tiny claws in an RSL club chocolate machine.

Kfepffphhhhhhh this is . . . ahhhh . . . mission control . . . we have ahhh . . . . . . dispatched and ahhhh . . . are on our descent now . . . over.

kffFfFFFpPhHhh . . . KffppHhhHhh ahhhhhhhh . . . this is ahhhhh . . . the ahh lower colon . . . we ahhh . . . . . . we are ready to receive the package when ready . . . over . . . kKFfpFOPFPE . . .

These hand-outs are courtesy of Stick, who is being extra generous after securing a nice load from Mr Rogers, the terminally ill cancer patient he has befriended and trades match tickets with in exchange for heavy painkiller medication.

Pulling my pants back up, I walk away from the piss-stained corner of the carpark to meet the others. Stick, Shaggers, Mud and Squidman are all waiting back by the car with their club suits on. Fucking ugly things they got us this year. Not even worth getting the emblem embroidered on the pocket stitched off. And while we're at it, fucking horrorshow ad they got the boys to do as well. Sad to think there'd be some actors or models starving out there while a couple of the ███████ Football Club's Golden Boys stare longingly into the distance in slow motion.

Shaggers: How was old Mr Rogers?

Me: The cunt's near dead.

Shaggers: Does it feel a bit like robbery, what you do?

Stick: No fucking way. It's a business exchange. He gets tickets, I get what I'm after. Fair's fair.

Shaggers: I doubt that bloke's using the tickets. He can't even walk.

Me: The poor cunt can't even get up and go to the bathroom. He just sits there with piss running down his leg all day and his little dog comes and licks it off.

Stick: Well maybe he just wants to spend some time with someone, eh? And I'm the only cunt decent enough to give him the time of day.

Mud takes a big whiff out of the amyl he's stashed in his inside pocket. I'm assuming he stole it from some unsuspecting stranger on a night out because I can't picture him going into a sex shop and asking for it. He's got an irrational fear of all things non-heterosexual and non-missionary.

He stays frozen as the blood is cut off to his head for about six seconds. Mud's also doubled up on the bullets because he reckons he can handle anything Stick can. In my expert opinion, Mud's set himself on course for destruction. Stick's tolerance is inhuman.

Stick: You right, cunt?

Mud (blood returning to head): Well my anus isn't as loose as you boys, so forgive me if I need a little bit of assistance.

Mud's bullshit washes over me. I take it as a sign that bullet might already be having some effect. That's why we've taken them after all. So that the bullshit of this night can't touch us. A thick, protective layer of disassociation is what we're fitting ourselves with.

Shaggers (trying to do his tie up but failing miserably): You got the cards sorted?

Me: Squidman and I prepared some of our finest work for this evening.

From my back pocket I withdraw several pieces of A5 paper, cut neatly, with a five by five table on each.

Mud (reading the card closely): *Wilko's granddaughter is there*, I fucking hope so.

Shaggers: Why, so you can stand in the corner and not talk to her?

Mud: Fuck off, I'll do more than talk to her.

Shaggers: No, you won't, cunt.

Mud: Fuck off, she was all over me at BNF last year. Was grinding away on me on the dancefloor.

Shaggers: And who'd she go home with again?

Mud: Fuck knows, I was off with other birds by then.

Shaggers: Course you were.

Mud wasn't with other birds. He was at the casino with me, convinced he could count cards before realising there was no card counting involved in poker.

Mud: Good riddance anyway, I wouldn't be able to look old Wilko in the eye if I fucked his granddaughter. Plus she's rooted enough of the boys. If anything, I dodged a bullet.

Stick, abnormally quiet, opens his car door and pulls out a large water bottle. He takes a sip and recoils at the taste.

Stick: This and the bullet take the edge right off. New trick I've found.

I've no option but to trust the cunt because when it comes to non-traditional medications, he should be considered the Subject Matter Expert. We each take a large swig from the bottle and Squidman, for whatever reason, takes several gulps.

Stick: You right, cunt?

Shaggers: Thirsty, big horse?

Squidman (recoiling from taste, impersonating our lead masseuse): Dawww, spose so.

The cunt sounds half-gacked already. We head towards the lift and wait for the little light to go yellow. It feels like that scene in *Gladiator*, where slaves are waiting for the gate to the lion pit to open. That's what this is. A feeding frenzy about to happen.

The door slides open and we pile in.

Shaggers (reading from the card): *Yellow-tooth Susan sexually assaults one of the young players.*

Stick: The old fucking chimney.

Me: Figure she'll have a couple of wines and get some photos with the boys and do her usual hand on the lower back routine.

Mud: She was my fucking sponsor last year. I reckon I got second-hand lung cancer from talking to her all night.

Shaggers: Yeah, well, she won't bother you this year. She goes straight for the fresh meat each year. You're used and abused. Consider yourself lucky.

The doors of the Used and Abused Express open to a full room. *Welcome to the Jeffrey Horn convention. How may we assist you today?* Every year we do this against our will. A big meet and greet with all of the Platinum Tier Fans. Fully blown nuffies. Teo from upstairs has tried explaining to us on a few occasions why these people matter. The summation is that they give money to the club and in exchange we put their name on top of a locker and piss in their pockets while some struggling university students dressed as hospo workers dish out hors d'oeuvres that none of us want to eat. At least the gladiators had weapons. This is more like a zoo: we're fucking caged animals and they've bought a VIP pass so they can come and be on the inside with us for a bit of stargazing.

Kiwi Kel, dressed in her usual power suit, gives us our nametags and the names of our sponsors for the night. Then we congregate in the back corner of the room, playing penguins until one of the sponsors spots their prey and moves in.

Shaggers: *Fangs gets taken first.* Tick.

Unfortunately, I am the victim in this case. We shake hands and this old guy and his wife stand and gawk at me like they're thinking of a way to tell me they're into threesomes and have a few feet of rope in the back of their car if I'm interested. I'd almost rather that than stand around and talk dribble. Dribble. Shit. I can feel some moving down the side of my face already. How potent were those things?

Sponsor: So, have you ever wanted to go sky diving? I can get you in a plane if you like.

Me (overtly conscious that I'm losing control over the right hand corner of my mouth): Oh no, that's not particularly of interest to me, you see, I have this terrible fear of heights. The sheer thought of it makes the palms of my hands and soles of my feet sweat. It's a bit like that Batman movie [Bingo card item: *Someone is able to mention Batman in a conversation with their sponsor,* that's the Shaggers special, I'm almost certain they're the only movies he knows] where he's climbing out of that big pit in the ground and he stands on the ledge and he has to forget that the fear is there in order to make the jump. That fear is unavoidable for me.

Sponsor (looking dumbfounded, forcing a smile): Right. (Another lengthy pause.) Have you ever read the book *The Barefoot Investor*?

While the cunt starts talking about separate income buckets, I feel like everything's bouncing off me. My eyes are getting heavy and I feel like I'm going to fall asleep standing up. Stick's stuff has more than taken the edge off. I am completely rounded. Smoothed down. DiCaprio in *The Wolf of Wall Street* slugging down the stairs. That's where I'm headed. I scope out across the room to see if I am the only one feeling said side effects. It would appear that I am not. Squidman has pulled his fake tooth out and is showcasing it to a small crowd of onlookers. I excuse myself from the one-sided conversation and grab Squid and usher him away towards the bathroom.

Me (adopting somewhat of a British accent): Are you right?

Squidman: Tickets?! Room passes?! You gotta be fucking kidding me, don't you?

He's looking at himself in the mirror, properly cooked. Poking his tongue through the gap where his tooth should be. He's lost the plot and I'm dribbling. Still, we've been worse. The door to the bathroom opens.

Shaggers (excited): There's a Hayley out there.

Squidman (imitating our lead physio, again): Finger tape?! You're not even worth the money we're paying ya!

For context, a Hayley is a particular breed of female. It's what we've come to call fit birds who make appearances at training nights or functions. They're a lightning rod for the boys' attention and the running gag is that at corporate training nights where they let us give out a Best on Ground award for the session, nine times out of ten—no, higher than that, *every time*—the Hayley will win the award. This is regardless of how many errant kicks she had, how little effort she put it, and how impressive other attendees may have been. A Hayley will always win.

The door opens again.

Mud (card in hand): What do we need for Bingo?

Squidman (loudly): BINGOOOOO!

Shaggers: Anyone seen any of the boys take a Coke Zero?

Mud: Steely did.

Shaggers: Well, all we need is either the Q&A to be hosted by a D-list celebrity or one of the boys to say 'training the house down'.

Me: I'm pretty sure I saw Sam Pang out there before, so I'd say we're a good chance.

Mud: Who?

Me: Exactly.

The Used and Abused Express has now relocated itself to the bathroom. Squidman doing his impressions of various club personnel, me still speaking with a somewhat British bent, and Shaggers and Mud hyperfixating on the bingo game we've got going on. There's a loud knock on the door and Stick walks in. He's looking completely untouched by the concoction that has destroyed Squidman.

Stick: The fuck's up with him?

Squidman: (Murmurs something. A low drawling sound.)

Me: You fucked him with that drink and the bullet.

Stick: Hey, I didn't force any of you cunts to have it. I won't accept any finger-pointing for drink-spiking around here. That's not my go and you cunts know it.

Me: Stick, what're you doing in here?

Stick: Oh, sorry, ladies. I was just about to give you the heads up that the Q&A was about to start, but I guess I'll go fuck myself, eh?

Stick walks back out. Full tilt, as usual. Ballistic cunt needs to see a therapist or twenty. Shaggers and Mud exit too, leaving just me and a half-inflated Squidman.

I guide him out to the back of the crowd that has formed for the Q&A. If we can get through this, then we are safe and secure. Post Q&A, I'll just steer him out and we can call it a night. But Squidman, of course, has other ideas. As recurring panellist on the Channel 10 TV show *Have You Been Paying Attention* and former *Logies* host, Sam Pang, tries to orchestrate the panel, he starts yelling out *BINGO! BINGO! BINGO!* Ever the consummate professional, Sam's response is to make a joke out of the interruption before asking another question to get things back on track. Feeling the closest to a sense of obligation to maintain the integrity of this club that I have in years, I do what I can to stop the noise and cover Squidman's mouth with my hand, but as I do I can feel the cunt poking his tongue through the gap in his teeth and licking my hand. I snatch it back and Kiwi Kel comes over and asks if everything's ok.

Me: Err, yes. Squidman's not feeling too flash hot after training.

She gives me a double take. The British twang in my voice is still there.

Kiwi Kel (who I'm sure is aware of the bullshit): Right, maybe it's best if you take him home. I'll take care of his sponsors and order you an Uber.

No further questions are asked. Thank you, Kiwi Kel. Thank you dearly. You're too good for this place.

I escort Squidman down the stairs in the same manner that one does a toddler. Giving him encouragement for the most basic of tasks. Good boy, Squidman. That's a good step. I'm unsure if I've ever been this disgustingly nice to him before and I don't intend on it happening ever again. I've walked in on him near death with gastro before and I wasn't this sympathetic.

The Uber arrives as we reach the base of the stairs. I continue to guide Squidman towards the car door, and he hops in and lies down immediately. I sit in the front seat and engage in a bit of chit-chat with the driver.

Uber driver: Ah, is your friend ok?

Me: See, that's a big question.

Squidman: (Emits the same low drawling sound that he was making in the bathroom.)

Me: Squidman, what are you doing?

Squidman: (Continues to make the sound.)

Me: Cunt, you've got to sit up and speak if you want something.

Squidman tosses his head and the drawl turns into a low sort of whirling sound, like a kid describing a hurricane. He's giggling to himself while doing it. If there's something funny, I'm not getting it.

I turn back and look at the lights. We're almost home. Just a few more blocks. Then we can call it a night and just tell everyone we were feeling a bit off. I'm planning the locker room routine for the following morning when I hear a loud thud. The driver starts yelling out in a dialect I don't quite understand. I look behind me and Squidman's no longer there. No, he's not even in the fucking vicinity. Out the window I see him scurrying across the road. Fucking hell. I jump out and start to chase him down.

Me: Squidman, what the fuck are you doing?!

Squidman: (Making louder hurricane noises.)

Me: Squidman! What the fuck!

Cunt. Don't get hit by a car. I highly fucking doubt that

car insurance covers collisions with prescription-drug-fucked footballers. And you would most certainly be at fault in this situation. I'm running down the centre line of the road. Headlights either side of me, cars beeping as they pass. You think I don't know I'm not meant to be running here?

Me: Come back you prick!

Shit. He's put a few metres on me and climbed to the top of a hill. I stop at the bottom and put my hands on my knees. These suits were not made for running, that's for sure. And trust Squidman to put on his best running performance of the year in a situation like this. I catch my breath and look up. Squidman has ripped the buttons off his shirt and is staring up into the night sky. As he stands there, bathed in moonlight, he repeats the hurricane sound he's been making all night, only this time, it suddenly becomes clear to me what he's trying to do. We are back on the same frequency. The drawling sound rises in pitch and becomes a quivering vibrato. It's an unmistakable call to the rest of the pack. *AwoooOOOoooh.* The unsanctimonious arrival of 'Squidwolf'. One silver bullet and he's done. Howling at the moon. There's a lot more to his demise than just that. But I get the gag. Not your worst, Squidman.

Sorry, Squidwolf.

THE WALLS ARE CLOSING IN

PUSSY PUSSY MEOW MEOW WHATSAPP CHAT

A screenshot of a Terry's Instagram post of them kicking the ball in the ressies game played earlier that day. The caption for the post is the 100 emoji followed by the flame emoji.

from Bubbles, 7:13 pm

Crook

from Windmill, 7:13 pm

Fuuuuzzyyy duuuuckkk

from Squidman, 7:13 pm

A photo of the stats sheet showing that the Terry only had one touch all game.

from Fangs, 7:14 pm

149

> Good that he got a photo of
> his one kick
>
> from Gatesy, 7:14 pm

> Virgin
>
> from Stick, 7:14 pm

A note on the current name of the group, which comes from an incident at a recent beer pong tournament.

After consuming half a bottle of Wild Turkey, Steely turned to Fangs (though, it is unclear if he meant to turn to Fangs as the comment that irked Steely was said by Stick and not Fangs) and asserted: 'Don't you talk to me about pussy, cunt!'

The line was said with a sort of visceral hatred that is rare at such events. The interaction came after Steely had left his Facebook logged into one of the club's computers, leading Stick to discover a message exchange between Steely and the club's receptionist.

At 1:24 am on a random Sunday morning, Steely had messaged the receptionist saying, 'Wot u doin?'

The message was read by the receptionist, yet no reply was given.

This is what Stick had said to Steely during the game of beer pong to stir his rage: 'Seen and no reply.'

After the night, the group chat was titled 'Pussy Cunts' before becoming 'Puss In Boots: Reloaded', 'The Octopussy Support Group' and eventually finding solace as 'Pussy Pussy Meow Meow'.

A photo from the Terry's Instagram posted three years ago of him at a ▮▮▮ game with the caption 'luv the footy! :)'.

from Shaggers, 7:15 pm

Luv being a virgin :)

from Shaggers, 7:15 pm

Luv sitting on the pine all game :)

from Gatesy, 7:15 pm

An image of one man giving another man a massage, and the face of the man giving the massage is edited to be the Terry's face, and the face of the other man is a poorly cropped football.

from Squidman, 7:16 pm

An image from Silly Sunday of Pricey sleeping on the couch with his cock hanging out of his jocks.

from Shaggers, 7:17 pm

151

An image from Silly Sunday of Pricey sleeping on the couch with his cock hanging out of his jocks, edited so that Georgey-Boy's face is where the cock should be.

from Squidman, 7:17 pm

An image from Silly Sunday of Pricey sleeping on the couch with his cock hanging out of his jocks, edited so that Pricey's face is his cock, and his cock is his face.

from Fangs, 7:17 pm

An extreme close-up of Pricey's cock where his head should be.

from Windmill, 7:18 pm

An extreme close-up of Pricey's head where his cock should be.

from Hally, 7:18 pm

T.S.C.R.I.W.C.H.

from Squidman, 7:18 pm

T.S.C.R.I.W.C.H. stands for 'The Shortest Cab Ride In Wan Chai History', which relates to the group's most recent off-season trip to Wan Chai.

Orchestrated by Hally, the whole trip was a trainwreck. The hotel they stayed at was chosen because it had a swim-up bar, however when the group arrived at the hotel the pool was empty and the bar was under construction.

Clutching at straws, they spent most of their time at a pub across the road called Misty's, which was 'Australian themed'— basically meaning it sold VB and had a few Australian flags scattered around. The bar was dingy, lifeless and devoid of any natural light. The only perk was that it allowed the travelling players to sneak in cheap Smirnoff Ices from the 7/11 next door.

The group did very little sightseeing on this trip. Every day they'd meet in the hotel lobby at 11 am and venture across the road to Misty's, fill themselves with drinks and then eventually stumble back to the hotel where late at night they would be swarmed by dozens of sex workers who would be waiting on the lounge by the elevator of their floor.

The aforementioned Shortest Cab Ride In Wan Chai History took place on the penultimate night of the trip when Pricey, having not slept in two days, sculled his beer at Misty's and then stumbled out of the pub and into a cab. None of the boys had said anything as it happened, mainly because Pricey was known to get a bit of a look in his eyes after a few drinks and, because of his size, was someone who you just let do what he wanted to do to preserve your own physical safety.

It was about twenty minutes later that a taxi pulled up on the other side of the road. It was Georgey-Boy who spotted it, crying out: 'Look, it's Pricey!' Everyone crossed the road, drinks in hand, and asked Pricey where he'd been. Theories were building that he'd either gone to a strip club or a rub 'n' tug. His response: 'I just asked the cabby to take me back to the hotel.'

No one knows for sure what happened in those twenty minutes, but the distance from the start to the end of the journey, a mere 12.5 metres, the length of two lanes of traffic and two narrow footpaths in Wan Chai, surely made it The Shortest Cab Ride In Wan Chai History.

A screenshot of Bubbles' two year anniversary Instagram post.
from Pricey, 7:18 pm

A side-by-side of Bubbles' girlfriend's face and Fangs' face. There is an uncanny similarity.
from Gatesy, 7:23 pm

A photo of Hally from the club's fan day. Hally has the tops of his ears tucked under his hat. It's unclear if he is doing this deliberately as some sort of sun safety mechanism, or if it has happened accidentally.
from Windmill, 7:26 pm

A photo of Windmill edited so that his neck is three times longer than it otherwise would be.
from Gatesy, 7:26 pm

A two-second video of Fangs in Bali on his first footy trip wearing a Jason Mraz straw fedora. He is looking down at his phone screen and when he realises the camera is on him he sticks his tongue out and screams at the camera.

from Hally, 7:27 pm

An image of Fangs in his first year, kissing a blonde girl at a nightclub with his eyes open and his hand up the back of her skirt. He is wearing an ironic Simpsons *tee that says, 'Everything's coming up Milhouse.'*

from Squidman, 7:27 pm

A photo of Dennis with a filter applied so that his face narrows around his nose and eyes.

from Fangs, 7:27 pm

A photo of King Curtis from the eighteenth episode of Wife Swap *USA's fifth season, 'Brown/Holland'. The image is from the part of the episode where King Curtis, while speaking about his faux mother for the week, who has just taken away his chicken nuggets, says: 'She can't run in those little high heels.'*

from Dennis, 7:28 pm

Chicken nuggets is like my family

from Squidman, 7:28 pm

She acting like she's the queen, and we're the sorry people!

from Fangs, 7:28 pm

I'm not smashin food . . . In my own backyard . . . end of story

from Bubbles, 7:29 pm

PISSANTS

A screenshot of a friend
request sent from Bubbles
to King Curtis on Facebook.
The request has been
pending for six months.

from Bubbles, 7:30 pm

:(

from Bubbles, 7:30 pm

lel

from Squidman, 7:31 pm

A screenshot of Hally
accidentally sharing a
random girl's Facebook
photo on Facebook without
realising.

from Gatesy, 7:33 pm

A photo of Gatesy at a strip
club in Hong Kong with
three bags of pretzels ripped
open in front of him to form
one monster pretzel platter.

from Windmill, 7:33 pm

An image of a bewildered
Shaggers with Tubigrip
around his left calf.

from Fangs, 7:34 pm

An image of a bewildered Shaggers with Tubigrip around his left calf.

from Hally, 7:34 pm

An image of a bewildered Shaggers with Tubigrip around his left calf.

from Windmill, 7:34 pm

An image of a bewildered Shaggers with Tubigrip around his left calf.

from Gatesy, 7:34 pm

An image of a bewildered Shaggers with Tubigrip around his left calf.

from Fangs, 7:34 pm

An image of a bewildered Shaggers with Tubigrip around his left calf.

from Stick, 7:34 pm

An image of a bewildered Shaggers with Tubigrip around his left calf.

from Mud, 7:34 pm

> *An image of a bewildered Shaggers with Tubigrip around his left calf.*
>
> from Gatesy, 7:34 pm

> *An extreme close up of Pricey's cock where his head should be.*
>
> from Shaggers, 7:35 pm

> *A turtle emoji.*
>
> from Fangs, 7:35 pm

It is well known that any comment featuring the turtle emoji is banned on ▮▮▮▮▮▮▮▮ Football Club social media posts.

This came after Sugar, one of the more senior players at the club, and his partner had posted a gender reveal for their unborn child online. In the video, the pair are standing side by side, smiles on their faces, as a series of blue balloons are released into the sky above.

On top of the usual swath of comments (two types: one consisting of clapping emojis, the other unsolicited feedback about the damaging implications of enforced gender norms), a series of vitriolic rumblings came from a group of animal rights activists who identified themselves as 'Turtle Life Warriors'.

The Turtle Life Warriors (TLWs) were outraged that Sugar (who was actually quite a big animal lover himself, having what many considered a small farm of domesticated animals at his home) had released helium-inflated latex vessels into the stratosphere that would eventually find themselves in the ocean where they would inevitably be consumed by baby sea turtles.

The turtles obviously couldn't defend themselves against

Sugar's thoughtless act of horror, so the TLWs took to social media to fight for their justice by commenting a torrent of turtle emojis on the post. The attacks on Sugar's account lasted for weeks. His inbox became flooded with turtle emoji after turtle emoji. Attention then moved to the main account of the ██████████ Football Club. No matter what was posted, turtle after turtle would drown out the entire comments section, completely ruining any attempt at social engagement and traction amongst fans. A social media meeting was held and the decision was made to utilise various platforms' comment restriction protocols, adding the turtle emoji to the list.

Amongst the playing group, the turtle emoji is now used to communicate any number of things, such as when entry to a nightclub is not permitted, when there is a fan waiting out the front of reception for autographs, when a group has already left a café after being asked if they are still there, and in this case by Fangs, that Shaggers has attempted to deflect attention from himself in the conversation.

> *An infamous image of a rugby league player performing a bubbler, edited so that Stick's head is the player's head.*
>
> from Mud, 7:35 pm

> *An image of Katy Perry at Sydney airport wearing a full black and white adidas tracksuit next to an image of Mud wearing the exact same tracksuit.*
>
> from Shaggers, 7:36 pm

*A screenshot from the
Courier-Mail Facebook page
of an article headlined:
'Police are hunting for a
man who ejaculated on
the back of a woman at a
music festival'. Hally's face
has been overlaid on top of
the composite sketch of the
perpetrator.*

from Gatesy, 7:37 pm

When are we heading down
for appearances?

from Sixty, 7:50 pm

SIXTYYYY

from Fangs, 7:51 pm

*An image of a marquee
women's rugby league
player scoring a try with
the head of Sixty put on the
defender chasing her.*

from Squidman, 7:51 pm

Hahaha

from Sixty, 7:51 pm

I think old mates waiting
at the back of the box for
us now

from Sixty, 7:52pm

*A low-angle photo of Scotty
Danks from the matchday
appearance team waiting at
the back of the player's box
with a clipboard in his hand.*

from Sixty, 7:52 pm

*A low-angle photo of Scotty
Danks from the matchday
appearance team waiting at
the back of the player's box
with a clipboard in his hand,
edited so that the clipboard
is where his face should be
and his face is his clipboard.*

from Squidman, 7:53 pm

*An extreme zoom in on
Scotty Danks' head as a
clipboard.*

from Fangs, 7:54 pm

*An image of a bewildered
Shaggers with Tubigrip
around his left calf.*

from Hally, 7:54 pm

An image of a bewildered Shaggers with Tubigrip around his left calf.

from Fangs, 7:54 pm

An image of Sixty with his arm around the shoulders of a super fan at the half-time signing table.

from Mud, 8:03 pm

An image of an empty line at the signing table.

from Fangs, 8:07 pm

This is real fun

from Fangs, 8:07 pm

Lol stiff

from Squidman, 8:08 pm

A photo of American middle distance runner Steve Prefontaine.

from Fangs, 8:45 pm

Oi PLAY!

from Stick, 8:45 pm

Play time

from Shaggers, 8:45 pm

Good boy, good boy. Play!

from Stick, 8:46 pm

Oi Stick, play?

from Mud, 8:46 pm

Yeah, play! Good boy!

from Stick, 8:46 pm

An image from Silly Sunday of Pricey sleeping on the couch with his cock out, edited so that his face is his cock, and his cock is his face.

from Georgey-Boy, 8:51 pm

A video from Silly Sunday of Georgey-Boy sitting on the floor with a Corona in his hand giggling while pissing on himself.

from Pricey, 8:54 pm

A video from pres of the boys singing the song of the opposition team who just beat the senior team.

from Fangs, 9:20 pm

> *A photo of Mud wearing Gucci loafers at pres.*
>
> from Shaggers, 9:22 pm

> *A screenshot of how much the Gucci loafers Mud is wearing cost online.*
>
> from Shaggers, 9:23 pm

> *A selfie of Fangs wearing his Uber driver's sunglasses.*
>
> from Fangs, 10:24 pm

> Fuck this lines long.
> Anyone inside?
>
> from Fangs, 10:59 pm

> Yeaaahhh G'dayyyyyy Mickey, it's Sam Canavan here mate, just wondering why you didn't touch the footy on the weekend?
>
> from Squidman, 11:00 pm

Sam Canavan was a fictional journalist that a group of the players had created to trick unsuspecting first-year players into giving away information that could be used against them in any number of ways (such as in fine sessions, the building blocks of a new nickname, or in Mad Monday outings).

The unsuspecting target player would be called and assured that everything had been cleared with the media manager of the club and that Canavan was writing a feature piece on the player to go on the official AFL website.

Some calls lasted longer than others. Often the target would pick up on the gag, or the player making the mock *Sixty Minutes*-esque voice would crack and give it away.

There was one instance, however, of the calls lasting for a full year. The night before every game, the group would call a first-year player by the name of Mickey Montief (a player who only lasted one year in the system). They would ask him the usual questions about how he was finding his new environment and ask for pieces of colour about his off-field life (What is your favourite meal? Lasagna. And favourite movie? *Kung Fu Panda*.) that Canavan said the readers adored. 'Mickey, fine details are king!' was a common phrase uttered by whomever it was pretending to be Canavan that night.

Excuses were made for the repeated calls. System errors deleting what had been written. Editors demanding more information. But there was a general reliance on Mickey having no clue how long a piece such as this took to complete. One time they had managed to keep him on the phone for a full hour as he explained the intricacies of training that day and had given away more about the game plan than should be given away. Especially by a player who himself had not fully grasped it.

One time, Mickey had explained that he'd had a meeting with the head coach earlier that day.

'What was said, Mickey? If you don't mind me asking,' said Canavan, played by Shaggers that night.

'Well, ah, he just kept talking about a penny or something.'

Shaggers muted his phone's microphone and the room full of boys erupted with laughter.

At Mad Monday, Mickey was asked on stage and was

interviewed by one of the players in the Sam Canavan voice. Even with it right there before him, he still did not understand what was going on. The penny, sadly, never dropped.

> *A blurry selfie with Sixty's head taking up the lower third of the screen and a packed dancefloor full of eighteen to twenty-one year olds.*
>
> from Sixty, 11:01 pm

> *A photo of Walshy standing by the edge of the dancefloor holding a tall glass of vodka Red Bull in both hands. There is a straw in each glass and both straws funnel into his mouth.*
>
> from Sixty, 11:02 pm

> where else can we go?
>
> from Mud, 11:06 pm

> Fuuuuuuzzy duck
>
> from Hally, 11:08 pm

> Fuzzy duck
>
> from Gatesy, 11:08 pm

> Fuzzy duck
>
> from Hally, 11:08 pm

Duzzy
from Gatesy, 11:09 pm

Ducky fuzz
from Hally, 11:09 pm

Ducky fuzz
from Fangs, 11:09 pm

Ducky fuzz
from Squidman 11:09 pm

Duzzy
from Hally, 11:09 pm

Fuzzy Duck
from Fangs, 11:10 pm

Duzzy
from Hally, 11:10 pm

Fuzzy duck
from Fangs, 11:10 pm

fucked up, gotta drink
from Fuzzy Duck, 11:10 pm

A photo of Fangs holding his finger up at Hally who is a few spots ahead of him in the line standing next to the group of girls he has tacked himself onto in order to get inside. In the photo, Hally is unaware he is being flipped off.

from Fangs, 11:11 pm

Oi PLAY!

from Stick, 11:14 pm

Where the fuck are u

from Fangs, 11:14 pm

We want to play Stick

from Mud, 11:15 pm

Square. Come cunts.

from Stick, 11:15 pm

A photo of Shaggers sitting at a table drinking out of the spout of a white teapot.

from Stick, 11:18 pm

Oiiii teapots! Good boy! play!

from Hally, 11:19 pm

A video of Walshy doing the Napoleon Dynamite *dance routine in the middle of the dancefloor. Several people look at him strangely but that doesn't deter him.*

from Sixty, 11:45 pm

A selfie of Sixty with the DJ who is giving him nothing.

from Sixty, 11:53 pm

Chicken nuggets is like my family

from Dennis, 12:01 am

Dennis come to Square!

from Stick, 12:01 am

A photo of the toilet bowl in the disabled bathrooms at the club.

from Sixty, 12:05 am

Sixty's had his two beers and is pissed

from Fangs, 12:05 am

Oi fuck up Fangs!

from Sixty, 12:05 am

Ooooo chirpy!

from Hally, 12:06 am

I remember my first beer

from Gatesy, 12:07 am

A video of Sixty drunkenly calling Fangs a virgin.

from Sixty, 12:08 am

mustn't have full strength piss in Canberra

from Fangs, 12:09 am

Anyone seen Windmill tonight?

from Gatesy, 12:09 am

Windmill's dead man I haven't seen him in years

from Hally, 12:10 am

Fuck up Gatesy

from Windmill, 12:10 am

Who's number is that?

from Gatesy, 12:11 am

Windmill any danger of having a crack

from Hally, 12:12 am

> *Photo of Windmill's neck edited so it looks three times as long.*
>
> from Gatesy, 12:15 am

> Bring back Richie
>
> from Hally, 12:15 am

'Richie' or 'The Vague Lookalike' is one of the more well-known Mad Monday outfits in recent memory.

It started with the switcheroo that Gatesy pulled off on a footy trip in Cairns a few years back. He'd seen a bird that he went to school with and smoke bombed off with her while Fangs, Stick and Windmill kept dancing in the backpackers club.

The following morning, the boys woke up in their hostel and saw the top of Gatesy's head popping out from under the covers. They had all wanted him to wake up so they could find out what happened the night before, but he wasn't budging. There were objects and abuse hurled his way, but no response. He could've been dead, for all they knew.

Bored by Gatesy's lack of response, the rest of the boys went and got brekky then came back and started talking about the night once more when, without notice, Gatesy got up, grabbed his things and left—only thing was, it wasn't Gatesy. It was just a guy who looked like Gatesy.

The 'switcheroo' Gatesy had called it, without explaining much more.

This planted the seed for what would be The Vague Lookalike costume instigated by Windmill, who sent a look-alike of himself to Mad Monday the following season. The real impetus was that Windmill was covering for the fact he was off doing a medical for another club, hoping to sign a new contract.

The bit confused a few of the boys initially. But the bloke—whose real name was Richie—didn't break character once and was very forthright in acting like everyone else was off the deep end for thinking he wasn't who he claimed to be, which was Windmill. Richie had gone full method. He knew everyone's nicknames, knew the rules of all the games and after nine beers started to walk around naked and windmill his cock in the air, which is what Windmill had very firmly instructed him to do. It was never concretely known if Windmill had deliberately found a bloke who had a similar cock to him, but it seemed too coincidental for some, who then imagined their teammate spending entire days auditioning blokes for the part by making them drop their dacks and spin their cocks in front of him before making his decision.

By the end of the formal proceedings, Richie fit in so well that the boys said they'd rather have him in the team than the actual Windmill.

Things changed a few hours later, however, when some of the boys found themselves at the only dive bar that would let them in. All they saw was a security guard grab Richie by the neck and push him towards the door. Gatesy reckoned Richie had groped a girl in the corner. His exit was deserved, they'd agreed, and as they all turned around, they heard Richie start screaming out again and again: 'I AM WINDMILL! I AM WINDMILL!'

Two days later, the police knocked on Windmill's (the real one's) door and handed him an ID card and asked if they could sit and have a chat. They told Windmill that they'd interviewed a young male the night before who'd been committing identity fraud, telling them all night that he was 'Windmill'.

173

When asked if he knew anything about it, or if he had any concerns for his own safety, Windmill simply shook his head. 'No,' he said, 'that's odd.'

No one has heard from Richie since.

Photo of Windmill standing on the subway in Hong Kong battling the demons of no sleep for three nights and two for 28 HKD Smirnoff Ice.
from Fangs, 12:16 am

Oi I just got kicked out where we at cunts
from Sixty, 12:32 am

Image of international cricket umpire Billy Bowden giving an out decision.
from Squidman 12:33 am

An image of Pricey at the bar trying to order drinks by holding up two fingers. The only thing is, it isn't the bar, it's the DJ booth, and the DJs are wearing Daft Punk helmets.
from Squidman, 12:46 am

Who's Seth? I'm Seth . . . let's do another one to me!
from Dennis, 12:51 am

PISSANTS

It's you . . . MCMUFFIN!

from Squidman, 12:51 am

Momma's makin' a pubie salad and I need some of Seth's own dressing

from Dennis, 12:52 am

Oi Dennis where the fuk r u

from Hally, 12:53 am

Wherever I wanna be

from Dennis, 12:55 am

A video of Sixty dancing with a cardboard cut-out of Tom Cruise on the lounge of the karaoke bar. The camera pans to a middle-aged woman, presumably the owner, in the doorway motioning for him to get down. The camera then goes right up to her face and flips so that her and Walshy's faces take up the screen. Walshy is still singing the song and tries to give the woman a kiss on the top of the head.

from Walshy, 1:02 am

A photo of Hally from the club's fan day with the tops of his ears tucked under his hat.

from Shaggers, 1:05 am

Walshy where are you

from Fangs, 1:06 am

Sixty changed the name of the group to 'Fangs is a virgin'

Fangs changed the name of the group to 'Sixty's contract negotiations'

Shaggers changed the name of the group to 'Heavy chat'

Stick changed the name of the group to 'OI PLAY!?!'

Hally changed the name of the group to 'goodboy play! Play!'

Fangs changed the name of the group to 'Mystery Dicks'

Gatesy changed the name of the group to 'Where's Windmill?'

Dennis changed the name of the group to 'Chicken Nuggets'

*Gatesy changed the name of the group to
'Paul Salmon Appreciation Society'*

Paul Salmon refers not to the prolific goal scorer who played 324 games for Hawthorn and Essendon across three decades, but to a marine lifeform which has become part of a Mad Monday tradition at the ████████ Football Club.

It was a duty bestowed upon one player each year. In the time between the group being kicked out of the first pub of the day and before arriving at the nightclub for the evening, they were to source a full-grown Atlantic salmon which would then be brought into the nightclub and placed in the centre of the dancefloor while all the surrounding players chanted, 'PAUL SALMON! PAUL SALMON! PAUL SALMON!' repeatedly.

The Paul Salmon tradition had led to the group being banned from a number of venues and was becoming increasingly hard to pull off with the constant presence of social media and every punter now being a guerrilla journalist. Still, it has a fond place in the hearts of those who have been a part of it before.

The last player to carry out the duties was Hally, who snuck 12 pounds of Atlantic Salmon into a heaving nightclub by concealing it in his pants. When he had purchased the fish from a Chinese restaurant it was still alive, and while waiting in line, Hally felt occasional flails from the fish. When placed on the floor of the club however, there were no signs of life. Still, the cries of 'Paul Salmon' rang out.

*An image of a bewildered
Shaggers with Tubigrip
around his left calf.*

from Fangs, 2:02 am

An image of a bewildered Shaggers with Tubigrip around his left calf.

from Gatesy, 2:03 am

An image of a bewildered Shaggers with Tubigrip around his left calf.

from Fangs, 2:05 am

A video of Walshy in the back seat of a cab in the drive-thru asking for a Double Quarter Pounder meal. The voice through the intercom says, 'Sorry, only breakfast right now,' to which Walshy responds, 'What, only breakfast?!' He flips the camera around so it's facing him and in the background of the shot you can see Sixty passed out with his head cocked all the way back. He gains consciousness for a brief moment to slur out the words 'Only bweakfast'.

from Walshy, 2:32

DUBLIN/GALWAY

Elliott
DAY 38

I used the green token they gave me at reception for a free beer from the hostel bar. Mariah Carey Christmas songs were playing for some reason and the bartender with blonde hair and lip fillers smiled at me and I gestured at the speaker and said, 'Really?' about the choice of music.

A youngish man sat down on the seat beside me and introduced himself. His name was Manuel. He was from Switzerland and travelling for ten days because he'd just finished his studies back home and was unsure what he wanted to do next. We got talking about his compulsory military service and how he speaks Swiss German.

'We speak Swiss German, but the Germans do not,' he said.

Eventually the man to my left, who was Australian, joined the conversation.

'You can't mistake the accent,' he said.

Michael, bearded and solidly built, has been in Europe

179

for six weeks on what he calls a 'career break'. He's been to Portugal twice so far to do ayahuasca.

'I probably shouldn't be drinking because I'm still coming down off the stuff.'

'When did you last take it?'

'Two days ago.'

I wasn't surprised. The way he talked was very slow and controlled.

'The way it works,' he said, 'is that you go on a retreat with the guides, and they build up your dosage each day until you take the full amount at the final ceremony.'

He explained to me that he didn't have hallucinations so much as 'experienced a different reality'. He felt there had been a 'fundamental change' since, describing himself as usually a pretty anxious person who felt like a life-changing experience had taken place.

'But I wouldn't recommend it to anyone who wasn't sure they could handle it. Stick to the beers if you want to take the edge off.'

He tapped his glass against mine, making a clink sound.

Manuel was keen to go out, so me, him and Michael finished our drinks and walked out to the street. A blonde girl from Boston and her friend, Albie, asked where we were going and if they could join. Sophie, another woman who joined us out the front, was from Brussels and had recommendations on where to go, so she led the way.

Our first stop was a typical Irish pub, except that it had a very loud dancefloor hidden around the side. These two young girls—eighteen at most—stood trying to get people to buy tickets and dance. I poked my head around to look and said to the others that there was nobody there. The young girls said, 'Buy a ticket then.' I laughed and said it didn't look worth it and they waved me away.

From there we went to a second pub where we ordered more drinks and watched these two men play pool. They were both in their late forties and handy players. I figured they were regulars. After watching five or so games we went downstairs and started to dance. I was drunk enough to dance but still aware of people around me. Albie and I danced a lot and when we went upstairs to smoke, Sophie seemed quite interested in me—though there had been many men who she'd seemed interested in over the course of the night. Then she said, 'Can I ask you something?'

'Sure.'

'Sorry if it's too personal, but are you gay?'

I raised my hands in front of me, 'No, no, I'm straight. Very straight.'

She said, 'Oh, I just thought that the earring meant that you were gay.'

DAY 40

I went to check into the hostel again and they said they were booked out. Niamh, the woman at the desk, was nice about it.

'The only room available is all female. You can try the Generator,' she said. 'They are a good hostel. I've stayed there myself.'

After checking in to the Generator, I walked towards the Cobblestone Hotel on the corner. There were no seats inside, so I walked to a back room which was empty except for a guy on a stool playing guitar. He was American, grey haired and singing songs about slavery. He tried to sell me his book for twenty euros and started saying how he was disappointed that the pub didn't promote his gigs. He said he'd done thirteen or so over the last two weeks, but no one had come to watch.

'It cost me one hundred euros a night to book the room and no one even knows I'm here.'

I thanked him for the song, finished my drink and left.

I ordered a drink from the bar and stood shoulder to shoulder with people in the main room. The band tucked in the corner played until close. At the end of the night I said thank you to them and the elder fiddle player asked where I was from and that started a conversation. I asked how they all knew what to play and then turned to Maeve, the younger fiddle player, and she said that there were songs that everyone knew, melodies that you just understood. One person starts and the rest know where it goes.

Maeve had blue eyes and dark hair. When I asked what the difference was between the fiddle and the violin she said, 'They're the same thing, it just depends on the type of music you're playing.'

I stood outside with Maeve and Robyn, the guitarist, for a while and talked about where I should go in Ireland.

'Dublin is not really Ireland,' Maeve said.

She took a drag of her cigarette and added, 'Go to Galway, that's halfway between this and the real Ireland.'

I told them I'd walked through Trinity College during the day.

'Only geniuses or fakes go to Trinity,' Maeve said.

Then I made a joke about Sally Rooney and communism and I think they found that funny.

DAY 42

Cliff, who played drums in Eliza's band before moving to America with his wife, said I should message a friend of his called Andy who lives in Dublin.

Andy said that there was a football game on; his team wasn't playing but he still wanted to go. We met at a pub, bought two tickets online and then walked to the stadium.

On the way Andy told me how Cliff was a friend of his brother who stayed with them when he was travelling over here last year. One day Andy came home from work and Cliff had made himself at home in Andy's parents' house.

'He is the kind of guy who makes friends with everybody,' he said.

Andy is dating a Canadian girl who lives in Belfast. Once a week she catches the train to Dublin and the following week he takes the train to Belfast. Over Christmas they are going to Canada together to travel for six months.

Inside the stadium there were flares going off. The supporters of both sides were covered in an orange smoke. The game itself was nothing special, we left before it was over and went to find a pub where there were traditional musicians playing. Andy told me what each of the songs was about and explained the significance of The Dubliners and Luke Kelly to me. There was one song that came on and Andy said that his dad would sing it to him and his brother when they were kids, and that his dad had also sung it at his grandmother's funeral.

We had a few pints and then went to go and get some food, American pizza by the slice. Andy bought a pack of cigarettes on the way and we had to shelter behind a corner of the building to get the things to light because the wind was so strong. Andy's mate Podge joined us. They said they were going to a gig and had a spare ticket if I wanted to join. I thanked them but told them I felt like going back to the hostel. I was at that point where the alcohol was wearing off and I knew the only way to keep feeling happiness, or numbness, I'm not sure what it is anymore, was to drink more. But if I did that, I knew it'd just make things worse.

When I got in I locked myself in the hostel lobby's bathroom and went on Eliza's Instagram. All the photos of me were still up and I watched the new stories she'd posted. All I could think about was her moving on. Her with someone else. I knew I shouldn't think about her, but I couldn't help it. I imagined her saying that she loved me. Imagined how it would feel to be back together. That all of this might be a bad dream. I could hear her voice and picture how she looked when we were having sex. I started to masturbate to the thought and felt like I was going to finish. Then her face started to change. Like a horrible metamorphosis. I shook the thought and tried to continue. But it came back. Eliza's face sunk in on itself, shrivelling until it was gone. Blank. No eyes, no nose. Only lips. Lips that took in a long gasp of air then slowly turned blue. Red, bloodshot veins surfacing on the cheeks spread themselves across the entire face which had withered skin. It wasn't a face. It wasn't Eliza. It was nothing. It was my mind playing tricks on me. My own self-hatred trying to stop me from having any joy. My mind trying to forget. I started hyper-ventilating. Threw my phone away. Sat against the locked door of the bathroom and put my head between my knees. I don't know how long it was before the knocking from the other side came and someone was asking, 'Is everything alright, is everything alright?'

DAY 43

Sitting in my hotel in Galway. The wind outside is very loud. When I walked through the town, I was pushed back by the gales several times and the water under the bridge was a torrent. You could drown in there easily. I'm sure people do. The television is on and the news is playing. Christiano Ronaldo has said something that is causing people to talk. I can't stop thinking how sad hotel rooms are. This place feels like a waiting room or something and I don't think it's good to follow that line of thought too deeply. I went to the Cliffs of Moher today and felt scared standing by the edge. I felt like I couldn't trust myself. On the small tour bus there were two other people, an American woman and a Canadian guy with a bald spot on top of his head circling a large mole. The driver was explaining the Irish Potato Famine and the woman from Florida kept saying how she felt like throwing up as we went around the narrow roads. I have the Canadian guy's number. I feel like I should go out. Message him and get a drink. I can't spend the night in the room. It's only 6:45 pm. I can't. I can't be alone with myself.

DAY 45

Father John Misty in my ear. My head against the bus window. A steady stream of cars going the other way. I shut my eyes and try to breathe slowly. Another airport. Another water bottle. I look through the books. I don't need another book. A woman is sleeping across three chairs. I haven't washed my clothes in a week. The guy next to me is typing something. I have two more weeks. Everyone is lost at the airport. I google things to do Edinburgh. It's all the same shit.

TRIGGERS

Social media

Bathrooms

Stress

Attractive women

Intrusive thoughts

Salivating

Heart rate increase

Increased sexual thoughts   Loud voices

Erection   Arousal

SIGNS

ORIGIN

Inadequacy/embarrassment

Year 5

Sleepover at Marks

Numb   Anger   Regret

Shame   Loneliness   Feeling down

Embarrassment   Guilt

AFTER EFFECTS

Addiction = narrowing of the things that give us pleasure

Fulfilling life = broadening of the things that give us pleasure

THE PSYCH'S WHITEBOARD

Yt.

Ed., two things on the peripheries not featured in my diagram of the Psychologist's Whiteboard provided above: 1. A clock which is set four minutes slow. The psych (peculiar character, more below) told me that he noticed setting the clock this way led to players staying a few minutes longer. He noticed that players would leave around the fifteen-minute mark of their sessions, based off the time shown on the clock relative to the nearest hour and not the actual amount of time spent in the session. Yt. believes the reason for the rapid movement of players in and out may be related to the contents of a bingo card which predicts to a concerningly accurate degree the nature of discussions with the psych.

In my role as embedded chronicler of the club, I had to partake in my own session with the psych. He had clearly just eaten a chicken, lettuce and tomato sandwich when yt. entered, as evidenced by the crumbs around his lips. The situation evolved into one of those scenarios where yt. thought to tell him about the appearance of said crumbs, but was overcome by a sense of second-hand embarrassment, which crippled yt.'s ability to utter the necessary words. Tactics then used were for yt. to wipe his own mouth in the hope of prompting some form of mirroring behaviour (which some psychs employ to instill a sense of comfort in client, e.g. crossing legs when client crosses legs). No such luck, however. The crumbs remained throughout.

187

2. An A4 framed photo of the drummer of the White Stripes, Meg White. Psych will often refer to his musical background and inevitably tell a story of attending a White Stripes concert at Selina's during the nineties after which Meg White threw her drumsticks into the crowd. One of these projectiles is now the psych's most prized possession, which is kept in his study at home and not the office at the club. The reason for the item's safekeeping away from the club is a long-standing mistrust between the psych and the club's nutritionist, who uses the room to conduct skinfold tests on players who have requested more privacy (reasons for distrust believed to be that the nutritionist has been known to order extra protein powder on behalf of the club, which she then sells in online strong-men groups to make extra money). The Meg White image is, as far as I can tell, used to infer a connection between Meg White's drumming and the psychology of the football club, i.e. that sometimes playing your part goes unrecognised by everyone except those in the band/team alongside you. W/r/t synopsis of lengthy discussion that circled Ringo Starr's drumming, redwood trees and much, much more: Meg White's drumming was four on the floor simple, but always, in the words of the psych, suited the song perfectly, allowing the perfect amount of space for Jack White (who pretended to be her brother, though the pair were married at the time) to noodle over the top with his guitar. According to the psych, 'Meg never let her ego get in the way of the part.' These sorts of analogies are extremely popular within the Four Walls. At times it seems the coaches and staff members might be in competition to see who can draw the longest bow; for instance, various connections have been drawn between the following and the game of football: the climbing habits of mountain goats in the Himalayas, Ernest Hemingway's iceberg theory, Nicholas Taleb's black swan

PISSANTS BINGO
PSYCH SESSION EDITION

Is midway through a chicken, lettuce and tomato sandwich when you walk in	Says, 'Good, good, good' more than three times in the session	Mexican stand off—he poses a question and stares at you until you say something	He is wearing chinos, a tablecloth-check shirt and brown leather RM Williams	He takes his glasses off when saying something serious
Notes from last session are still on whiteboard when you walk in	4-minute mile	Tells you to download the mindfulness app and goes on about it like a used car salesman	Mentions that he used to play an instrument	'So, who do you live with again?'
Venn Diagram	Has a pair of quirky graphic design socks on		Asks if you've read a specific book, proceeds to check his bookshelf for the book and says he'll lend it to you, but can't find the book	Has a plastic cup of water ready for you when you walk in and the cup is filled below the first line
Stands up and opens the door for you when the session ends	Jokes about how his second job is to look out the window and yell out when the parking inspector is coming	There is a weights session going on next door and the sound of barbells thumping on the ground repeatedly ruins his train of thought	MEG WHITE	Makes a self-deprecating comment about his own physical conditioning
Makes you do the same personality test again	There is a light blue box of Kleenex tissues in the centre of the table	Blatantly forgets your name and calls you 'Champ', 'Mate', 'Bud' or 'Legend'	Mentions that he went backpacking in his twenties	Has just had a snooze in Ricky's bed

theory, and, perhaps my favourite of all, Jackson Pollock's abstract expressionist paintings. The last example came during an interaction with head of GPS data ('Scuba Steve') who showed yt. a transparent overlay of all of the GPS data from a game and then directly afterwards a printout of Jackson Pollock's 'Number 1', observing the similarities between the two. Of which, to yt., there were either many, or none.

Ed., I attained a 'bingo card' from a group of players (see attached), the elements of which are mostly self-explanatory. Though some may require more detail. For instance, the reference to '4-minute mile' is when a player is able to get in and out of the psych's office within four minutes—not a common occurrence, though it is possible.

Things such as the psych blatantly forgetting a player's name happens far more commonly than expected. For instance, last week a group of players congregated in the physio room, which is beside the psych's office. The psych, attempting to build some rapport with the wider group, entered into a conversation the players. By way of entry, he proceeded to mention everyone's name one after the other, however when he reached Pricey, he simply said, 'Big Fella.'

Furthermore, 'Has just had a snooze in Ricky's bed' is a rather interesting point. The psych is known to take afternoon naps in the SleepTech Sleep Pod, which is referred to within the Four Walls as 'Ricky's bed' and has a rather low usage amongst the playing group due to a significant design flaw.

From the SleepTech website: 'The pod's access mechanism is a seamless sliding door system, employing precision-engineered linear bearings for smooth and quiet operation. Integrated touch-sensitive controls, utilising capacitive sensors, allow users to adjust interior lighting, temperature, and even ambient soundscapes to create the perfect sleeping environment tailored to individual preferences.'

What is not mentioned is how the access mechanism can be overridden. Exit from the SleepTech Sleep Pod can be effectively prevented with the right amount of Elastoplast ankle tape, of which there is no shortage in the adjoining physio room of the ███████ Football Club. The inability of the Sleep Pod's designers to foresee such debauchery as inevitable, and their failure to account for it, is the main reason that none of the players at the club use the SleepTech Sleep Pod.

'Ricky' refers to Ricky Rogers, an American recruit delisted from the club three years ago. An interesting case that perhaps explains why, amongst the playing group, the greatest fear is being late, and why on several occasions yt. has overheard players debating whether or not they would deliberately T-bone their car if they were ever running late to training or a meeting.

Re: Ricky—reportedly, things started off well for the American. In Ricky's first month at the club, a clip of him was shown in the team meeting. HC stood up the front and said, 'What do we notice here?' He circled the green dot of his laser pointer around Ricky's running pattern, then turned and spoke to Ricky as though he was the only one in the room. 'Ricky,' he said, 'that's really good, really good.' Ricky nodded his head and in the weeks that followed there was an aura of excitement about him as a prospect within the group. Six foot ten, built like only American athletes could be built, and agile.

'Tulips' is Tulips after a video of him was shown in a team meeting and HC said that it looked like he was 'tip-toeing through the tulips', even going so far as to mimic to the playing group what that would look like.

Spoiler alert: the wheels fell off.

The first instance was when he'd been put on the field with Tulips after Tulips was returning from injury. Ricky was told to stay away from him on the field, as the last thing the conditioning staff wanted was collateral damage in a marking

191

contest between two teammates in a reserve grade game that didn't count anywhere near as much as Tulips, on a very lucrative contract, being right to play. Sure enough, in the first marking contest of the game, the big yank went up for a mark and broke two of Tulips' ribs. All week Ricky walked around the club saying, 'I broke two of Tulips' ribs, man. I'm done for.'

There were various other training mishaps, a lack of development and a waning desire to improve. But it all culminated one morning when the team was scheduled for a recovery session at the beach. There was the usual headcount as the clock ticked towards 8:30 am. The players who had been out the night before had all messaged each other to make sure everyone was up and someone retold the story of how Gatesy had used his oven timer as an alarm clock after he'd lost his phone on a night out. As the time grew near, mumbles within the group intensified. By 8:30 am, the yank had not shown. The team walked to the other end of the beach and did their swim and stretch routine. As they walked back to their cars, they saw a figure in the distance. It was the yank. When he got closer he put he put his hand up and stopped the whole group. 'Hey guys, that one's on me. I gotta own that one,' he said. There was a look in his eyes, a searching for an extended arm or forgiving comment from anyone. A life raft. Someone who would understand. But no one gave him anything; he was dead in the water before he'd even arrived.

A few months later, he had his end-of-year evaluation. Ricky walked out and said to Squidman, who was waiting by the lift, 'They said they don't want me no more, man.' The club had cut the second year of his contract and Ricky returned home the following week, where it is now believed he is a police officer.

It was shortly after this that the SleepTech Sleep Pod was purchased for what many assume to be roughly what the second year of Ricky's contract was worth.

> The ▓▓▓▓▓ Football Club seems to be a beacon for travelling salesmen claiming to have developed revolutionary methodologies for Improved Performance. Since yt. has been within the Four Walls, there have been: 1) BlueView Performa-Wear: Blue light glasses that players were to wear for two hours before bed each night. ('BlueView Performa-Wear: Your Nighttime Game Changer for Daytime Victory.') 2) OxiGum: A chewing gum that supposedly improved aerobic endurance. ('OxiGum: Unleash Your Breath, Elevate Your Game.') OxiGum was trialled one session during pre-season and abandoned after low GPS times and HC complaining that players were chewing too loudly during the huddle. As a result, several boxes of OxiGum Mint Blast Breeze reside in the property steward's storage cupboard and are often used to position sodden boots in front of a large fan when they need to be elevated and dried. 3) Visual-Eyes Game Ready: An augmented reality program that allows players to 'walk' onto grounds on the nights before games and visualise their moves. ('Visual-Eyes: See Tomorrow's Victory Today.') The issue was that that the players could only walk on to the ground and not perform any of their usual playing actions such as kicking. Several players also noted a disturbing pattern in the 'crowd' that filled the 'stadium', where a series of four movements were repeated on a loop with perfect synchronicity by the entire 'crowd' (all modelled off one character design) and that these movements were quite close to a certain raised arm movement associated with a particular time in history that many wish to forget. 4) Rohash Strooker: An art salesman who created large acrylic splash paintings that he claimed created relaxing settings. ('Rohash Strooker: Using Art to Unleash Your Team's Potential.') Strooker wanted to position a 3 × 2 metre canvas in the reception area of the club that would activate the pre-frontal cortex of the players' brains, thus enabling higher order cognitive functions such as decision-making. However, the piece he produced was removed shortly after being mounted following several complaints (including one from the club CEO) comparing its appearance to that of the bleached anus of a cow. 5) Zenith Athlete Performance (ZAP): A four-player game that was introduced to improve players' reflexes and to build a sense of composure under pressure. Each player was connected to a console and given a buzzer to press after a light in the centre of the console turned from green to red. A leader board was set up in the changeroom to encourage uptake. However, the playing group soon identified that a certain configuration of settings in conjunction with the removal of one screw from the battery compartment would cause the device to malfunction and 'zap' the loser. Its uptake surged but was subsequently banned by the club after several players reported 'numbness' along their playing arms.

TIME TRIAL

MUD

Alright, brus you ready for this? Shit, the fact that you have to ask means you're probably not. But fuck it. You're here now. You're ready. You're good. You're good, brus.

Simple shit. When you go down the gravel, let your legs fall over themselves, use that as a small recovery. That's using your brain, brus. And sit behind Gatesy, just on his tail. Use him as a little windbreak, fall into his slipstream like one of those cyclists. The type with the lycra and those special shoes that make them walk like they're holding onto a massive shit.

You got this, brussy. Focus on Gatesy's heels. Keep up with his heels. Then when you get to the oval, kick. Not too much though, brus. Just a bit. It's 500 m from there. What's 500 m? Fucking nothing, brus! Five 100s. Shit, the last one doesn't even count because you're not going to stop 100 m out, are you brus? Once you're 100 m out you got no choice but to finish. Your mind gives up before your body. You've just got to keep going. You're fucking Goggins man. David Goggins. And Nedd Brockman, brus. Get comfortable being uncomfortable. That's the shit. Yes brussy, that's it. Get to a

194

point of pain where you just can't take it anymore and then break through. Then you'll keep going. Who's gonna carry the boats? Uncle Mud, that's who.

This is ten minutes of your life. You can hold off that fucking voice in your head for ten minutes. Don't cunts go walking on hot coals? And swim laps in ice-cold water? The human body is fucked. Today is your day, brus. Today is your day . . .

The moment between ready and go. Here it comes . . . and . . . go brussy, go . . . stay strong . . . hold your line . . . cut right . . . Fumbles will take the lead . . . let him go . . . who's on your right? Shaggers . . . How the fuck does a guy with that body run faster than me? . . . Whatever, let him go . . . Where's Gatesy? Not in front. He must be behind. Piss Boy's gone out like a fucking maniac. Nah brus, don't do that. He'll die at the end of the first lap. Stay cool and calm. Be like that Greek fucker, Marcus Aeriolas, live in the present brus. Live in the present . . .

Fangs is somewhere over my back shoulder. Breathing heavy. It'll be the same story with him, brus. Throws in the towel when it gets a bit hard . . . better than Stick though, saying his tendons are too sore to run . . . this pace is good . . . I feel good . . . every step takes me a metre closer to the end and every step is a piece of piss brussy . . . I could run like this all day . . . I could keep this pace comfortably . . . who's gonna carry the fucking boats? Me, brussy, me!

Focus on the breath. One breath every four steps. Don't think about the steps too much. Focus on the breath. It's coming in easy. It's coming in easy and going out easy. In brussy, out brussy. In brussy, out.

Coming up to the hill. Let your legs fall . . . Shaggers is still beside me. Gatesy's beside him. This is a good group.

Windmill is a bit in front. This is a good peloton to be a part of . . . try not to be wide when we come to the oval. Fall into line. Ideally behind Gatesy . . . and then watch his heels . . . coming up to the gate . . . what's the watch say . . . 3:30 . . . what's that . . . first kilometre in 3:30 . . . first lap will be close to 5:00. It's heavy grass though . . . bit of Stewy Dew about . . . probably 5:05 . . . you're ahead of where you should be, brus. And you're feeling fresh. Fresh as fuck. This is *good*. This is really fucking good.

Hold this pace and then you've got an extra ten seconds saved up. Money in the bank. It's alright if Gatesy creeps out a bit. Ten seconds. Give him fifty metres. That'll still keep you on track . . .

. . . five ten split . . . lost a bit there, brus . . . after six minutes you've only got four left . . . well, five left . . . but the last one doesn't count . . . You've already done one and a half times that when you get to the final four. You've done what's left plus another half. It's fuck all. Just have to hold on for this minute, brus . . . Ok, there goes Gatesy with his little kick. Hold onto him . . . hold onto him . . . he is speeding up . . . he's definitely speeding up . . . fuck it . . . dig in a bit, he'll slow down at the top of the hill . . . stay . . . stay . . . stay . . . get to six minutes. Get to six minutes. The last four is easy. That's one three minuter and the break after . . . you smash out six three minuters easy, brus . . . Sure, you drop off in the last two . . . but you can do four fucking consistent . . . hit 880 each time . . . or 880, 850, 845, 820 . . . Just dig in. For one three minuter. Like your life depends on it . . . fuck . . . Shit, I don't know if I'm going to finish if I keep this pace up . . . I've got to go down the gravel then round the trees then the last lap. I need to save a bit up . . . slow up a bit . . . save some tickets . . . Gatesy's going . . . you'll get him with your kick . . .

196

he doesn't kick at the end . . . you can make up fifty metres on him easy at the end . . . if he gets 100 in front of you then you can chew up fifty when you get to the far point post . . . just ease up a bit . . . take deep breaths . . . fuck who's that behind me? . . . Hally, cunt's humming in the second lap . . . I should try that next time . . . cruise the first lap and then when I've got my second wind I'll be able to pick it up in the second lap . . . I'll be in a more positive mindset then, knowing that I have the energy left . . . It'll feel like I'm downhill skiing . . . or maybe I go fucking hard and try and hold on . . . no . . . I can't do that . . . that won't work for me . . . Piss Boy's done that today and he's cooked himself . . . If I sat at the back I'd get a kick each time I overtook someone. I could mow them down . . . get to the next one . . . then get to the next one . . . Shaggers? Cya. Fangs? You too, cunt. They've made their beds, they can lie in them. Not me though. Ticking them off as I pass, that would keep me focused and motivated . . . getting overtaken or trying to hold on isn't good. It's fucked me mentally. Fucking hell . . . don't look at your watch . . . don't look at your watch . . . what's a song . . . sing something in your head . . . distract yourself . . . don't look at your watch. Who's gonna carry the boats, brussy? Who's gonna carry the fucking boats? Don't look at your watch. There's nothing good that can come from looking at your watch now. Don't look at it . . . just wait . . . wait till you get to the oval . . . then look . . . wait . . . wait . . . FUCKING TEN MINUTES. FUCKING FUCK BRUS. That's one minute to do the final lap . . . I'm going to run over eleven here. What the fuck . . . go . . . kick now . . . don't get over eleven . . . Shaggers is ahead of you . . . The prick isn't slowing down. Fuck . . . do you want to be here? Why didn't you do the running you were meant to . . . Don't give the Big Fella or High Horse Shaggers another chance to say it . . . that you're not a good trainer . . . fuck them . . . that prick hasn't even played a game yet . . . at least my name's on the board . . . a hundred to go . . . I can't feel my legs . . . 10:42 . . . i'm not going to make it . . . I'm not going to make it . . . I feel like I'm about to die . . . 10:45 . . . Who's gonna carry the boats? Who's gonna carry the fucking boats . . . there aren't any fucking boats here, brus, you're on a fucking field . . . Brus, it's a metaphor and shit. Fuck that . . . keep going . . . keep going . . . 10:52 . . . fuck you . . . fuck you . . . fuck you . . . fuck you . . . fuck you . . . 10:55 . . . 10:56 . . . 10:57 . . . 10:58 . . . 10:59 . . .

OUR HAPPY PLACE

Stick

Ah, wakey wakey, hands off shnakey. Where the fuck am I?
I feel like I've eaten a bucket of cement and it's set in my
head. Could this be CTE? Or whatever the fuck all those old
cunts say they have, trying to squeeze money from the game.

Fuck me dead. Check out this view. Right over the fucking
ocean. Get your telescopes out, boys, and behold my cock!
Ah, hang on, what do we have here . . . our first piece of
evidence from the night in question. Two sets of handprints on
the window. A successful night was had by Sticky Stick then.
I've got no recollection of the deed being done, but the DNA
evidence does not lie, does it? My sausage fingers and her long
elegant ones. And she must be a bit of show pony, wanting it
in front of the window like that. Wonder where she's got to?

And here is our second piece of evidence. Exhibit B: a nice
wedding photo on the bedside table. Bit thick through the
arms and legs but gee she has a pretty face on her. Mr and
Mrs Pearly Whites. Shame that I have come between such a
glamour couple like I have, but who knows, maybe I was doing
you both a favour. Maybe Old Stick should hang around, get

himself a little sugar mummy in a nice pair of Juicy track pants. A place this nice, she must have a bit of cash—or the cucked husband does, but we can knock him off and I'll just move in, no questions asked. Take my place in the Taj Mahal. Hell, I'd suck on her James Nitties every night for a little bit of pocket money in return.

Ooooh, tell you what, there's something foul brewing in my guts right now. I'm going to have to use your bathroom, dear. And it ain't going to be pretty. Not one bit.

Well, looky here, our next piece of evidence—a couple of raincoats floating in the toilet. It would appear that once was not enough for her, eh? Not only that, they look proper full too. Sure her bloke would be a bit sus if a coupla kids pop out that don't look the faintest bit like him. Better to be safe than sorry. Horny little minx. I shall dispose of the evidence for you with a simple flushy flush. I must say I'm surprised I could get it going twice.

Geez, tell you what. I can feel that. She must've slipped a pinky up there. I feel like it got right kinky last night and a bit of pink in the stink is all fine and well with me. A modern, sexually liberated man. Maybe I should fuck blackout drunk more often. Maybe I've got some sorta Johnny Sins alter ego which emerges after twenty-five drinks.

Alright Stick, pull it together. Get that brain back in your head and away from your cock. What actually happened? For pres we had a balcony party at Mud's. Gatesy was walking around with a cape on and the beer bong. Windmill's house-mate drove us to the club in his chip van. In the back were me, Squidman, Fangs, Shaggers and I think Big Sexy. Gatesy and Windmill were on the floor before we left. Windmill was curled around the toilet bowl, I remember that clear as day. Poor cunt. Then what? I remember getting kicked out for trying to pour a drink down that bloke's saxophone. That would explain this shirt I'm wearing that says, *i love* ████. A quick change of attire is usually good enough to trick the few combined brain cells of most bouncers. Then from there . . . Hmmm . . . Think Sticky, think . . . Ah, the hens' night! That explains why I'm here. That's right. The pink sashes and a tiara. Cock straws. Unmistakeable. It's all coming back to me now. I told them I'd give the bride-to-be a lap dance. Turns out one of her friends had a different idea and stole me for herself. Do you take this woman to be your one night stand for the night, to love and to cherish? To that, I say, I do. I truly do.

Alright, let's have a little looky look around the house now. See if there's any secret sex dungeon or if we kept it to the room with a view. Ladies and gentlemen, the first door on the left contains . . . an array of children's toys and a little table painted like a ladybug. I suppose the kiddie mustn't have been home last night. Mum must have cashed in some coupons for a night to herself. It's one thing to bring a drunken buck home so you can fuck his brains out, but another thing altogether to do it when you've got a kid in the next room. Maybe Mr Room With a View has shipped out and taken the kid, or maybe they're at a sleepover with a little pal. Hope it went a bit better than my first sleepover. Jesus. Silver Fox Serge and his little Argentinian pecker poking out the bottom of his robe running in to check on me and little Matty.

Ok well, the sight of the ladybug table has sent me completely flaccid. I've sunk faster than the Titanic. No morning after quickie for me. Oh fuck . . . I can hear a car pulling up in the driveway. Maybe I can go another round, if you insist. Back to the window we go. Oh, there she is. All dolled up and everything. I must've been out cold, too gone for her to wake me with the hair dryer or a blow—Oh, I see, we have a bit of a situation here. It's the husband as well. This is not something I care to be in right now. He punches me. I punch him. She slaps me. I boot the kid across the room. It's a mess waiting to happen. Abort mission. Get out now! Oh god, too late: footsteps. Fuck! Think, Sticky, think. Christ, my cement head is really getting in the way right now. Now I'm just thinking about fucking her in front of the window while all the sailors out at sea get an eyeful. Come on, get your shit together. That's it. Hide in the closet . . . It's a tight fit, nestled between her dresses. Sequins against my cheek. Meow, little kitty. Who's a naughty girl? Now just don't breathe or sneeze or make any sort of noise. God, those footsteps are too heavy. It's the geezer. The cuck. Fuck. I can hear the shower turning on. This is my chance. I'll jump out, run downstairs. Give Mrs Room a little kiss on the cheek and get the fuck out of here and no one will be any the wiser. Ok, three, two . . .

'Oh, hey there.'

Christ, what? He looks mortified. Like he's about to start crying. Like his head's going to go full OceanGate and crumple in on itself. What the fuck? Is he going to hit me? I bet he's a pacifist. Well, that's why your missus is out finding young blokes like me. Now he's looking away. Oh, fuck. He's locked the door. Maybe he's going to kill me in here. Maybe this isn't the first time this has happened. Shit. Up you get, Stick.

'Look mate I—'

'What the fuck are you still doing here!?'

Oh. He's in my face. Got me by the neck. Long fingers. Why does this feel—

'You were meant to fucking *leave*. I left a note that said you had to be gone by twelve. Are you fucking *serious*?!'

The handprints.

'Fuck, put one of these shirts on. FUCK!! She's going to know it's happened again. Fuck, you idiot.'

Two raincoats.

'Just follow me and keep your mouth shut.'

Sore arse.

Fuck.

My hands are shaking as I button up the shirt. I don't want to know. I don't want to know. The hens' party left. I was at the bar on my own. Then he bought me a drink.

'You on your own, sailor?'

Oh god. Don't think about it, Stick. Just walk down the stairs and get out. You were never here. Say it again. *You were never here.*

'Hey honey, sorry, forgot to say that Mark was here just finishing off some of the reports for the team. Mark, do you need anything before you head off?'

My mouth is too dry to say anything. I feel like I'm going to be sick. The only thing I need is to get the fuck out of here. Deny. Deny. Deny.

'Alright, well, thanks a lot Mark. I'll see you in at the office tomorrow morning. Great work with everything again.'

The door shuts behind me. The doormat says, *Our Happy Place.*

The shouting on the other side of the door suggests it might be anything but.

A MONDAY MORNING MEETING

Time: 0900h
Location: Centre of Excellence
Mood: Post-loss

Coach Mac	Fangs
... no one can tell ... no one can tell. No one can tell ... the Big Fella can't tell ... you're fine ... just ... just get through your reserves review and then you can slink to the back ... fuck ... I'm coming down hard ... why am I fucking shivering ... it was just coke ... maybe speed ... fuck fuck fuck ... no one can tell ... just get through this meeting then no more ... no more coke the rest of the year ... it's not good for your head ... it's not good for anything ... you can stop using ... delete all the	Abandon all hope, ye who enter ... Ok, what have we got in here today for the Monday *Mourning* meeting? Lethal in or is he too busy smoking darts out the front? No, there he is, tucked in the back corner. Hardest cunt on the face of the earth. And they've shipped him down to the IT department because he was having PTSD fits around the other coaches. Shame the bloke types with two fingers. Gee, hang on, Stick looks like he's seen a ghost. Unlike him to be sitting up straight like that without pointing his finger in someone's

numbers . . . that's step one . . . remove the temptations and the triggers . . . step two . . . stop drinking . . . drinking leads to poor decisions which leads to coke . . . all roads lead to coke . . . my god I can feel my teeth grinding . . . Ok, focus . . . is Piss Boy wearing a new pair of glasses? He is. Christ . . . They don't look great on him . . . If only he wore them on the weekend, maybe the cunt would've been able to hit a target inside 50 for us . . . what's the bet he comes into my office after this to ask for some more feedback only he'll push back against everything I say . . . Lay a tackle Piss Boy . . . *I couldn't get there* . . . Work harder on your fitness . . . *I haven't had a proper pre-season* . . . Don't get injured . . . *I can't help it* . . . Excuse after excuse . . . shit ok, I'm up . . . Alright boys, reserves review from the weekend. Not the result we wanted, but not a bad result, if we're being honest about it. What it really drives home to the group is that we need to be consistent over four quarters. That it's not good enough to do it for ten- or fifteen-minute bursts, that when we cross that line we don't switch off until the job's done. I've just got a couple of clips to show you that highlight some

face and giving them a bake. What's up his arse?

Look at Quadey standing up the front of the room there. He's the single piece of tape that holds everything to do with a computer together inside these Four Walls. But for us players, never to be seen when you need him: *404: Quade not found.* I still can't take the cunt seriously after Round 1 last year. Rocked up to the game with a hangover, then printed off the wrong stat sheets at quarter time. Craigy just threw a pen at him and said, 'Count every kick, handball and mark the old-fashioned way.' As in, write them all down. That's a mare as it is, but it only got worse. Must've been the smell of coffee coming down the aisles of the flight home that triggered some sensory recall from the espresso martinis he was having the night before, but all I see is poor old Quadey jump up and try to make it to the bathroom at the back of the plane. Shame his timing couldn't have been worse—he found himself caught between the trolleys at either end. Ah, poor Quadey. Fell to all fours and threw up all over that woman's shoes. The Scooby Doo's match day crew has never been the same since. The Big Fella gave them a big talking to

205

of our better efforts and some where there's room for improvement . . . Quade, if you could just click play . . . thank you . . . Ok . . . shit shit shit which clip is this? . . . Fuck did I upload them properly? . . . Why the fuck was I—ok thanks, pause it there . . . So that right there is an example of us getting our defensive shape right. We've got good layering on the inside and outside and a really good press from Bubbles to come forward. Bubbles, are you in here? Great, there you are . . . what helped you to go forward the way you did there? . . . Please say voice cunt, just say voice . . . yep, ah huh . . . ah huh . . . and the voice? That's exactly right. The voice from behind makes the decision for you. It's something that we as a ressies and development group need to keep improving upon. We can't be quiet out on that field. The voice acts as an extra player for you . . . Ok, so next clip . . . Fuck am I sweating? . . . Shit, shit . . . is that my nose going? . . . Oh fuck . . . wipe quick . . . wipe it away . . . sniff it up . . . *** *** *** shit there's still some in my nostril . . . ah fuck . . . I can taste it . . . I can taste it going down my throat . . . my lips are numb . . . ah huh . . . ok . . . Quadey . . .

about PROFESSIONALISM and STANDARDS. They've only gone up in my books though.

Ok, what's Mac got for us this week? Looks a bit shaky today. Heard something about him as a character. Very suspicious, how he wound up here after all that shit with his old mob got swept under the carpet. A full investigation that just went *poof,* nowhere. Shaggers may be on the money when he says that Mac's godfather is on the board here. Nepotism, that'd be about right. But you're up the front and I'm here so let's do the Stanford Prison thing. Mac, you have my undivided attention. Let's see what you deliver, just don't strip me down and throw a bucket of shit over me.

Oh, this clip. Bubbles almost cooks it and just guesses which way to go. I guarantee Mac will use this to drive home one of his familiar points about voice and trust and structure. There's a reason he's got the audio muted while showing the clip, because it'd be abundantly clear that there was not a single word spoken to Bubbles during that passage of play. Shootsy, who's just behind him? Never utters a word, and Big Sexy is still learning his lefts from his rights half the time. Cunt can pause it . . . pause it there . . . yep . . . that's good . . . ok . . . so . . . so . . . sorry . . . so what did we notice in that clip? . . . Anyone? . . . One of the boys that played . . . how about . . . Fangs, what's happened there? . . . Come on, cunt . . . be good for something for once . . . no more sooking around . . . please . . . ah huh . . . ah huh . . . yep . . . exactly . . . that's exactly it . . . what happened was that we didn't get our defensive running right which meant that on turnover, we weren't in the right spots offensively . . . so offence starts with defence and vice versa . . . we have to do our work early, slide down the ground and defend and that way when our defenders win it back, which happened a bit on the weekend, they look up and see us on the outside shoulders . . . we didn't see it there and it led to us turning the ball over again . . . ok . . . I think I'll leave it there . . . overall, not a bad effort from the twos boys . . . plenty to rock on . . . work on . . . sorry . . . and we'll be better for it next week . . . fuck, rock on . . . and my nose is going . . . they've got to notice . . . I can just shoot off to the bathroom quickly . . . Big Fella is doing his spiel . . . I can duck off . . . down the hall . . . down

kick a ball, but he's got no idea about much else.

Shit, what's going on there? Has he got a bit of a blood drip going? Christ, he does. Naughty boy, Mac! Turns out there may be truth to those rumours after all. I wonder how deep the trail goes? Uh oh, he's thrown it out to the group. Shit. Hide. No, I'm in the crosshairs. I'm done for. Meeting voice on. Clear the throat.

Me: Yeah, so basically that one's on me. You can see me just drifting there and ball-watching. I've got to push down another five or ten to get space on my man so that I can get used on the way back out.

There we go, that should suffice. It's not hard. Just pick the stock phrase, rinse and repeat. If all else fails, just say you can't remember that one.

Shit, tune back in. Slightly more relaxed now that the Big Fella's on, talking about the Big Boys' Game, but he's no stranger to a rogue call-out either.

Oh wow, the Big Fella has got it going frame-by-frame here. He's going super slo-mo, fucking *Wide World of Sports* 2,400 frames per second. Poor Hally's got his balls under the microscope here, and it ain't pretty. Shit, they're looking a bit deformed, unnatural to a the hall . . . shit . . . that coke in my nostril has hit me . . . it's got me good . . . ah . . . head noise . . . not good . . . I'll be back down soon . . . no . . . just delaying the crash . . . I can't crash today . . . I'm here without any supply . . . it's ok . . . I can just text one of my numbers . . . they'll get here now . . . I can meet them down the road . . . NO NO, don't do that cunt . . . no more . . . you said it before . . . no more . . . we're off it . . . just . . . STOP! STOP! Delete the numbers . . . get rid of them . . . look up the number for that rehab clinic . . . fuck . . . what's it called again? . . . The doc was talking about it . . . maybe go down and see him . . . hey doc, just wanted to see if you had the number for that rehab clinic? . . . No, that sounds fucking dumb . . . crazy . . . don't do that . . . just . . . just . . . get through the day . . . get through today, and tomorrow you'll be ok . . . start your recovery from now . . . start meditating again . . . in for four . . . hold . . . hold . . . out for six . . . you are a leaf floating down the river . . . your mind is not your mind . . . your mind is a thinking thing . . . view your mind . . . observe your thinking . . . what *colour* are your feelings? . . . Label them . . .

degree where unnatural no longer seems a strong enough word. Mutinous. Hiroshima level toxicity ballbag. Spiderman, but bitten on the balls so his superpower is shooting out testicular beams of energy. Pew. Pew. Pew . . .

Alright, who's he going after now? Who's next to fuck up? Which of the whipping boys will it be . . . It's Georgey-Boy, having a little snooze on the field. Now all he has to do is say the magic words and all shall be forgiven. Say it Georgey-Boy, say that it's *fucking shithouse*, that you were wrong. Utter those magical little words. Uh oh, Georgey-Boy has gone silent. He's shrunken down. He's going for a little standoff. One Mississippi. Two Mississippi. Somebody say something. The Big Fella's head looks like it's about to explode and for those of us in the first three rows, there are no raincoats on offer. *Rambo III*. There will be blood. Guts. Gore. That is one brain whose contents I would not like to see. The word 'efficiency' would paint every inch of every wall. That and a list of the pricks in this room whom he wishes he could give the axe. Cunts who can then go join the grave-yard of names gone by. Who will feature as In Memoriam-looking now picture that little yellow orb floating from the tips of your toes to the top of your head, warming you as it does . . . now stop shaking . . . stop shaking . . . fucking hell get back down there and front up and get through the day . . . no more . . . no more . . . just STOP!

social media tiles. White ghosts floating up to the sky, thanked dearly for their contribution to the ▓▓▓▓▓▓ Football Club and told they are part of the *family* forevermore. You know who else had a 'family'? Charlie Manson. That didn't end too well, did it? So I hope it does not come to that. For fuck's sake, somebody say SOMETHING!

THE ONE THAT GOT AWAY

Shaggers

Kick ons and we've ticked off the usual topics. Gruggsy our goal-kicking coach and his double family situation back in the eighties. How he managed to keep them separate until a phone call from one of the wives asking him to pick up their kid from school. Must've been a big day for Gruggsy because he said, 'Which one?' and of course, the wife calling said: 'What the fuck do you mean, Gruggsy? We've only got the one kid!'

Stick's just run off on his tangent about whichever player's sexuality he's currently fixated on, saying they've been offered a contract here and that the club pitched to them a full PR plan saying they'd support them coming out of the closet.

Of the various things Stick said on his rant, none make the podium for homophobic remarks this year. Would be hard to knock off Walshy's joke at induction drinks: 'How do you get four gay guys onto a bar stool?'

Went right into shock and apologies when he found out a couple of the senior boys had gay brothers.

This topic, as usual, leads to a back and forth between Fangs and Stick over how many gay players are in the comp.

My view: who gives a fuck? And if a prick is gay, I don't blame him for staying in the closet. Why subjugate yourself to all that extra attention? The whole world just wants to wheel you out like a meat puppet to get their own agenda across. You're no different than any other player, except you are, because they'll make you a fucking spokesperson when you probably just want to get a kick like the rest of us.

But try getting in any of that when Stick and Fangs are solving the world's problems. Fuckheads.

Somehow, and I don't quite know how, but the conversation has now turned to the one that got away. I've obviously not got much to say on the matter. Gee and I have been together so long that we've started to look like each other. I'd never say it to her, but if you didn't know, you'd be forgiven for thinking we were just a very close sort of brother and sister. Foot rubs on the couch, keep the bloodlines pure. Crook.

Stick's got the floor. The speaking baton is the collar of Pleb's deceased dog. Henry. Poor thing had a heart condition that none of us knew about when we took him on a little adventure. Went too long without taking his meds. Pleb was distraught about it, sent out a PSA over socials asking for all our supporters to help him look. But there's nothing that could be done without the meds. Henry would've gone sooner or later. When viewed this way we're able to live with clear consciences at least. Well, clear*er*.

Gripping the red collar, Stick's blabbing on, trying to act like he's not in denial about Tay leaving him. It's been a year now. It was after a night out and he went back to theirs fuck-eyed and they got into a Matty Rowell. He says she was already on the way out when he went into the kitchen, pulled out two pieces of bread and slapped his cock between them. Reckons he said, 'Sure you don't want dinner one last time?' and then she walked out. He is the sort of cunt who would say that, the sort of cunt who would bury himself so far down that there's no chance of redemption. The punchline to the story when he tells it is that, as she walked out the door, he yelled out that they were all out of tomato sauce. He's in denial, I tell you.

Fangs gets his turn and starts telling his story, which I've heard before. Twin sister of his best friend in school. She left him waiting in the bushes one day after school, so they broke up. Stick yells out, 'Broke up? How old were you, like ten?'

The new addition to the story from Fangs is that the bird moved somewhere around here not long ago, and asked him to help her with a fridge or something.

'What'd you say?' says Mud.

'Said I was busy.'

'Worried she'd stand you up again?'

'Nah, just didn't want to help her with the fridge.'

If there was an image to describe Fangs, then waiting in the bushes would be it. Waiting. Always waiting. He's going to die waiting. Love the bloke, but he's a victim of the universe now. He's given up trying. I just want him to wake up and realise it, or just to give a fuck for once. The one that got away . . . could be the title of a movie about his career. A short film, more like it. Shit, he'd go see it. Cunt loves his movies and his books more than he loves his footy sometimes. That copy of that lobster book in his bag is his most prized possession of late.

Mud takes the collar and then starts talking. He's got his sad eyes on. Happens to him after a few drinks, when he drops the arrogance.

'I did English with this bird in Year 12. Shinelle. Me and her were the only kids in the class who were normal.'

'There's no way you did Year 12 English!' says Stick, almost jumping out of his chair.

'And there's no way you're considered normal, cunt,' adds Squidman, giggling to himself as he does.

Mud does have that sort of book-smart-but-dumb-as-dog-shit vibe about him sometimes. No common sense. I've seen him cut Glad Wrap with scissors to cover a plate. I think his mum, who happens to be a great sort—so much so that Mud gets weird if you start talking about her, which of course, we do—was real hands-on with him.

Fangs pulls everyone back into line by saying, 'Shut up, cunts, he's got the collar.'

'Can I continue, pricks? Ok. I messaged her one day asking what her marks were or some shit like that, and then we just started talking online every day after school. Never talked to her in person or anything, but always online and we'd smile and shit at each other in class.

'Anyway, the thing is, Shinelle had cancer. Like fucking terminal. The shit that gets you, brus. She had this walking stick at school and she had trouble getting around.'

I look at Stick, who bites down on his tongue. He wants to say something about them both having peg legs and being the perfect match. But he keeps it down for once and just sucks on his beer.

'One day the school told us it had escalated but she was still going to do her exams. Like, fucking hell, imagine being told you were going to kick it? The last thing I'd be doing is fucking school exams. I'd go to the Colosseum or the Eiffel Tower or something. But I dunno, maybe she just wanted to be a normal kid. Whatever the fuck normal is.'

I can see in Mud's eyes that he's building up to something. Never seen him like this before. Fucking hell, these drinks have got us in some kind of mood.

'She did her exams and then I didn't hear from her for

a while. I started training here just after that and when we got our marks back I messaged a few people, including her. I never heard back from her. I messaged her at like 8:15 in the morning, just before training, and then I found out she'd passed away earlier that morning. The funeral was a few days later and her mum was up the front saying how it was like she'd waited to get her marks back, and then she could leave. It was my first funeral. Well, the first one that I cared about. We all went outside and let all these balloons off into the air and I remember watching them fly all the way up. All these white balloons. And I just stood there thinking how no one fucking knew that we had this friendship, you know? Like her parents would've had no idea who the fuck I was, brus. But her and me had this connection. Maybe it's all bullshit but I think there was something there. But yeah, she's gone now.'

We all sit kind of silent looking down into our bottles. Squidman looks desolate. Like he might be digging up his own baggage. Same with Fangs. Heavy chat. As the sole participant without baggage, or with the least amount of carry on, I speak.

'That sucks, Mud,' I say.

He looks up at me, makes eye contact for half a second. He's got puffy eyes. I haven't seen him like this before. Sooky, sure. But this is something else.

'I went into the car after the funeral and just didn't move for like an hour. It was freezing and I had no heater or nothing, but I just sat there while the windows frosted over. I was reading our old messages. I still got them. But yeah, fuck I don't know. That's it, hey.'

When one of your mates starts talking like they've got a heart it does something to you. Something that nothing else can do.

INSIDE/
OUTSIDE

A REAL BULLDOG

Becoming a Real Bulldog. That was what they called fucking Belle Thompson. Belle was the quote unquote sister of the male playing group at the Craigstown Bulldogs. The incestual sister who everyone messaged on a night out and wanted to fuck after a few drinks.

She had played juniors with the boys growing up and still trained with them once a week. She was now twenty-two and it was well known that she had slept with a few members of the playing group, some of them multiple times. But she maintained a rule: she would never *date* any of them. It was only sex. She'd known for some time that men were a bunch of pretenders, and if not for the thing between their legs and the continuation of the population, then women could take off and start a better civilisation on their own. But that was a while away, and if there were boys who wanted to fuck, and there were boys who wanted to be fucked by her, then so be it.

This familiar thought runs through her head as she is seated between two of her club's male players at the ▉▉▉▉▉ Football Club match.

She was aware of the phrase, Becoming a Real Bulldog. She liked the power it gave her over the group, so much so that in the notes app of her phone she had a running list titled: Boys I've made Real Bulldogs. Sometimes she changed it to say 'Men I've made Real Bulldogs' but when she looked at it, the word 'Men' didn't seem quite right.

She's been drinking for some time today, to get herself to the point where she could maybe add another one to the list. It was Ladies' Day after all, and if the footballing world would put her on a performative pedestal once every 365 days, then she would take it.

And take it she had. When the club board asked the girls if they'd like to be the showcase game on Ladies' Day, Belle was the loudest to veto the idea. She petitioned that their game should be the earliest of the day, so that they (she) could start drinking as soon as possible after the game and be drunk by the time they made it to the stadium for the ████████ Football Club game.

To her left, Boof. Belle has always known of Boof's romantic feelings towards her. To him, she was the girl next door fantasy. Their families were close, and they'd grown up five minutes away from each other. They'd carpool to training and when Belle started working behind the register of the local IGA, Boof would find any excuse to go down and buy something from her register. On those occasions he would say only a few words and make minimal eye contact. Perhaps it was this lack of eye contact that had prevented Boof from seeing the truth: that Belle just wasn't interested in him.

To her right though, a different story. Belle knew from Instagram that Flynn was in another relationship, however she also knew that there was a chink in the armour. This she interpreted from his flame reactions to her Instagram stories over the previous two Saturday nights.

There was a history between the pair. The first time had been three years before. They had been out for the club's fiftieth anniversary. While they were sitting in a group, Belle had asked Flynn to kiss her on the cheek. As he leaned in, she turned her head and made sure their lips met. She looked at her friend Sarah, who she'd bet earlier in the night that she would kiss Flynn on the lips, and raised her eyebrows to show that she was in charge.

At a party a few hours later, Flynn followed Belle into a bedroom. They looked at each other for less than a second, then locked lips. Flynn put both his hands on Belle's ass and squeezed, then pushed her onto the bed and started to feel under her dress. He whispered that he was going to put his thick cock deep inside her and Belle let out a shaking flutter of breath. She could feel herself getting wet. She loved dirty talk. She grabbed Flynn's hand and directed it around her clit. She'd learned that the boys weren't great at knowing where to rub and how. Rather than stroke their egos, she stroked herself. As he pulled down her underpants, Belle felt a sense of panic. She thought she could see figures standing in the corner of the room. She felt clumsy stabbing fingers between her legs. She wanted an out. She didn't want to add another name to the list. Thinking quickly, she pushed him away and asked Flynn about his girlfriend, his now *ex*-girlfriend. It was enough to kill the heat of the moment.

She wondered if Flynn had ever told his ex-girlfriend about the night. Probably not, she figured. Then she wondered if tonight his new girlfriend would be cause for him to avoid her advance. Testing the waters during the quarter-time break of the game, she'd scooped the ice cubes out of Flynn's drink.

'What are you doing?' said Flynn.

'You don't like ice cubes, do you?'

'Guess not.'

It wasn't her best work. But she knew that none of the boys cared about her chat. Boys were idiots: hormones on legs with a few brain cells telling them to eat, fuck, drink and shit.

Deep into the third quarter, Belle returned her focus to Flynn. She tried another tactic.

'You wouldn't finish that drink, would you Flynn?'

'No I wouldn't. Well, not yet.'

Not yet. There was hope.

'So, how's your new girlfriend?'

'She's good.'

'That's good.'

As the three-quarter-time siren went, Belle felt the moment was dead once more. Flynn had been drinking himself silly all game. She could smell the alcohol seeping out of his pores, which were frustratingly clean. She had three separate skin creams to keep her face clean. Flynn most likely used nothing at all. How was that fair?

Even if his conscience did waver, she doubted he'd be any good to her tonight anyway. So, all things considered, Belle left her seat and walked out of the stadium. She could no longer stand the drinks being spilled on her by the boys around, nor the lack of stimulation beyond a humdrum conversation about the game being played.

Belle found a spot outside the stadium where she took a seat and began to vape. She pulled out her phone and read the list of Real Bulldogs. Some of the names on there she hated. The men's head coach. That was a night she wished to forget. It was a good thing he was no longer welcome back at the club. Also, some names she had forgotten about, erased from history if not for the list.

Alone in her thoughts she was disrupted. *What the fuck was that?*

'Shit, sorry.'

She looked up and saw a figure wearing a ███████████ Football Club polo shirt. He was clean shaven, looked about her age, not unattractive but nothing to write home about. Maybe that was just bumps and scratches on him from a game of footy earlier that day. Fucking men. Can't even walk straight without causing destruction.

'Watch where you're going, fuckwit.'

Oh yeah, Belle Thompson had a way with words.

'Woah, Christ. Sorry to disrupt your precious vape time.'

She looked him up and down. He seemed familiar. Or he just had that wanky aura that all men his age who go to footy games have. At least he didn't have the mullet and that shitty bowl cut on top. And if she had to see one more group of boys wearing jean shorts and tablecloth-chequered shirts, she'd grab the nearest fork/chopstick/sharp utensil and give herself a full frontal labotomy.

She took a deep breath in of her vape and blew the smoke out the side of her mouth. Smoke? Vapours? Chemically demented aerosol? Whatever it was that was inside these things that she had become slowly reliant on over the last two years.

'Why are you in such a rush, hey? Game's not done yet.'

'I just thought it would be more fun to come out and be berated by a random stranger sucking on a vape.'

'This a regular occurrence for you, is it?'

'Oh yeah, only sometimes it's not lychee-peach vape. It could be any number of options.'

Who the fuck says things like that? She couldn't remember the last time a guy had said something to her that she couldn't have scripted herself. Shitty compliments or backtracking comments after seeing they'd dug themselves a hole. Worse yet, the ones who dug deeper, doubling down and talking to her like she was a confused little girl with a confused little brain.

'You're a player, aren't you?'

'What makes you say that?'

'You've got that look about you.'

'That look?'

This was more entertaining for her than the game inside.

'Yeah, you look like a rapist.'

Like an animal playing with its food.

'Shit, what gave me away?'

'The teeth. You have *rape teeth*.'

There was nothing in particular about the players' teeth. It was just that 'rape eyes' had been overused. The comment seemed to irk him however. Belle was used to some men not getting her humour though.

'Dental interrogation from someone hocking down peach flavoured battery acid. Much appreciated.'

'Well, you are all rapists, right? Or just like some of you?'

'Oh yeah, the whole lot. That's where I'm off to now actually, the big rape convention we have every year.'

'Do you all jack each other off at it as well?'

'Yeah, it's one big circle jerk. Fingers crossed I get a good spot this year. Last year my partner had carpal tunnel.'

She laughed. Sometimes they were good for that too. Men. A laugh.

The player checked his phone and turned to walk off. 'Enjoy watching the rest of the game from out here. Try not to make too many friends.'

'Enjoy the rape convention.'

'Enjoy a slow, peach-flavoured death.'

Their voices grew louder as the distance between them increased.

'Hey, you're the rapist not me.'

'And you're the one spending your Saturday night watching the rapists run around.'

'I didn't pay for my tickets, you dick.'

'And I didn't rape anyone.'

'Yet!'

The player turned away and crossed his fingers, holding them up to her. The siren from inside the ground went. Followed by a loud cheer. On the back of the player's backpack Belle saw his playing number. The same as hers.

Happy Ladies' Day, she thought, imagining that the cheers coming from inside the stadium were for her.

A NUFFIE'S SPRAY

Spray (*noun*): A severe scolding of players by their coach.

ARTHUR McALISTER

Awright, bring it in boys. Let's get one thing straight right now: last week is in the rear view mirror, Ok? We've put that behind us. Today we get the chance to come out and respond! Today we get to send a fucking statement to the rest of the comp and say hey, we are HERE!

Now I want to share a little story with you all. Hey, Razor! Bring it in, listen up. Ok, boys, I was out at the ▇▇▇▇ ressies game on the weekend. I would've been the only one in the crowd but let me tell you something, those guys play like their lives bloody dee-pend on it!

Those blokes, they really give a shit, and they're not getting none of the credit or car deals or money. They just do their job! That's the attitude we need to take into the game today. Do your job!

Like, they got this big bloke called Squidman, tall drink of water. He's had a few injuries and played a few senior games

224

here and there, he's got every right to go chasing cash else-where but he's committed to earning his spot. I caught him after the game when he was coming out of the changerooms and I asked him how they stayed so roofless when they were up by so much! And he told me that the bus driver had asked him the same bloody thing! They just keep going, he said! Brushy, Plugga, I can garrontee those boys aren't sooking around because they're not getting a game. They're working their assess off and trying to grab the oppertunity!

Awright, back to us now. I'm telling you, these blokes rate their chances today. They would've seen the score from last week and gone these blokes are cherry ripe to be picked. What do we think of that? Boys? Scrub, what do we think of that? It's fucking bullshit, that's what it is!

We know we can do it, we know that *our best* is *the best*. That's fucking clear, isn't it? That our best is *the* best. But it's not just gonna happen today. We need everyone buying in! Caddy, where are ya? There y'arr, Caddy. Mate, you're the biggest bloke in the competition. No one can tackle you. I want you running through packs today. You get the footy and then you use your big frame and your legs and break out of the stoppage all day. You're a big bloody bull and today I want to see it!

Spongey, where's Spongey? Spongey, there. Mate, you've got the best peg in the comp. See it. Hit it. I want to see you changing the angles. I want you to be the one that gets the ball moving for us all day. See it, hit it. I'm never going to bake anyone for missing a kick here; that's not what we're about.

Righto, who's ready to go out and make a fucking statement today? Bring it in close. Grab a jumper. In real fucking tight. Hey, we owe these pricks one from last year still. Remember that? We fucking owe them one, big time. And we fucking hate these cunts, we really fucking hate 'em. Make no mistake about it. They're out there thinking that they've got us pinned this year, well they haven't faced pressure like ours! If we bring that, I garrontee they won't want a bar of it. They'll put their tails between their legs. But you have to want it! And you have to be the one to start it! You can't wait for anyone else to do it. You can't just step back and expect your mate to do it. You've got to be the one. Set the tone with your first contest and then we pull each other along! Think about your first contest, your first chance to hit someone out there and be physical. They're a physical team, make no mistake about it. But we do it harder! We do it harder and we do it for longer. Harder for longer! Fucking harder for longer and then we come off at the end of the game and we know we've had a crack! We fucking know!

Awright boys, out ya go. Out ya fucking go!

*

. . . Jesus, Spongey, what the fuck was that kick? Suddsy! Suddsy! Can you send a message out to Spongey. That's one shocker early. Go out there now, Suddsy. Let him know . . .

. . . Fucking hell, how about that grab from Bathmat! The big boy's got some mitts on him. Playing with a bit of confidence. Fuck, he's missed the kick, though. Don't worry about it. Don't worry about it, Bathmat, head up . . .

. . . Jesus . . . Jesus . . . Jesus, what the fuck are our mids doing?! Suddsy, what are the mids doing? Why do we have no one playing on a man?! Brushy doesn't want to be here again. He's really packed it in. What the fuck is he doing? Suddsy! Suddsy! Can you go out to Brushy and say if he doesn't want to play on a man he can come and guard the fucking bench, I'm sick of him doing it, week in week out. Fuck me dead . . .

. . . GREAT WORK WET JOCKS! Great spot. Super. Geez that's good play, that's exactly what we want. Hey boys, did you see that? Yeah, exactly, he didn't even hesitate!

. . . Plugga's got to go here, he's got to go . . . PLUGGA! What the fuck was that! You've got to give something! You can't just fly by like that and then go to deck. Fucking hell. Suddsy! Suddsy! Get Plugga up forward!

. . . Fuck me dead, these umpires are kidding 'emselves, that was holding the ball! That was holding the fucking footy! Jesus, they've gone fucking quiet. Swallowed their fucking whistles . . .

. . . Awright, good quarter boys. Real good. What did I say, if we play our brand of footy, then they won't want it. And look at that quarter. We can tick that one off. We can say that was a quarter of good footy. But that's only one quarter. Remember what Squidman said? Remember how to be roofless! Job's not done. Job's nowhere near done. Awright. Look at the board, boys. Let's get out there and fucking give it to them . . .

. . . Fuck me dead, is Head and Shoulders any chance of soft hands when he's tapping? He's got fucking cinder-blocks on the ends of his arms. Soft hands, mate! Fucking soft hands . . .

. . . Suddys, what's that winger doing? We told them to go man on man. Why the fuck is Loofah drifting?! He's got to stay right next to his man! Fuck, he's giving nothing so far. Can we throw him forward? I know he gets lost forward. Fuck. He gets lost all over the ground!

. . . What the fuck is Two in One doing there? He's in no-man's land. You've got to drop back, mate, you can't just fucking sit there because . . . because that'll fucking happen! Fuck me dead, straight over his head . . . Jesus, he's having a fucking shocker. We need another key. I can't keep playing the bloke. Every week he has five fuck-ups that cost us. Can someone put an advert in the paper, or up on Facebook marketplace or whatever the fuck you're all using? I want someone who's six foot four and can catch a ball. No kicking needed, just give the handball. That's all. Is it too much to ask? Suddsy, Suddsy, can you run out and ask Two in One if he's finished the washing up from last night because from where I'm sitting it looks like he's still holding onto a couple of dinner plates! . . .

. . . Fucking hell, they've got two quick ones now. Every fucking week this happens to us. Every fucking week. We let teams get these run-ons against us. That's what we're getting known as. A team who can hear footsteps and shits the fucking bed! Look at them, they're up and about now. They reckon they've got us pegged. Look at them. Look at the body language. Can somebody fucking do something? Can one of you useless cunts take a stand and say not today!? Fuck me dead. Throw it on the boot . . . throw it on the fucking boot! FUCK ME, WAS ANYONE TALKING TO HIM THERE?? . . . THEY'VE GONE MUTE AGAIN . . .

. . . is Rubber Ducky any fucking danger of competing in the air? If you were a steak at the Royal I'd send you back to the kitchen for god's sake!! That's how bad it is! Suddsy, Suddsy, get out there and ask Rubber Ducky if he's waiting for a flight or something, and then say, SO WHY THE FUCK IS HE CARRYING AROUND ALL THAT BAGGAGE WITH HIM NOW?! Fuck me dead!

LOOFAH!!! LOOOOOOFAH!!!! . . . How . . . many . . . FUUUUUUCKING TIIIMESSS DO I HAVE TO FUUUUUUCKING TELLL THAT CUNT TO FUUUUUUCKING RUNNNNNNN! CUUUUUUUUNT! FUUUUUUUUUUCK MEEEEEEEE!

PISSANTS

CUUUUUUUUUUUNTS! CUUUUUUUUUUUNT! FUCCCCKINGGGG CUUUUUU—

. . . WHAT'S THAT, BARB!? DINNER?! NO! I'LL BE OUT IN A SEC! JUST, GIVE ME A COUPLE MORE MINUTES. JUST SHUT THE DOOR IF IT'S TOO LOUD! YOU KNOW I'M SUPER-SUSPICIOUS ABOUT THESE THINGS. JUST GIVE ME A SEC! YES, I KNOW IT'S BIN NIGHT, I'LL DO IT! IT'LL GET DONE! I'VE JUST GOT TO FINISH OFF THIS GAME . . . YES, I'LL PUT PANTS ON FOR DINNER! JUST GIVE ME A MINUTE!

Awright, fuck, where was I . . . ah, bring it in boys . . .

JASMINE RICE

Fangs

I'm waiting under the lights of the establishment that has just kicked me out, for reasons unbeknownst to me, awaiting my chariot. Various forms and qualities of alcohol running through my veins, coke—if you can call that white powder *coke*; fairer to say baby powder—congealing in my left nostril.

Jasmine with an S, who is not to be confused with Jazmine with a Z, who I also have some fraught psycho-sexual relationship with at this current point in time, is en route.

No, do not be confused. This is not some sort of Romeo and Juliet type number. That would be several acts too long . . . You see, Jasmine with an S has come over three times to the chateau of Squidman and myself and each visit has been rather underwhelming for all involved. The whole thing has been rather sus from the get-go. I got a random text message saying she got my number from a friend. Not much of a story to tell the kids. But ignorance is bliss with regards to my number potentially floating out in the ether. Anyway, one thing led to another and I invited her around to watch

230

Netflix in my room. (*Superbad*, that's the movie I tend to watch with the girls who come over of late. Intimacy usually occurs around the time that Fogell, aka McLovin, says, 'It's 10:33' in the school hallway.) During our first encounter, Jasmine with an S had me paralysed with nerves and I didn't make my move till we got to the end of the movie. Then, and I know this sounds like an excuse—an embarrassing one, at that—we engaged in sexual activity and I lost all control rather quickly. Ladies and gentleman of the jury, I swear! It just came out of me and I found myself saying that phrase, that awful phrase, *I swear that's never happened before*, and she just looked at me and rolled her eyes, like, sure it hasn't, buddy. No words needed.

Despite that, we are on tonight, apparently, and I am hoping that the amount of alcohol I have consumed will help me last longer than the usual thirty seconds—though even that sounds generous. To date, two pumps, ten seconds, is all I've managed on the three occasions she has come over. Though I am worried I may have drunk too much and may encounter another issue.

Jasmine: I am one minute away.

Me (discretely tapping my cock to see if there's any life in it): See you soon.

I think briefly of making light of the situation and saying, *One minute is thirty seconds more than I need*. But perhaps it's best not to highlight my shortcomings—*fast* comings— right now.

There is a sign of life from downstairs and I feel the right amount of faux confidence to sustain deadpan sex for at least ten minutes. Then we can move on and all will be forgotten and for the rest of our lives I'll just have fifteen drinks before we engage in any kind of sexual activity. Mummy, why is

Daddy always drunk? Well, son, he loves Mummy very much and the only way he can sustain himself sexually is to numb himself to the point at which he has no idea what is going on. Run along now.

The love bus pulls up and to my surprise there is another body inside.

Me (confused): Hey.

Jasmine (on her phone): This is Sarah, she's staying at mine tonight as well.

Me (less confused; now slightly optimistic): Hey Sarah.

Sarah (also on her phone): Hey.

Jasmine (taking a momentary break from her phone): We aren't having a threesome if that's what you're thinking.

Me (optimism rescinded): Not at all.

Well, that is not the complete truth, Jasmine Rice. The thought had flashed though my mind. I'm still yet to find out exactly how sexually perverse you are. Thirty seconds, total, is not enough time to allow any kind of hypothesis. Perhaps you like it from behind, on top, windmill kamikaze style. We are dealing with Schrödinger's erogenous kitty cat, but tonight, with luck, we should overcome that.

I get into the car.

Me: So, how're everyone's nights going?

My question is met with no response. Guess I'll go fuck myself. At least I'd know what to expect . . .

Then, as if she had to wait for her brain to reboot before speaking, Sarah responds.

Sarah (still staring down at her phone): Good.

Talkative bunch we have here.

Jasmine: Sarah's boyfriend gets back from Malaysia tomorrow. So she's preoccupied.

Me: Holiday?

Sarah: Work.

Don't ask if he works in sex tourism. Don't ask if he works in sex tourism.

Me: Is he in the army or something?

Sarah (finally putting the fucking phone away): He is! But I'm not supposed to tell anyone.

Jasmine: He's killed people before.

Sarah: Jasmine!

Jasmine: What, he has.

Sarah: Well, yes, he has, but I'm not meant to say that. I'm not even meant to say where he's serving. He's had his phone off this whole time.

Me: That must be tough.

Sarah: Yeah, but he's almost back and—

Jasmine: And they're going to fuck like crazy.

Sarah: Jasmine! You bitch.

During this conversation, a truth is revealed to me. The substance in my nostril must indeed have been baby powder and much of the alcohol watered down, because I can feel no discernible effect. The numbness I had anticipated is not forthcoming. And now, as the white lines on the road rush by, shooting themselves towards me in a steady stream, I feel trapped. Fuck. Hold on boys! Not all at once! This forebodes an anticlimactic evening.

Things couldn't be worse, until they are.

Jasmine: How long do you and your boyfriend have sex for, Sarah?

Sarah: What? Like on average?

Jasmine: Yeah, how long does it last?

Sarah: Ah, I'd say at least twenty minutes.

Jasmine: (Laughing.)

Me: (Staring out the window, wanting to open the door

233

and jump out, but figuring that we're going forty kilometres per hour too fast for that to be a viable option.)

Sarah: That's normal, right? How about you two?

Jasmine: Try thirty seconds.

Fuck, she's being generous.

Sarah: What?

Me: (Realising that it is a viable option, opening the door, and jumping out.)

Jasmine (sound receding with the car): JESUS CHRIST!!!

I hear a scream, but the car keeps moving. We are, after all, on a busy highway. However, miraculously, my tuck and roll is performed expertly and there is not a single scratch on me. If this gig doesn't work out, maybe there's some stunt double work in my future. What are your skills and expertise? Can you arrive on time to shoots? No. I'm always *early* . . .

The issue now is that I have no idea where I am, nor where we were headed. And there is only a tiny sliver of battery showing on my phone. Damage control. Do I order an Uber, or throw a Hail Mary somewhere else? Who in my contacts list would give me a chance tonight? Who? Bec? Olivia? No, neither want a bar of me. How about *Old Random Creep*? Who the fuck is that? *Lani from El Camino*? Ok, at least that's a bit of information but not enough to put a face to a name. How about . . . Alexa?

Ah, yes. Alexa. I could try her. Or is it too weird that her sister was in my grade and that she was four years below? I don't know. She'd be eighteen now. She kind of looks like her sister. Fucking hell. I wonder if she knows her sister asked me to give her head up the back of the movies when we were in Year 7? Thirteen-year-old me didn't have a clue that girls could receive head themselves. If we'd ever got past talking on our phones, I would've been in all sorts at the back of the cinema when she asked me to go down on her. *Down where?* I doubt Alexa would talk to me if she knew that her sister was almost my first random sexual experience. Or maybe she would. Maybe she hates her sister. No one's heard from Tahlia for a while. She's gone AWOL, off the grid, full unyoked. I think she had a kid, actually. She doesn't have Instagram or anything, but I'm like ninety-five per cent sure she had a kid and got engaged. Christ. Kids. No thank you. The dad brigade at the club are always going on about how everything changes. It's some chemical thing. I'm inclined to believe some of them because I've seen the kids and they're nothing to write home about. But like sure, they'll tell you it's the best thing ever so you have a kid too and then when you do they're all AH UH, GOTCHA, YOU FUCKER! Then you're trapped with these little blobs of shit that you have to feed and dress and take to the doctors when they do that stupid little kid cough where they don't know what to do with their tongue.

So, all things considered, let's just get an Uber then. Save myself the effort. There will be no gratification tonight, so I have saved myself the thirty sec—

Jasmine: Where are you I'm coming back.

Me: I don't know.

Jasmine: Just stay where you are.

Me: Ok.

Huh, shit, maybe those thirty seconds were really good for her. Maybe she's in love. Or maybe she just wants a little blob of shit and is using me to get there. Fuck it. I'll go along with the ride tonight. Consider me passenger 1A. Business Class, perhaps. Hot towels? Why, thank you. Maybe a quick visit to the Mile High Club? They wouldn't even notice, that's how fast it'd be. The light on the door wouldn't even change colour.

A car's arriving. The door opens.

Jasmine: Get in.

Me (climbing into the back): Thanks, I don't know what came over me.

Jasmine: You're such a drama queen.

Me: No arguments here.

There is a silence in the car that brims with what could be considered sexual tension. But as my feeble male brain processes the quiet, it feels more like indifference, perhaps even disdain and frustration. It seems that any sexual activity tonight won't take place under the guise of friendship, romance or love; more like an aggressive interaction of necessity with Passenger 1A not taking any lead. I am strapped in and awaiting further instruction. Break glass in case of emergency—so long as the emergency doesn't last longer than the aforementioned thirty seconds. Tick. Tick. Tick . . .

We have arrived at the suburban home of Jasmine with an S. No cars in the driveway; her parents must be away. When we walk in, there is a young girl sitting on the couch. Jasmine does the small talk intros and then says she's going to go to the bathroom. There really is no right way for one to be in this situation. I feel equal parts predatorial and awkward. The girl's eyes are firmly fixed on the television screen. She's wearing fluffy pink slippers and wrapped in a bathrobe several sizes too big. She really has made a night for herself. Here's hoping I will too.

Sister: You know she really likes you.

The Baby Bjorn can talk.

Me: Oh, that's nice.

An awkward silence persists. She's watching *Gilmore Girls*.

Me: Ah, do you have a boyfriend?

Shit. What the fuck kind of question is that to ask?!

Sister (turning her attention from the screen to me): Oh my god, I can't choose between two boys.

Me: Ah, spoilt for choice. Wha—

Sister: Max is really nice and he sends me all these cool messages and he got me a flower for Valentine's earlier in the year. But then, Zihad, well, Zihad is really hot and I just get this feeling when I think about him. Like, everything inside me is all warm and, I don't even know, it's amazing!

Take the batteries out of this thing would you.

Me: Sounds like you like Zihad.

Sister: Yeah. That's exactly what I keep thinking! But it's so hard you know because sometimes he's really into me and stuff and then other times he doesn't reply and I know he sees my messages because it says he's opened them!

A woman on the big screen starts crying. She's really letting it all out.

Jasmine (entering the room): Come with me.

Thank god.

Me: Well, bye, kiddo.

Sister: Good luck.

Good luck? Shit, does she even know about my little problem? Was that her way of pumping me up for the night?

Ok, here we go. Soldiers, prepare yourselves. This is Normandy. But hold on. Await instruction. Do not go early into that good night . . . Fucking hell.

Jasmine: Sarah's in the spare room so, there, that's where you're sleeping.

The couch she points towards doesn't look big enough for two, and without the need for speech, I deduce the inference here. I am a stray dog that a guilty conscience looks after for the night. In the morning, it will be off to the pound.

237

In her pocket, I can see the outline of what could be a small flashlight or, more likely, a vibrator. It would seem that those minutes in the bathroom have been well spent. In five years, we men will no longer be required. As sexual pleasure technology evolves, it will not be the people at home with their VR headsets who will benefit most. It will be the women who have never had an orgasm who triumph and no longer need to rely on fleshy sacks of XY chromosomes for satisfaction. Our time has come, brethren. It has come *too soon*.

The light goes off. I take my place on the couch while *Gilmore Girls* plays in the next room. The blanket is too small to cover my torso. This is what I deserve. At least I can sleep in peace now, knowing that the hole won't be dug any deeper. At ease, men. We are off the hook for the night. Blissful solitude . . .

Jasmine (breathing heavily): Just stay there, baby.

Me: What the . . .

Jasmine: That's it, baby, that's it.

My hand is gripped by another and moved in circles.

Jasmine: Just like that. Just like that. Just . . . like . . . *that*.

The body on top of mine tenses and there is a scream that is muffled by the blanket it is made into. The legs between mine shake and spasm. The moonlight comes through the window just enough for me to make out basic shapes. The sound of breathing intensifies, as does the grip on my hand. My hand which is wet with self-lubrication. I try to pull my fingers away, but they are interlocked and it feels not even the jaws of life could release them now.

Jasmine: Yes, baby. Yes, yes. *Yes*.

Passenger 1A knows better than to say anything else. Lie still. The score now reads 3–1. Some goals just require more preparation than others.

ENGLAND

Elliott
DAY 50

On the way back to the room in Leeds I walked past a guy who'd just come back from a run. We both said hey. I asked if he was Australian and he said yes. His name was Liam and we sat in the kitchen talking for a bit.

He started rolling a cigarette and offered to roll me one.

'I just finished a book on how to quit, clearly it didn't work,' he said.

On his eighteenth birthday, Liam's dad told him he'd stop smoking as a gift for him. Liam laughed and said, 'So now I feel like a piece of shit.'

We went out to smoke and then walked to the Aldi nearby. Dinner was a two-litre bottle of Taurus cider and a microwavable chicken korma.

On the walk back, Liam followed me on Instagram. Then he said, 'So how do you know Madeleine?'

I started thinking that maybe he was one of her

ex-boyfriends, because she did say they were Australian, but I couldn't remember their names.

He explained that he'd been away with her and her friends for a week in Italy and I told him that she'd showed me photos of that trip and the Airbnb they stayed in.

'Small world,' he said.

Two more people joined us in the kitchen area. Hostel workers that I recognised from the front desk. They said they were going to a Wet Leg gig and had a spare ticket if either Liam or I wanted to go. Liam had never heard of them and said I could have the ticket if I wanted. I said we should buy one for him online too and that I'd split the cost.

We sat for a while drinking with Lulu who was from Vancouver, and Tony, who had been here for a week and was on his way to work at a ski resort in Scotland. He's twenty-eight but looks seventeen. Lulu asked him, 'How does it feel to look the youngest but be the oldest?'

'It's the best of both worlds,' Tony said.

On the way to the gig I asked Lulu what she does.

'I work at a bar,' she said.

'Serving drinks?'

'Guess again.'

'Security.'

'Guess again.'

She looked me right in the eyes and held my gaze for a while, sort of smiling at me.

'But I don't make any money,' she said. 'Because all the punters want is some skinny blonde bitch and that ain't me.'

She showed me a photo of her with a shaved head, then one of her with a pixie cut and another of her wearing a jacket that looked like the one I've been wearing this whole trip.

PISSANTS

Liam and I stood up the back with our drinks and danced a little before going out to smoke. We talked about Ian Curtis and Joy Division. How much it would have sucked that he couldn't tour because the lights from gigs would give him seizures. Liam said he wants the song *Anthem* by Leonard Cohen sung at his funeral.

Then he asked what I was doing over here and when I went to answer he said, 'No, what are you *really* doing over here?'

I feel like I could've given him a big spiel and tried to convince myself of things but I just said, 'Fuck knows. Trying to get over stuff.'

We walked to another pub and sat in the courtyard out the back. Tony from the hostel was there, pretty drunk. I looked over at him when I went to the bar. He was sitting on his own just staring out into space. I couldn't think of anything to say to him.

DAY 51

I got the train to Liverpool from Leeds. It took a few hours and I was standing the whole time. Walking to the hostel I realised it was in the middle of the city; the noise from the pubs and cheers from people on the street grew louder the closer I got.

The hostel seemed full of locals who were probably staying there because it was cheaper than trying to get home. The door to one room was open and a group of women a bit older than me were in there doing their makeup and drinking out of brightly coloured cans.

My room was tiny, six bunks in total, bags on two of them but no one around. The window beside my bed opened out

241

onto the street and across the road was a packed pub already heaving at 2 pm. I stood for a minute and could hear racket from places down the road and under the hostel and all around and I knew I would not get a good night's sleep.

I went downstairs, searched for an Airbnb and paid the reservation fee straightaway. While I waited for the approval, I FaceTimed with Tammy, a girl from back home who I followed on social media but had never actually met. She was going through a divorce and posting about it. We'd been messaging each other the past two days after I replied to one of her stories. She was drunk and was getting undressed while we chatted. She said she'll be in ███████████ when I get back and we should catch up.

'So tell me about your night?' she said.

'It's only two in the afternoon here.'

'And where are you again?'

'Liverpool.'

'*Liverpool*, that's so cool of you.'

A group of people walked past me in the stairwell. I lowered my voice. Tammy turned the camera around and showed me the mattress on the floor of the apartment she'd just moved into after having to sell the house she lived in with her ex-husband.

'He's been a real cunt about it,' she said.

When the Airbnb approval came through, I said bye to Tammy and went to get my bag. I left my key card on the bed and snuck out the fire escape to avoid having to tell anyone I wasn't staying.

I had a quiet night in and watched *Drive* on my laptop. The bed was flimsy and the base barely held my weight; one of its plastic slats broke during the night. There was a fake plant in the corner of the room and a small desk with an ancient doily on it. I heard the door open and shut a few times; there were two other rooms that were available in the house.

DAY ?

I realise I've been here for six hours now. Somewhere in Manchester. Near Manchester. Some random pub that was empty. It's pitch-black outside. Phillip is telling me that he tried to hang himself once and that he doesn't really do drugs but tonight he is because I'm here. Then he tells me a story about Paul Scholes being the best midfielder of all time and how he put the ball on the ground in front of Ronaldo and hit a target 60 metres away and said, 'Do that.' Now I'm in the cubicle with a key up my nose and I'm just trying not to think about it all too much. I'm just trying not to think about anything. I do another line. And another bump and another drink and I get an Uber so I can check into my hostel before 11 pm. I'm paranoid about getting back by then or they won't let me in. The guys call me when I'm in the Uber and Louis keeps saying, 'Man, it's so crazy that I saw you in there tonight. We're like family, man.' He says that a few times. Family that just met tonight. I ask the Uber driver if he's ever been heartbroken. He says no. He's got a wife and two young boys. He is a year older than me. He says that it's just a different stage of life when you have kids. It's not better or worse, but different. There are difficulties. There are things you miss out on. But he loves his kids. Then I ask if he had a partner before his wife. He says he had two girlfriends. But you said you were never heartbroken? He laughs and says they weren't that serious. At the hostel I ask the guy at reception for the wi-fi password. I ask what he does and he says he's a security guard most of the time. I ask how he gets through the night shifts and he says that he just puts on Netflix and relaxes. Nothing much ever happens at night. Except for one time there was a fire alarm that went off because somebody burnt some toast. Now I'm in bed and there's no one else in the dorm. I think. Then I hear someone cough. Someone else is in here. I can't sleep and my nose is fucked so I have to breathe with my mouth open all night but that makes my mouth really dry so every few minutes I have to take a sip of water. I check my phone and its 4 am and I don't think I've slept at all. I don't think I've slept but it doesn't feel like time is going that slow and I go on my phone and I check Eliza's Instagram and I think how awful this is going to feel tomorrow but I need to sleep and I just can't get comfortable. I drink more water then go and blow my nose in the bathroom but it doesn't do anything and I can see a long black hair coming out of my right nostril and my phone is going off with notifications from people I don't really care about and I'm thinking about the day before we broke up and the car ride and how she said I can't talk to her like that and how I had pushed her away and how I always fucking push people away because I'm a fucking terrible person who hurts people and I deserve what I fucking get and I'm back in bed lying on my side with my mouth open and my lips so dry so I turn over to try and find a comfortable spot and all of a sudden I hear cars outside or trucks and there's a crash of bottles in the hallway and it's 4 am now and checkout is at 10 so the most sleep I will get is six hours if I go to sleep now and I don't know if that's going to do me any good because I don't feel tired well my eyes don't feel tired but my body does and at least my jaw has stopped swinging and if I close my eyes I can try and sleep but it doesn't work and the other person in here coughs again and then I think to set the alarm on my phone to remind me to throw out the bag that's in my wallet otherwise I'll forget and go through customs at the airport with it.

DAY 53

If you stare down into it, the centre is empty. Around it are rings, black rings, most likely. They spin around at an even pace but they never touch the centre. The void at the centre that is never touched, that is loneliness. That is why I want to text you and tell you how it's been going. Because that void is unfathomable and the feeling of that emptiness so strong that it makes me want to cry.

THE CONTENTS OF PISS BOY'S OVERHEAD LOCKER

Yt.

Ed., the ██████████ Football Club maintains that none of its players have a 'problem' with gambling and that it has structures/guardrails in place that prevent the most harmful effects of gambling on its playing group. Yt. recently observed one such protective mechanism: an 'Off-field Intervention Session', conducted once a year by the club's wellbeing officer.

```
          ***TabBet***

Den W vs. CHI $2.19
Wash W vs. Sea $1.54
RSOX Over 4.5 HR $1.10
LIV total corners over 6.5 $1.12
-------------------------------------------
Total bet $50
Return $423
```

During the session, Wellbeing Officer posed scenarios like: 'You're at the races with a group of friends and one friend is seeming [sic] more anxious than usual, what do you do?'

Actual responses from playing group for this particular question: 'Don't bet on what he's betting on', and 'Tell him to chase his losses'. Laughter ensued after both. For reference, the correct answer was: 'Pull him aside, talk to him and tell him to stop betting for the day.' Snorts and murmurs indicated playing group's gripe with this oversimplification.

After the session, the playing group completed a five-minute survey on their phones. The average rating for Wellbeing Officer was 'Exceeds expectations'.

Note: Despite this positive feedback, there is currently a sense of distrust held by the playing group towards Wellbeing Officer. Story relates to an incident last Mad Monday where Officer attended and partook in the usual wrestling that occurs in the late afternoon. It was mentioned by several of the players that Wellbeing Officer attempted to forcibly stick his thumb into their anus while wrestling them. The reason for the overwhelmingly positive feedback may be in the design of the online form, which placed 'Exceeds expectations' as the first option the surveyed party saw.

The average time taken to complete the five-minute survey was roughly twenty-seven seconds.

The ████████ Football Club's anti-gambling stance is amicable on the surface. The ████████ Football Club states

Note: The club has an anti-gambling sponsorship ad that features during games, however, the club explains that players are free to 'Do as they choose with their own money—just don't endorse it' and that 'They're people as well as football players. They have free will.'

Note on note: Standard Playing Contracts stipulate that players cannot at any point: ski, snowboard, bungee jump, sky dive, ride a motorbike or ride in, or occupy, a 'Monster Truck'.

it will accept no direct sponsorships from gambling companies. They have even actively criticised other clubs via their social media channels for accepting money from betting partners. However, there is a level of fraudulent hypocrisy here as they themselves exist within a broader competition and business that will and does accept large amounts of money from gambling sponsors and that this money is vital to their own existence. Furthermore, the TV networks and radio stations that broadcast their games and the stadiums that host their games also line their pockets with sports betting money ('Now it's time for the BetterBet quarter-time break!'). Of the publications who print stories on the ██████████ Football Club, Publication 1 (who published the story '██████████ Football Club Says No to Betting Agencies') has full-page betting advertisements on a large insert cover on their weekday editions, within each of which are four total pages dedicated to 'Sports CODE Bet-O-Sphere' featuring, among other things, a weekly 8-leg multi, usually for some less popular sport, e.g. South African Indoor Volleyball. There is also Publication 2, who recently published a comprehensive expose of sports betting partnerships. At the time of publication, Publication 2 featured advertisements for gambling outlets on both their online and print editions, as did their parent company. Today on the website of Publication 2, an on-page ad for the 'Top 20 Gadgets You Must Have Now' clicks through to another webpage featuring gambling advertisements down its entire right-hand side.

Ed., the easy approach is to condemn gambling sponsorships, to criticise the impact they have and to call for them to be banned from sports altogether. I fear we are too far gone in this regard. But I ask you for a moment to step back and ponder how the gambling industry is distinguished from other partners of the ██████████ Football Club, such as BullRun©, a digital stock exchange platform with a very heavy crypto arm, with whom they have a sponsorship arrangement.

WELCOME BULLRUN© TO THE ███████ FOOTBALL CLUB

The ███████ Football Club is proud to announce its new and exciting partnership with BullRun© Online Crypto and Stock Exchange.

With a strong track record in sports sponsorship, BullRun© is a natural fit for our club. This collaboration marks a dynamic step forward as we continue to expand our reach and connect with the next wave of passionate football fans.

When you're at one of our games, we want you to be cheering on the teams with your BullRun© Crypto Clappers!

BETTING ON GAMES? NAH MATE, NOT HERE.

The ███████ Football Club believes that gambling doesn't have a place at our games.

Going to the footy should be a family-friendly experience.

When you're at one of our games, we want you to be cheering the results for the right reasons.

When it comes to betting on games? Nah mate, not here.

*If you or someone you care about needs support or advice, please call StopBet on **1800 155 322** for free and confidential help and support 24/7.*

W/r/t gambling vs. investing, the main difference in public perception seems inextricably linked to the idea that one relies on hope and the other on intelligence.

There is undoubtedly a class-based attachment to the distinction between the share market (suits, ties, Wall Street, the Oracle of Omaha Warren Buffet and the compounding impact of snowball investments, etc.) and gambling (local TAB, drunken dads, violence, etc.) and this distinction preserves the social acceptability of one more than the other. In some ways, not that I argue this point too strongly, Ed., but it is worth saying that gambling is a safer platform than crypto investment, which is rife with pump-and-dump schemes, rug pulls, and fake projects that disappear overnight. This is more heinous and damaging than a gambling loss, as there is an added layer of deceit and duplicity around the safety of investment, which is more often than not encouraged as a responsible financial investment.

Other items affixed to the inside of Piss Boy's locker include:

Not pictured, but also present at time of inspection: the aroma of coffee, specifically, a full cream milk latte. On average, Piss Boy will drink three large takeaway coffees a day equating to $15.60 (unless he tries to pay with a $50—a trick employed by many of the players—in which case the café's owner will say that he can just pay next time he comes in, by which time the owner has usually forgotten the debt owed). This averages out to $93.6 per week (he will never drink coffee on game day). As his caffeine tolerance increases, a fourth cup looks likely in the near future. The return on investment for this is unsurprisingly zero dollars. Furthermore, it has been noted that on days when Piss Boy does not consume his morning coffee, he is: irritable, short-tempered (more so than usual) and prone to picking at the nail beds of his fingers such that they bleed. So bad has this bleeding been in the past that the only way he could take the field to train was by placing Band-Aids around the bloodied tips of his fingers and then wearing a pair of gloves. During these gloved sessions, Piss Boy would be known as 'Mittens', 'Two-stroke' and/or 'Burner', which was short for 'Cockburn'.

▮▮▮▮▮ Football Club Framework

Run and Carry
Outside Shoulders
Defend to the Death
Inside/Outside
United

Hally's playing badge from his second year

Memo to the playing group:

Please ensure that all club associated paraphernalia is signed with your <u>correct</u> signature. To the best of our knowledge, International DJ Calvin Harris is not part of the playing group.

Piss Boy,

Like I said last time, CHASE ME!

Sincerely PT x

PT = Opposition player who Piss Boy played on in Round 1 this year. There was a clip shown in the team review where Piss Boy was chasing PT but unable to get him. According to various sources, Piss Boy looked like he was on a treadmill. Handwriting on card matches that seen on Fangs' and Squidman's fridge.

MAC'S WORST NIGHT EVER

Coach Mac

. . . the Cointreau is kicking in. I'm feeling relaxed. Feeling like I can talk to someone without embarrassing myself. Ok, the girl we are looking for . . . she has short blonde hair . . . Is that her? Fuck, I should really be wearing my glasses. But I look like a right prick with those things on. Alright, let's give that woman a little half wave and see if it's her . . . and . . . donuts. Fuck, that's embarrassing. That's not her. Shit, there she is over there. I think. That's definitely her. Let's just hope she hasn't seen me wave at that woman who kind of looks like her . . . Hey, Lisa, how's it going, nice to meet you. Oh, that woman . . . yeah, she's an old friend of mine, can't remember her name though, super embarrassing. Oh, this is your friend? Hi, I'm Mac, nice to meet you . . . Oh, that's very kind of you to offer but I'm all good for food, you can keep your left-overs . . . Oh, no, not at all, you wouldn't be intruding . . . you can stay and have a drink with us, I wouldn't mind . . . Can I get you one? . . . Oh, just around the corner? Right, well, don't let us keep you, it was nice meeting you, hope you enjoy the rest of your night with your Thai food . . . Lisa, are

252

you sure you're ok for a drink? . . . Ok sure, sure . . . I'll be back in a second . . . ah, fucking idiot. You fucking moron . . . that was a fucking trainwreck . . . a friend whose name you can't remember? Fuck me . . . she's definitely going to think you're some sort of fucking creep . . . and her friend was definitely waiting with her to make sure you weren't some psychopath . . . at least I passed the first test I guess . . . Hey there, can I just get a . . . fuck it, can I get margarita, thanks . . . ah, what's the difference? . . . Oh I see, just a classic then . . . fancy place this with all the choices . . . Ok, thanks . . . Back we go . . . pull it together . . . So what are you drinking there? Oh, prosecco, that's nice. Fancy drink. So, what's been going on today? Oh, writing a script? That's interesting . . . what's the script about? Oh, really . . . wow, that's incredible . . . Geez, this guy really is playing all the hits, hey? Doing my head in a bit . . . Can't really sing either, can he? Maybe we should go somewhere else? There's a nice place just down the road . . . yeah, that's the one. That's where I was going to suggest we go if this place didn't work out . . . No, no, I think this is going great so far. Do you? Yeah, agreed . . . ok, let's finish these drinks and then walk up . . . No, no rush . . . I'll go to the loo quickly before we go if that's alright . . . Ok, keep your shit together . . . you've salvaged it somewhat, she seems nice, she seems interested . . . maybe you don't need to do the whole bag now, just a little dab . . . just a key . . . ★★★ ★★★ ★★★ Yep, that's nice, that's a nice little bump. That's good shit . . . Fuck . . . That is GOOD SHIT . . . Woooo . . . Fuck . . . Ok, back we go . . . Shit, she's looking good . . . Maybe give her a little kiss on the cheek . . . No, no. Don't do that, you fucking idiot . . . just wait . . . Ok, ready to go? Great . . . So, how long have you been on the apps for? Yeah same, not long . . . they're pretty terrible . . . yeah . . .

Yeah . . . shit, she's reaching for my arm already, linking her fingers between mine . . . This is the joint here, right . . . yep . . . never actually been here before but always thought it looked nice . . . Hey, is there any room for two . . . no, we don't have a booking . . . no, I don't think we're eating, just after a few drinks . . . Thanks, we don't mind, we'll sit anywhere . . . Here? This is perfect . . . Thank you . . . To start? Ah, do you want to choose a bottle of wine for us, Lisa? I'm easy. I'll drink whatever . . . Actually, what do you recommend, mate? Ok . . . Ok . . . so one tastes like cardboard and one tastes like cat's piss . . . and you think the cat's piss one is nicer? Ok, we will grab a bottle of that . . . thank you . . . Hey, Lisa, I have to run to the loo again . . . sorry, I'll be back in a sec . . . Thanks . . . Ah, fuck. Look at the size of those pupils, you're fucked mate . . . Fucked! As if she won't be able to tell . . . Just a little bump now . . . Just one little *** *** *** AHHHHH FUCK, that's good. Shit, that burnt going up . . . Ok, maybe this is cut with something else. Fuck it, though, it's doing the trick right now. Feeling good. Feeling great. Yeah, yeah, baby . . . Hey, sorry about that. What's the wine like? Oh, yeah, that is nice . . . Doesn't taste like cat's piss at all . . . Oh, sorry, I didn't realise I hadn't paid you a compliment yet . . . you look lovely . . . Sorry? Oh, yeah, sorry, that is the best I can come up with at the moment . . . Sorry, you do, you do look lovely . . . Bathrooms? Just down those stairs . . . careful though, they're a bit steep . . . Ok, see you in a sec . . . Fuck, fuck, fuck. She's off me . . . She's fucking off me. She can tell I've had gear . . . Idiot. Fucking idiot . . . No more rack . . . Stay present . . . Hey, that was quick, I'm sorry about before . . . you have really nice hair and a lovely face . . . I like your jaw and you have nice eyes . . . that top, it's really nice too. It matches your eyes . . . That tattoo on your finger, what does it mean? . . . Ah uh . . . ah uh . . . so it's your lucky number . . . that's cool . . . do you have any other tattoos? Oh, if I'm lucky I'll see them later, hey? That's good to know . . . Shit, what is she doing . . . oh, ok . . . that's nice . . . yep, her tongue is in my mouth . . . these people beside us must be wondering what's going on . . . shit . . . how long are we going to do this for . . . Oh, hey, ah, no I don't think we are going to order any food, mate . . . If we don't order food will you kick us out? Sweet . . . just a top up would be great then, thank you . . . You want to come back to mine? Oh I'd love that . . . yeah, yeah, how about I order an Uber . . . you're paying for the wine? Yeah just bring the rest of the bottle . . . Ok, I'll go wait out the front . . . actually shit, I might make one more run to the loo . . . yeah, it's crazy I have the world's smallest bladder I reckon . . . ok, see you in two secs . . . Fucking hell, look at yourself . . . look at those pools of black you call eyes . . . ok, just a tiny little top-up . . . *** *** *** FUCKKK ME *** *** *** JUST A LITTLE MORE . . . *** *** *** Oh man, I'm fucking good. I am g double o d good. Good good good. Shit . . . my teeth are chattering now . . . oh yeah, grindy grindy . . . fuck . . . Uber's on its way . . . I'll send the driver a message, tell him he's a great bloke . . . Yeah, that's a nice thing to do . . . Ah, should I get more gear . . . maybe . . . this bag's almost out . . . *Rockshow Rockshow Rockshow* . . . *AAA Tickets* . . . Yeah, can I get one please . . . Address . . . We'll be home in fifteen . . . I'll give them the home address . . . ETA twenty-five minutes . . . perfect . . . Ok . . . Let's get going . . . Hey, I'm all good to go, you ready? . . . Uber should be out the front now . . . there it is . . . I'll get in the back with you . . . Shit, the driver's going to get a little peep show here, she can't keep her hands off me . . . Shit, she's really grabbing for it . . . Yeah baby, I want to fuck you so badly . . . I can't wait to be deep inside you . . . Man, this coke's wearing off quick . . . oh fuck, there's some head noise coming . . . fuck . . . fuck . . . Hey, driver, do you mind if we change the location . . . I've just got to pick something up . . . it'll take two seconds . . . I swear . . . Ok, the new location is in . . . fuck, I hope the doc's left his door open . . . otherwise we're cooked . . . Wait, fuck, what time is it? Ok, 7:20 pm . . . there shouldn't be anyone there . . . Sunday night, they'll all be at home resting up . . . except for Sixty . . . fuck, this is his time of the week . . . he'll be in there doing his extra touch session . . . just him and the cleaners . . . He really should take a day off . . . fuck . . . he'll be downstairs though, I can just sneak up to the doc's office and get what I need to take the edge off till the bag gets delivered . . . Yeah mate, just here is fine, thank you . . . I'll be back in two seconds . . . Quick quick quick . . . In and out . . . no sight-seeing . . . Come on, please be open . . . Please be . . . YOU FUCKING CUNT . . . Shit . . . Ok, no Valium, you're alright. You're fine . . . Just fifteen more minutes . . . you can hold off . . . Get home . . . pour a drink . . . relax . . . Hey, sorry guys, I'm good to go now . . . Just back to the original location. Thanks . . . Oh, sorry, I had to run in and set up something for work tomorrow . . . Yeah, sorry . . . It's all good now though . . . We're not far from mine . . . So what else should I know about you? Modelling? What was that like? Oh, I'm sorry you feel like that . . . that's awful . . . yeah, I think we all have a fear of being replaced if I'm being honest . . . I reckon modelling and football are similar that way . . . short shelf lives . . . Oh, wow, that's impressive . . . with Ryan Gosling? But you didn't get the tape off in time? That sucks, I'm sorry, that would have been a big break for you I imagine . . . Ah uh . . . Ah uh . . . Yeah, that's cool . . . Pete Davidson? Yeah . . . that is true . . . I can't imagine a woman doing that either . . . being a sex symbol without being good-looking . . . Yeah and no woman is allowed to be like that, well what about that bird, what's her name . . . Schumer? Yeah, you're right I guess. She's not much of a sex symbol . . . Ok . . . Oh, you actually know Pete Davidson? . . . Oh, you know someone who knows him . . . a complete star fucker? Right . . . Fair enough . . . Huh? No, I'm not cold, sorry, I just get chattery teeth sometimes . . . I'm ok . . . So, tell me about your last boyfriend? Ah huh, ah huh . . . he sounds like a real piece of work . . . he was just going on benders the whole time wow . . . that's not fair. And you broke into the Airbnb with a rock? Shit, that's . . . that's . . . that's really impressive. I guess that's your inner criminal coming out . . . Hey! Here, this is it . . . just let us out here . . . thank you, thanks heaps . . . Sorry about the stairs here . . . it's up a few flights . . . good cardio though . . . Ok, here we are . . . this is my little chateau . . . Yeah, sure . . . you can use the bathroom . . . Just around the corner there . . . Ok, take your time . . . Shit, three new messages . . . WHAT THE FUCK THEY CANCELLED THE ORDER . . . Fuck you . . . Fuck you . . . I need something . . . anything . . . this is hell . . . Jesus . . . my body feels like it's made of fucking . . . I don't even know. It feels like I'm about to explode . . . EXPLODE . . .

E X P L O D E

E X P L O D E

E

X

P

L

O

D

E

257

E
P
X
L
O
D
E

exxxxxxxxxxxxppppppppplll
llllloooooooooooooodddddde

E

XXXXXX

P
L
O
D
E
X
P
L
O
D
E
E
P
X
X
L
O
D
E
L
O
D
E

X   P
L
O   D   E
E . . .

AH . . . ah . . . ahhhhh fucking hell there's got to be some in here . . . TRAVEL BAG . . . there's got to be some in my travel

bag . . . I always leave shit in there . . . ah . . . ah . . . ahhhh . . .
There's gotta be something to take the edge off . . . where is
it . . . ah . . . it's in my fucking car still . . . fuck . . . fuck . . .
go outside . . . check the car . . . check the side pockets . . .
there's gotta be some in there . . . fuck, this is unhealthy
now . . . just stop . . . that's the obvious thing to do. Totally.
Totally . . . ok . . . out the front door . . . quiet . . . quiet . . .
don't slam anything . . . I . . . ah . . . ah . . . ahhh I need these
fuckers . . . I'm so awake . . . so fucking awake . . . and the
coke's wearing thin . . . Jesus . . . ok . . . open the boot . . .
Ah. It beeped . . . fuck you . . . fuck you stupid motherfucking
car . . . ah . . . ok . . . side pocket . . . nothing. Nothing . . .
other side pocket . . . ah . . . empty . . . empty . . . nothing . . .
front pocket . . . come on . . . this is where I'd put it for
sure . . . ahh . . . ahh . . . AHHH. WHAT'S THIS FUCKER?
POWDER! POWDER! CRUSHED TABLET POWDER . . .
It's . . . it's . . . fuck it could be from a magnesium tablet . . .
what's it smell like . . . nothing . . . taste . . . ah . . . that tastes
a bit like magnesium . . . but maybe it's not . . . it looks a bit
too white for magnesium . . . it could be codeine . . . it could
be Forte . . . for sure . . . I just have to collect it all up . . .
and I'll snort it off the ledge in the boot here . . . I'll just . . .
like that . . . and . . . and . . . ahh . . . *** *** *** that fucking
burnt . . . ah . . . ah . . . ahhhh . . . no way . . . that was just
fucking magnesium . . . I can tell . . . FUCK maybe I should
call the doc? Tell him I need something to get to sleep . . .
Jesus, my head's spinning . . . this is crook . . . this is grim . . .
I'll call the doc . . . he'll have something for me . . . he will . . .
and where's he live again? . . . Not far from here . . . I'll call
him now . . . it's ringing . . . ringing . . . FUCK NO THAT'S
A HORRIBLE IDEA DON'T CALL THE FUCKING
DOCTOR DONTCALLTHEFUCKINGDOCTOR THAT'S

SUCH A BAD IDEA. THAT'S SUCH A BAD IDEA. Jesus . . . Does he get a notification if I hung up? . . . I'll say it was an accident . . . I was . . . I was reaching to turn my alarm off . . . and . . . yeah . . . yeah . . . that'll work . . . he won't ask questions anyway . . . if he does I'll tell him to fuck off . . . fuck off cunt . . . Fuck . . . there'd be someone who has a supply . . . Stick . . . hundred per cent . . . I can just go to his and explain my situation to him . . . he'll understand . . . Hey mate, it's just one of your coaches . . . yeah, do you have any painkillers for me? . . . Fuck, no chance . . . idiot . . . dumb cunt . . . say you pulled something . . . he'll have the goods . . . Jesus, he's worse than me with his problem . . . way worse . . . I'm not even bad with them . . . I just . . . I just need them to help me sleep now . . . it's not like I'm doing meth or anything or heroin . . . those are problem drugs . . . shit, Lisa's calling me . . . Hey, sorry, I just had to grab something from my car. I'm coming back up now . . . Shit, shit, shit, she's sus on me. Fuck . . . Ok, deep breath before going back inside . . . Fuck, maybe I should just come clean to her . . . Yeah, that's a great idea . . . Hey . . . this is a bit rogue . . . but . . . shit . . . tell her . . . say it . . . ask for help . . . this is the time . . . Lisa, do you have any coke on you? . . . I . . . Yeah, I'm . . . Oh, wow, that's fucking awesome. Can I have some, are you sure? . . . Fuck . . . You want a bump too? Sure? Ok . . . Just me then . . . *** *** *** Woah that's . . . ah . . . That's interesting stuff . . . *** *** *** Are you sure that's . . . Huh, what are you saying? . . . Wait . . . What the . . . that's . . . . Woah, shit . . . fuck . . . Wait, who are you guys? . . . What the fuck? . . . Lisa, where's Lisa?

What the fuck? Lisa, what's going on? . . . Look at the photo? Oh shit . . . What the fuck? . . . Jesus, no, don't . . . how did you . . . fuck don't . . . don't do that . . . what . . . what do you want? Do you want money? . . . I have money . . . I can go and get you some right now . . . No? Well, what do you want? What . . . yeah, that's where I work . . . Who? Yeah . . . I know that guy . . . Well, yeah, I know of him . . . we're in the same circle I guess you could say . . . So . . . You want his details? I can . . . Yeah, I can find out where he is . . . I can . . . I can get you access to him . . . No problems . . . Just get rid of those photos . . . Please . . . Please, yes . . . Ok, I'll get you his details . . . I'll get you his location . . . Yes . . . I promise . . . I promise . . . just don't show anyone those photos . . . That wasn't me . . . That isn't me . . .

PROFESSIONAL DEVELOPMENT TIME

The Pissants meet every Wednesday night in what is designated by their place of employment, the ██████ Football Club, as PDT, or 'Professional Development Time'.

It is during PDT that the group tends to several key matters they consider vital to the normal functioning of their lives. The first is to play FIFA.

Of the Pissants, Stick—a high-functioning painkiller addict with a limited footballing skillset centred around lockdown defence—is the most skilled joystick voyeur. His proclivity for the game was discovered, honed and refined while recovering from his numerous and severe injuries, when he spent countless hours in front of his 60-inch plasma TV, high on oxycodone, with a PlayStation controller in his hand. He'd mastered one-touch passing, timed runs forward to perfection and could jockey between defenders then strike for the ball at opportune times, of which there were many, given his usual lacklustre opposition.

As expected, he (Stick) had also perfected the ability to talk shit to someone in the opposite corner of the room while his eyes stayed fixed to the screen. His mouth, a barbed pendulum delivering incisions that cut through the thickest of skin, was his not-so-secret weapon.

Between Stick and the remainder of the group there was daylight, though each of the Pissants had a copy of the game for themselves. They were freebies scored by Fangs—a medium-sized forward too slow to be considered a genuine small, and too weak to be considered a third tall option, saved only by an ability to occasionally pull goals out of his arse—who had met the head of FIFA endorsements at the ▉▉▉▉▉▉▉ Football Club's Ladies' Lunch one year earlier. Fangs had saved the suit and tie in his phone as *Jules FIFA guy* after they shared an Uber home, and had forgotten about him entirely until one night, while drunkenly searching for the number of a romantic love interest, he (Fangs) messaged him (Jules) asking for free copies of the latest game. The following morning, Jules invited Fangs and the rest of the Pissants to the launch of the latest version of the game. What he (Jules) didn't realise was that the boys would roll in hot off the back of their bye-round bender, and take advantage of the free frozen margaritas on offer while ramshackling the attempts of all other attendees (social media influencers, other footballers from various codes) to film suitable content for their social channels. It was, according to Jules in his exit interview, the biggest mistake of his career. In the background of all photos from the night you could see the Pissants huddled, pointing their fingers at one another, veins popping from their necks, cords of spit spraying from their lips like bungee jumpers about to be retracted. It's worth noting that also present at the event were a series of NRL players, who the Pissants saw fit to towel up in two-on-two games. It was clear that the NRL players were rattled by the loudness of the Pissants. They were the recipients of the visceral spit and scorn which was normally reserved only for other Pissants, and they didn't like it one bit. When the Pissants left, it was Stick who remarked, 'How about those virgins?' No one could disagree.

When the Pissants converge on Wednesday Nights, the rules for FIFA are as follows:

1. Playing partners are assigned by pulling names from a hat.
2. For each game that is played, International Teams are to be used.
3. Teams are selected at random by one member of each player-pairing facing a member of the opposition player-pairing while tapping the square button of their controller repeatedly, as a mutual third party counts down '3 . . . 2 . . . 1'.
4. If you are not satisfied with your team, you are given the chance to press square once more. This is your new team, which you cannot change.
5. 'Team Management' is heavily frowned upon and considered against the spirit of the game.
6. 'Parking of the bus' is not permitted.
7. You cannot look at your opponent's controller while they are taking a penalty shot.
8. If the game is tied, it goes to golden goal extra time.
9. If there is no score in extra time, then the match is re-started and the first goal wins.
10. If the opposition goalkeeper scores against your team by running the length of the field, you are not allowed to participate for two weeks.

These rules are scrupulously upheld. Which is why, on this particular night, Stick is paired with Shaggers and Fangs is with an honorary Pissant, Hally, while Squidman sits in the corner on his laptop, searching Amazon for a new set of speakers for the changerooms.

The previous week, Squidman, playing as Brazil, had allowed the 72-rated Lu Kun-Chi, goalkeeper of the Taiwanese National Team, to waltz through his entire defence, dribble around his 92-rated goalie, and plant the ball in the back of the net.

The move came late in the game and, as star player Neymar went down with a calf cramp, he (Squidman) complained about the absurdness of the game's hyperrealism.

'Why the fuck are they getting cramps in a video game?!' he yelled, button bashing the square in an attempt to strip the ball from the Blue Wings' keeper.

'Get the pickle juice, boy!' screamed Stick, while he manoeuvred his lowly-rated goalie around some of the best players in the world.

The suspension of Squidman, however, is good timing for Hally, who has just broken up with his girlfriend of seven years earlier in the week and is searching for social opportunities wherever they come.

According to him (Hally), talk had turned to marriage, and he couldn't fight the doubts he'd been having about his former sweetheart. The Pissants all consoled Hally, but in truth were glad to see his missus go. At a house party a few years before, some of them (Fangs and Squidman) had trashed his room. The culmination of the upheaval was the tipping of an entire tub of Choco Buzz Hyper Max Whey Protein powder into a suitcase belonging to Lucinda, who was visiting for the weekend. Hally, who after playing senior footy back home since the age of fifteen knew a thing or two about footy clubs, had tried to talk Lucinda down, saying that it was just how things went. But his words were to no avail. A letter was written to the club's player welfare manager explaining the situation and the following day, a notice was issued to the playing group, reading:

> **Attention: Playing Group**
>
> Please refrain from destroying the property of others. While we understand that you enjoy one another's company outside of training hours, this does not have to come at the expense of others.
>
> Thank you.

When Hally picked up the memo from his pigeonhole, he shook his head. He knew what was coming and braced for the onslaught. By the end of the day, over thirty of the memos had been stuck inside his locker. He never said a word about it to Lucinda until the breakup.

Wednesday Night FIFA was the antidote to such situations. The trials and tribulations of life within the Four Walls are felt more keenly by the Pissants than perhaps any other subgroup—at least that's what they tell themselves when they gather together, discussing who was the biggest whipping boy of the week to the sounds of plastic buttons clicking frenetically beneath their thumbs. It was their solace. Their stress ball. Their outlet.

*

Before the first game of the night takes place, however, there is always another, more vital, matter to attend to, which is why the group are huddled like Emperor penguins around the fridge in Squidman's and Fangs' apartment.

PISSANTS

The tradition started on Silly Sunday in Fangs' and Squidman's first year, when Stricksy, a departing senior player at the end of a three-day bender, insisted that all the boys who had not yet revealed themselves in the showers during the year stand in his driveway while he hosed them down.

Stricksy, a well-respected journeyman of the competition, said that there was only one unforgiveable sin in footy change-rooms, and that was to be a Mystery Dick.

Since then, some three seasons earlier, the Pissants have gathered on the night of the Draft to watch their club select its future from a series of pimply eighteen-year-olds with untamed haircuts and skinny rigs. Like cattle buyers at a sales yard, they assess their new teammates, not just as players, but as future participants in the Mystery Dick Stakes.

What you didn't want was someone who looked like they'd played a bit of senior footy, someone a bit thicker in the torso, who would've already been told by some wily old operator who knew how things worked that it was unnatural to hide behind a pair of togs in the showers after a game. And what you did want was someone best described as a 'project player'. A wiry frame with 'potential' that had to be protected from the bigger bodies of senior local footy. Someone who would head home from games with the dirt still on their knees, if you catch my drift.

Once the Draft was over, the television would turn off and the Pissants would hold a draft of their own: the MD Stakes. Between the end of the Draft (the actual one) and the selection process for the MD Stakes, the Pissants were allowed fifteen minutes to do further research on the players their footy club had just selected. During this time, they would scroll through their social media and contact any common threads, skirting around the issue of whether the bloke showered with his

267

cock out or not, by asking innocuous things such as, 'What's he like?'

When the fifteen minutes were up, the proceedings were formalised with the current Chair standing while the rest of the room fell into silence. The Chair (selected on a rotating basis) would announce the Pissants one by one based on their finishing position in the previous year's MD Stakes.

Each Pissant would then pick one player he believed would not reveal themselves to the rest of the club for what they hoped to be the longest of times. While standing in front of their peers they would give a short spiel about their pick, regurgitating lines like: 'We're very excited about this prospect,' and, 'We think he'll fit in well at the footy club.'

Every subsequent Wednesday night, the Pissants would gather around the magnets on the fridge and share intel. If a player was known to have completely revealed themselves to their teammates, their name magnet was moved left and they were eliminated. The aim was to have your pick remain on the board while all others were mourned with a moment's silence.

There was complete understanding within the Pissants that all information shared was true and they solemnly agreed that no tampering was allowed. Nobody was allowed to hide the togs, jocks or budgies of a first-year player. Nobody was allowed to counsel them about their shower etiquette; to do so would be grounds for immediate elimination.

To win the Mystery Dick Stakes was an obscure, internal honour. Sure, there was no prize except the validation of the group. But the MD Stakes was the antithesis of existential meaninglessness: nothing turned to something through the imbued sense of worth by those who bought in.

On this particular night, there are two names left on the fridge. Sixty, the hard-working kid from Canberra whose shower routine is to wear what he calls his 'lucky' blue-and-white striped budgie smugglers; and Jenko, a country boy whose puppy-fat is yet to show any signs of acclimatising to the world of professional football after almost a year of daily training.

A stalemate lasting the better part of three months has evolved between the two remaining unwitting participants, as all other contestants have revealed all at one point or another while in the presence of one or more Pissants.

'Alright,' says Squidman, standing in front of the fridge, 'does anyone have any updates to the Mystery Dick Stakes for week thirty-six?'

Silence reigns, broken only by the auto-tuned vocals of Bad Boy Timz that accompany the FIFA pre-game menu screen.

Confused by the situation, Hally crosses his arms, thinking best not to ask any questions that he doesn't want answers to.

'If it's taken this long, I don't reckon either of them have a cock,' says Stick.

There's a quick glance between Fangs and Squidman. They both hold down the Pavlovian urge to laugh, as this comment sits up, awaiting a sharp retort. Sadly, however, the usual suspect to take advantage of such an offering, Mud—a second-year player with a fearlessness bordering on stupidity when it comes to taking all-or-nothing kicks who, after a string of Best on Ground performances in the reserves, has been presented with the opportunity to abscond from the Pissants—is absent, preparing for a senior game interstate the following night. As a result, what remains unremarked this time is that Stick himself is, from time to time, a Mystery Dick. It happens without rhyme or reason, those times he wears his togs into the showers and takes them off when facing the corner. This is one tactic used by those who have a foot in either camp. Another is to go into the cubicles before a shower and play with their cock for a few seconds so it gets slightly larger than usual, but not so aroused as to make it hard. There are a handful of players who are known to 'warm up' before showers.

'Well, it hurts that Jenko never showers with the boys,' says Fangs, who is the owner of Sixty, looking at Shaggers, who is the owner of Jenko.

'He's a fucking myth of a human being,' says Stick, bending his knees and propelling himself up as he does to intensify the volume of his comment.

The conversation continues, but the talk of Jenko's social exile from the rest of the playing group is white noise to Shaggers, who is mulling over the plan he's been hatching since the previous Thursday night.

Heart pounding, Shaggers speaks. 'Well, actually,' he says, then pauses . . .

For what happens next to make sense, you have to know that Shaggers has been on the phone to his manager all week. The good news is that he's getting a contract for next year, on slightly more coin, with a few match incentives and some bullshit ones surrounding club BNF that he knows don't have a chance in hell of paying off. But the bad news is that it means there's little to no chance of his best mate Fangs getting an offer.

'There's no spot for him,' his manager said when Shaggers asked if he'd heard anything. 'But that's good for you, mate. Bloody great news,' he'd added, biting down on his usual chicken Caesar wrap so obnoxiously that the crouton crumbs almost made their way through the phone.

Since the call, Shaggers has tossed and turned at night, fluctuating between a hatred of the club for not giving his mate a chance and a hatred of his mate who had done nothing to prove he deserved one to the club. Some mornings when brushing his teeth, he would find himself spitting into the mirror, pointing his finger at an imaginary version of Fangs and saying, 'You did this to your fucking self! You don't want it! You don't fucking want it!'

He would stare into the mirror until his face shook, his heart rate elevating rapidly in a visceral response. Sometimes the anger gave way and sadness took its place. In those moments he wanted to sit down and ask his mate what was going on. Why had he given up? But there was always something stopping him—like a weight inside his chest that blocked his vocal cords from the inside.

As Shaggers stares at the magnets, he thinks once more about his plan. The past few weeks he's let Fangs get a few wins over him, sensing the situation at hand. He'd gifted him their usual pre-training goal kicking comps and in last week's FIFA match, he'd looked down as Fangs was about to take a penalty and deliberately moved Albanian goalie Tommy Strakosha the wrong way to cost himself the game. Maybe it was because he'd had a year or two in the real world before coming to the club, maybe it was that he'd grown up without the effects of private schools that blew smoke up everyone's arse or the kind of wealth that made you take everything for granted. Whatever the reason, Shaggers had this overwhelming sense of empathy, or sympathy, one of the -pathys, he would tell himself, and when he thought about his mate Fangs, it kicked into overdrive.

After opening his mouth, he looks at his mate and the feelings kick in again. The sad ones, not the angry ones that manifest as trails of toothpaste and spit above his vanity.

'Well, actually,' he says.

Squidman, Fangs and Stick all take a step towards Shaggers.

'I had a shower after my rub Thursday night and I shit you not, Jenko showered full starkers. It rattled me.'

All eyes widen around him, as much for the revelation as for the fact that this was an act of self-sabotage by Shaggers. Honesty was encouraged, but to cost yourself a shot at the Stakes was a phenomenon never encountered.

'Story time!' says Stick.

'Story time!' says Squidman.

'Story time!' says Fangs.

Shaggers gathers himself. He looks at the three mates in front of him, unable to stop himself from noticing the space created by the absence of Mud. He feels the hole turning into a vortex, sucking them all in, and tries to fill it with his words.

'Well, it was just me and him, Thursday night after a rub, and he was already in the showers when I walked in. He wasn't hiding it or cupping it or nothing.'

The story wasn't completely untrue. Shaggers had had his usual Thursday night appointment with Steakhands, which had ended up being a forty-minute treatment of his left hamstring followed by a quick flush through his right hammy, lower back and glutes after Steakhands had become immersed in a conversation with the new masseuse, Sally, about his time rubbing ass for the Welsh mountain bikers when they came to Australia for the Commonwealth Games. And yes, Shaggers and Jenko *had* showered together after their rubs, that part was no fabrication. But the lie was in failing to reveal that Jenko had kept his navy blue Bonds undies on the whole time. The lie was in obstructing the truth in the same way that the tattered cotton produced in China and Vietnam obstructed a clear view of Jenko's mysterious cock.

'So that's it then?' said Squidman.

'Guess so,' said Shaggers, feeling a sense of pride in his falsehood as he sees the faintest of glimmers in his best mate's eyes.

Squidman moves aside and says, 'Well, do you want to do the honours, Fangs?'

The group watches as Fangs approaches the fridge. He places his index finger on the fridge door and drags it slowly from right to left. Jenko's magnet is moved to the side and lined up with the other names in the graveyard. Beneath the black marker banner reading 'MD Stakes' one name remains: Sixty. The unwitting winner will never be crowned.

The group bow their heads in silence.

It's Stick who breaks first, saying, 'Alright, let's play!'

UNITED

LAW AND ORDER AT THE RAMSGATE FOOTBALL CLUB

Ralphy is crawling around the room with a domintarix named Kai on his back. She is whipping him repeatedly as he scrambles down the home straight.

The congregation screams out:

'YOU FUCKHEAD, RALPHY!'

'GO, CUNT! GO!'

'THAT'S WHAT YOU GET, YOU DUMB CUNT!'

The boys of the Ramsgate Football Club are further impeding his movement by throwing beer at him, blurring his vision. This combines with the residue of black hair dye used to 'fix' Crackers' red hair earlier, to create a thick layer of Sasquatchian sludge on the floor, further hindering his movement. The disorientation resulting from this ad hoc sensory deprivation and the intensity of Kai's attack on his bare arse puts Ralphy into a cosmic abyss of woe.

At the front of the room, Judge McKinlay presides over the scene, wielding a rubber chicken dog-toy as his gavel. The judge is wearing his wife's best dress, which, to his credit, does showcase his pins quite well. Beside him, being secretary for the occasion—for the third year in a row—is Jarvo.

In the twilight of his career, Jarvo is the principle organiser of Kangaroo Court and is unwavering in his belief that it forms the foundation of the football club's culture. One day he will be gone, and he doesn't want to see the club to which he had devoted so much of his life dwindle away.

He didn't trust the younger players coming through to maintain the sense of club tradition that had been thrust upon him when he was their age and that he had bled for. It was becoming increasingly hard to maintain a sense of community. The kids displayed the worst kind of narcissism in the brief moments they looked up from their phones. It was all Steve Jobs' fault, Jarvo thought. Get a few cans into him and he'd tell you how Jobs would be remembered as a greater villain than one Adolf Hitler.

So Jarvo came up with something he believed would halt the inevitable demise of club spirit for at least a few more years. It came in the form of a slideshow reminiscent of a Grade 8 Geography project: Calibri, size 16 font; no backgrounds; large headings; simple body text and the occasional fade transition. It was known as *Law and Order at the Ramsgate Football Club.*

Ralphy, the first subject of a Law and Order hearing for the year, crosses the impromptu line marked out in masking tape at one end of the demountable changerooms. His punishment for the crime committed last off season.

J: Mr Secretary, the defendant please.
S: Ladies and gentlemen of the court, I call
   to the stand Mr Richard Flannagan, aka,
   Ralphy. Ralphy, the charge put before

you is the ramshackling and disorderly organisation of Kerry's buck's party in February of this year. Now before we get to the verdict, a few questions are in order. Judge McKinlay will now commence the hearing.

J: Thank you, Mr Secretary. Now Mr Flannagan, were you or were you not the person responsible for the organisation of Kerry's buck's party on February 2nd this year?

R: I was, Your Honour.

J: And what did those responsibilities include?

R: I had to find an Airbnb, organise a bus and make sure everyone paid their money.

J: Interesting. And where was this Airbnb located, Mr Flannagan?

R: In Newcastle, Your Honour.

J: Newcastle, interesting, very interesting. Good night life, in your opinion? Maybe see some of the Newcastle Knights boys? Get a photo with Kalyn Ponga? It *is* known as the coke capital of Australia. Understandable choice.

R: Yes, Your Honour.

J: What would you say was the motivation behind Newcastle being the destination of choice?

R: To ... to see the sights, Your Honour.

J: Oh, the sights! I didn't realise we were engaging in obscurities, Mr Flannagan. Please, do be more specific. What was it about the date of the 2nd of February

that made you particularly keen to see the
sights in Newcastle?

R: Well, Your Honour ... there were ... there
were races on that day.

J: Races, you say? Of the equine variety?

R: Yes, Your Honour. Horse races.

J: Oh, I see. A day at the races up in
Newcastle. Very interesting.

R: Yes, Your Honour.

J: Now tell me, how *were* the races on that
day, Ralphy?

R: Well, Your Honour ... the races ... they
weren't ... they weren't actually on.

J: Oh? What? Were they rained out, perhaps?

R: No, Your Honour.

J: A bout of horse flu strike down all the
ponies?

R: Not that I am aware of, Your Honour, but
perhaps.

J: Or is it more likely, that you, Ralphy,
had made a mistake in your administrative
processes? Is it more likely that you got
your dates confused when you looked at *last*
year's calendar, when there were in fact
races on the 2nd of February, and designed
the whole trip around seeing a horse race
that was not even on?!

R: That's ... it's true, Your Honour! It's
true.

J: Hush, hush. Order! Order in the court!
Pull yourself together Mr Flannagan. Now
as for the rest of the buck's, I believe

that no further reminders of those details
are required. Those present in the court
today are all familiar with the case of the
Seaside 7 and the forty-five-minute deep sea
fishing expedition.

R: Yes, Your Honour. Sorry, Your Honour.

J: So, as to the charges laid before you. The
ramshackling and disorderly organisation of
the buck's night. How do you plead?

R: Guilty, Your Honour, I plead guilty!

A raucous cry breaks out among the crowd.

J: Order in the court! Order in the court!
Very interesting, Mr Flannagan. Dismantling
a man's last free weekend as a single
soul before he enters the more responsible
stage of his life. It is a most heinous
crime. Most heinous indeed. Now, ladies
and gentlemen of the court, I do believe,
as always, that correction is in order.
Mr Flannagan, you said that you had hoped
to see a horse race on that day. Nay,
that you had *promised* Kerry and his buck's
attendees that *they* would see a horse race.

R: Yes, Your Honour.

J: And Kerry, in fact, did not see a horse
race of any kind that weekend.

R: It's true, he did not.

J: Well then, ladies and gentlemen of the
court, it appears that the ledger would
read one horse race owed. Bailiff, please

bring out the saddle, and what sort of
horse race would it be without a jockey?
And who better to whip him down the
straight than an old friend of ours?
That's right, ladies and gentlemen of the
jury, I present to you our dearly beloved
Kai Bennett!

Law and Order at the Ramsgate Football Club was a system of skewed justice. Lady Liberty held the scales blindfolded and weighed up the evidence presented while copping a knee in the back. The defendant was always given the opportunity to speak, and to present evidence that refuted the charges. In all the years of hearing, however, there had only ever been one successful acquittal.

Clae Sharply, who between the hours of nine to five during the week was a corporate finance lawyer, had prepared a PowerPoint presentation defending himself against the charge of calling for pickle juice in the first quarter of a game early in the season. He had cited scientific research papers suggesting that the early ingestion was the best way to prevent the onset of cramps, which hindered performance later in games. When the team then tried to adjust his fine for cramping, he cited the biophysical reasons behind the condition and his increased exertion on the field as being for the betterment of the team. 'If we start fining people for the betterment of the team, then we are going against the fundamental values of the team and therefore anarchy will ensue.' He had presented the court with an entanglement. His point was concise and clear and worthy of acquittal. Clae Sharply, however, did not manage to argue his way out of a fine.

First to achieve this feat was Ribsy Callaghan, who went

straight after Clae, citing a woefully non-existent defence of 'fucked if'—as in 'fucked if I know'—against a charge of sixteen missed wet weather sessions during the season, which earnt him the suspension of the sentence. There were clearly ulterior motives to infuriate Clae with the decision, as the same defence has been tried to no avail every year since. To this day, Ribsy was still the only player to successfully overturn a fine with a defence.

Another year, another round of fines, another string of petrified payers. The Secretary calls for the next defendant.

'Ladies and gentlemen of the jury, the next defendant is Mr Tom Bedford. Bailiff, could you please escort Mr Bedford to the dock?'

TB started racking his mind about what he was going to be charged with. He was a notorious airhead, but this year he'd made considerable effort not to be late to training or games. He'd double-check the ovals so he didn't arrive at the wrong ground (something he'd been found guilty of the previous year, and as such, had to spend a night handcuffed to Shane-o at Ark in the Big Smoke, seeing things that could never be unseen).

It was worse not knowing what he'd done. It meant that either he had been found out for something he had tried to hide, or that he had done something whilst so intoxicated that he did not remember the crime. Pleading the fifth, also known as the 'Blackout Drunk Defence', was not an option at the Ramsgate Football Club. It only worsened the punishment—and he did not have the stomach to down a beer bong of Guinness, Absinthe, tomato sauce and whatever else could be found within arm's reach.

'Mr Bedford, relax, there's no need to be nervous,' said Judge McKinlay, registering the obvious dread on TB's face. 'Or is there?'

He chuckled to himself. TB was a simple bloke, but that was to his advantage on the football field. The only instruction Tommy needed was 'See Ball Get Ball', and he'd go out and do that and be the best player on the field. He came from a good gene pool, did Tommy. He was the younger brother of ██████████ Football Club player, Mick Bedford, who was known by the moniker of *Stick*, and the son of Rex Bedford, a local footy icon in the Murray-Riverina region, having amassed five flags and several league medals in his illustrious career. The fact that Rex Bedford never played beyond the local leagues had always astounded those who'd seen him play. His height, or lack thereof, was the main knock on him as a junior. After his first league medal he was given an opportunity to trial for teams down in Melbourne, but a night out before one of the sessions led to him turning in a poor performance on his first day. He left at the end of the week and was never called back. It stung Rex, what had happened, stung him dearly.

'Mr Bedford,' said Judge McKinlay, in front of the impromptu courtroom that had been set up in the clubhouse. 'Any idea why you're up here today?'

'No, Your Honour.'

TB thought hard. He was off the dating apps, so there were no skeletons in the closet there—it wasn't worth the risk. Two years before, three of the boys had been caught sexting a Tinder account that ended up being run by one of the players. They had to get up in front of everyone and read out the conversations they'd had without realising that the person whom they had told they wanted to fuck repeatedly was standing right before them. Parmy was the hardest done by. His conversation was a trainwreck, turning from gentle flirtation, to aggressive pursuit, to three photos of his erect cock after a few too many Bundys. It was after that that Parmy became Eggplant. Not because of the size of his cock, but because in just two weeks of online conversations, he'd sent eighty-four eggplant emojis.

'Mr Bedford, tell me. Have you ever had thoughts of joining the army?'

'Ah, no, Your Honour.'

'Never thought about becoming a sergeant?'

'No, Your Honour.'

'How about SAS?'

'No, Your Honour.'

'Well, that's funny, because we seem to have evidence of you'—Judge McKinlay pauses at this moment for effect—'going commando.'

Tommy was confused. What did that even mean?

He looked out at the congregation, who were clutching each other in explosions of laughter while adjusting the wigs, dresses and undergarments they had donned for the day. He thought about why they might have been laughing at him and went red. Why wasn't he in on the joke? Tommy then saw that some of his teammates were pointing at something to his right, with tears in their eyes. He slowly turned, and there on the big screen was an image of him running down the wing, ball in hand, with his cock hanging out of the left leg of his shorts.

'Mr Bedford. That is you, correct?'

'Yes, it is, Your Honour.'

'No two ways about it. Clearly that is you Mr Bedford, in all of your glory. Now tell me something, do you remember that game at all?'

Tommy felt a jolt go up his spine. He was hoping that the image was it. Surely no one had found them? Surely not.

'I . . . I do not, Your Honour.'

'Oh Mr Bedford, please, don't lie to me. Don't lie to the courtroom.'

'Ah, I guess . . . that looks like the Wests game.'

'Very good Mr Bedford. It *was* the Wests game. A handy game from you as a matter of fact. Oh, it's ok, Mr Bedford, you can agree with me there. You can say you played a good game.'

'Yes, Your Honour.'

Tommy felt himself paying increasing respect to the judge. He knew he had something to carefully protect, something that he would never live down. A landmine he had to avoid. He kept repeating the words to himself. No one had found them. No way could they have been found. *No one had found them.*

'Mr Secretary, could you reveal Exhibit A for us?'

The secretary reached beneath the trestle table and pulled up a large Ziploc bag. The contents were not immediately clear to anyone except Tommy—and the person who had found them. But Tommy knew. Tommy knew full well they were the shit-filled jocks that he had discarded behind the toilet before the Wests game. He recalled the moment he had felt himself lose control of his bowels in the warm up, and how he had run up to the rooms to take them off. Now, all these months later, they were a mummified version of the steaming wet jocks he had hidden that day.

'Mr Bedford, do you recognise the contents of this bag?'

'No, Your Honour.'

'Secretary, please take the bag closer to Mr Bedford, as I do believe he is being untruthful to the court.'

The secretary pulled out two lace gloves, which they gently placed on their hands, before picking up the bag by one corner and dangling it like dead rodent in front of Tommy's face.

'Now, Mr Bedford, I will repeat my question. Do the contents of this bag look familiar to you?'

Tommy froze and then thought of the advice his older brother Mick had given him when he was a raw recruit about how to survive in a footy club.

'Don't resist, Tommy, it'll just make things worse,' he'd said.

Those words rang in his ears. He suddenly knew he'd heard those words before, when he was a kid, spoken in his dad's voice behind a closed bedroom door. He'd also remembered the bruises on his brother when they were growing up, but never on him. He'd wanted those same bruises, but Mick would always say he didn't want them, that they weren't nice.

Tommy struggled to swallow.

'Yes, Your Honour. I do recognise the contents of the bag.'

'And what do you recognise them as?'

'They are underpants, Your Honour.'

'Ah, very good, Mr Bedford. Your honesty is well received by the courtroom. Now, can you tell me what exactly is wrong with this particular pair of underpants?'

'There's ah, there's . . .' Tommy held. Maybe if he said it wasn't shit, they'd let him off. Stand still and a T-Rex won't see you. The game he and Mick had played growing up, in the backyard after the lights went off inside. But then he remembered Mick's words.

'There's shit in them.'

Judge McKinlay raised his eyebrows.

'Well, yes, Mr Bedford, there *is* shit in them. But, show me a pair of jocks around here that doesn't have a bit of shit in them. If *that* were the crime, then the entire courtroom would be on trial right now. To varying degrees, of course. No, the correct answer, Tommy, is that there is nothing wrong with these underpants at all. So, one wonders why you have thrown them away.'

Tommy felt a relief. He was over the hill. The tension in the room had dissipated.

'So, that being said, I believe that you should put them on. Waste not, want not, Mr Bedford. That is the current state of affairs.'

You were never over the hill in Kangaroo Court. But this, this he could do. *Don't resist. You'll only make things worse.*

As Tommy started to pull down his underpants, a red g-string that he'd bought the week prior in anticipation of the day, he was interrupted.

'No, no, Mr Bedford, you're already wearing a perfectly decent pair of underpants. I believe that these go somewhere else. Let's allow the jury to rule where Mr Bedford should put his second pair of underwear?'

As the room rang with cries of 'HEAD' and 'MOUTH!' Tommy B started gagging. The stench from the now unlocked Ziploc bag elicited pure repulsion. The stink of sewage inside his nostrils. Burning. His eyes watering. He had played good that day. Thirty disposals and two goals if he remembered correctly. Go there now, Tommy Boy. Go there now.

PARIS 2

Elliott
DAY 55

The first thing Emily said to me when I saw her again was that she's an insomniac and didn't sleep last night. Then she added, 'So I won't sleep with you tonight.'

She said the same thing at Soho House a few weeks ago.

I asked how her date went with that guy after we last saw each other and she said he was nice but 'too much', and not great in social situations.

'You have to see what a guy is like in a social setting before you date him,' she said.

Now she wants to focus on her career and go on Hinge dates and 'sleep around'. She said she saw Tom Holland working out at Soho House last night.

'I didn't recognise him at first—he was just a cute boy wearing a hat. It's hard to tell because the rooms are dark there because some of the members are famous. He went to put weights back and we crossed paths. He was very polite.'

She said I looked tired and I told her I haven't really slept for the last two nights.

'Why did you go to Manchester?'

'I don't know,' I said. 'I just did.'

She pointed to the skyscraper behind us and said that it had our initials on it.

'Oh wait,' she said. 'We don't have the same initials.'

DAY 56

Emily and I sat on the couch for most of the night. She's reading *Malibu Rising* and I'm reading *Naked Lunch*. The inside of the front cover is inscribed: *I can't wait to spend more time lounging around and reading books with you, you make me so happy—Mills.* When I asked who Mills was, Emily said it was her housemate's ex.

'They broke up not long ago,' she said. 'It was pretty sad.'

'No shit,' I said.

We both started laughing and then she snorted, which made us laugh even more. I haven't laughed like that in a while. So that was nice.

We read for another hour and then Emily asked where I'd prefer to sleep, on the couch or next to her, and I said it was up to her.

'You can sleep in the bed, but I have work in the morning so don't keep me awake.'

'So, no sex then?'

'Ha ha ha.'

I brushed my teeth and got changed and said thanks for giving me a place to stay and then we both went to sleep.

DAY 57

Emily, her housemate Franky and I all went for a drink after
Franky got home from work. Emily was wearing an oversized
blazer and saying her tooth was sore.

'I grind my teeth and go through fillings every few months,'
she said.

Franky said if she can wait then his mum will sort something out, but Emily said, 'No, it needs to be done soon.'

Franky's response: 'Let's get fucked up, that'll help.'

We went to a pub called the Cow where I ordered the first
round.

Franky is a chef who works at a new restaurant nearby.
When I asked how long he's been a chef he said eleven years
and seemed surprised by the answer.

'There is nothing better than making a meal and seeing
someone enjoy it,' he said.

He checked his phone. A girl called Tilly was sending him
photos; she is nineteen, blonde and attractive, and works
at the restaurant too. He said that he needs to stop getting
so fucked up and fucking the waitstaff, then he laughed
and went to take a piss. We ordered another drink and he
said he falls in love easily. Emily said she doesn't want to
fall in love for a while. They both turned to me, awaiting a
response.

'Love fucking sucks,' I said, and they cheersed my drink.

'To acceptance!' said Emily.

'To endless possibilities and women!' said Franky, and
Emily hit him for saying that.

We took the Tube to Soho House where Emily had reserved
a table. We sat by the pool and ordered a round of drinks and
then Franky started laughing and said that he'd sent Tilly to

the wrong Soho House, but it was ok because he'd ordered her an Uber to get here.

'I'd never let a guy do that for me,' Emily said. 'On principle.'

Tilly came in about half an hour later. Wearing red shoes. The first thing she said was: 'Sorry I look like such a twat.'

She sat down and we had a few cigarettes and went to go play pool. Franky was quite drunk and said that if Tilly made a shot then she had to kiss him.

After a few games Emily said she had to go and I offered to walk home with her.

A few hours later Franky knocked at the front door, saying he couldn't figure out how to get in. He was on his own. I went back to sleep then opened my eyes again. Emily was in the hallway saying how the kitchen was full of smoke because Franky put a pizza in the oven and forgot about it.

'I'm never drinking with him again,' she said.

DAY 58

Purple velvet chairs. Wonky love heart latte art. 'Cleaning in Progress' sign—yellow. Porcelain 'Dogs Welcome' sign. American woman on phone organising flight to Toulon: 'I never got my reservation number so I don't know how I'll check in.' Stairs to the bathroom. Pub across the road. Football on in the corner. Mexican flag next to television. Fake plants in water. In my bag: Vaseline for tattoo. Book on table. The sound of fork scraping plate. Conversation in corner: 'I think I've become more like that. You know British people are usually more polite?' Raynor hygiene truck. Blue sky. Dead trees. Damp leaves on footpath. Sign on a bus: *This is a banker*. Walk to a different place. Down a canal. Past a bike rider. Past a couple in matching hats. Past more dead leaves. Inside people booking Christmas parties. An L-shape in the corner works best and it's a ten-pound deposit per person. Some shitty pop playlist. Every song about breaking up. It happens to everyone. Red candle on table. Salt and pepper shakers. Phone charging. Guy walks in and replaces all the flowers. Bartender blond, earring in his right ear. I'm biting my nails. Biting the skin around my nails. I've had one drink and I feel warm again. I feel like I can't be sad right now. The sad thoughts are still there but they don't hurt any more. I am going to walk to another pub after this and have another drink and then I will book a hotel in Paris, near the airport.

DAY 59

Sitting on Emily's balcony with the book *Elephant* in my lap. Garbage trucks come around the corner. A woman is calling out for her dog to stop and it doesn't. She stamps her feet. Whistles. The dog still doesn't stop and then it does. The truck honks, drowning out the sounds of the hockey games being played on the oval I am looking at through the trees. The sun is high in the sky and the glare makes it hard to look up. I see green moss on the roof and cardboard boxes in the window to my left. I go back into the apartment. Emily is on the phone to somebody asking about a cheque that needs to be cashed and then I hear hold music. I walk into the living room and she says to sit down and do whatever because she's just got a million things going on but it's fine. The hold music is intense, Latin, not usual elevator stuff. She says once more that she's never drinking with Franky again. Apparently he owes her money because he was getting drinks at Soho and he didn't pay for them.

'They must've been putting them on my tab,' she says. 'I swear to god if I lose my membership because of him, I'm never forgiving him.'

I sit for a while and say that I'm about to order my Uber to the station. A group of school kids pass by outside and we can hear them laughing and it makes Emily smile. I say, 'Enjoy it while you can, kids, because life is relentless.' Emily laughs and says, 'Yes life is relentless,' and then my Uber arrives and I get my bags and give her a big hug and say goodbye.

★

When we come out of the tunnel I can't help but think how the sky really is a different type of blue over France. I have a new Carver book (*Will You Please Be Quiet, Please?*) on my lap. In the bookstore I bumped into a young woman who worked there while picking it off the shelf. She stumbled into a display and a few books hit the ground. I said how sorry I was and then after I paid we walked past each other again and I said we should be very careful and she laughed. The train has been black most of the trip as we pass through tunnels. Most people are on their phones watching Netflix. A group of American girls to my right are saying how you should never mention an insecurity because then people notice it. The comment sticks out and for the first time in a while I find myself thinking about the footy club and what it would be like if I was still there. I stop thinking about it. It's in the past. I tune back into the conversation. One of the girls is explaining how big her ears are and the others say they never noticed her ears before. One has had a birth mark removed by laser and one has an eye mask on and a travel pillow wrapped around her neck. I can taste last night's cigarettes all of the sudden and I could quite easily fall asleep right now at 5 pm.

DAY 60

I meet Madeleine at the station, and we walk to get food but first she pulls me over to a café and orders us a mojito. I tell her my trip highlights and she tells me about a guy from Cairns who she went to school with who called her up the other day. The story goes for almost twenty minutes. He went into hospital because he could not move his shoulder.

'He was a pilot,' she said, 'so the Air Force was paying the bills.'

After a few days his wife and child had not come to visit and when he called she said she never wanted anything to do with him again, and took all of the money out of their joint bank account. There's a lot more to it, like the fact he and his wife had been on the rocks for a year and that the baby wasn't his, or at least the lawyer he saw said that they didn't believe the baby was his and his mum said yes I never did think the baby looked like you. Then it was also that the pain in his shoulder was cancer and the Air Force had stood him down and were no longer paying his bills because his partner had alleged he abused her. So, that's why Madeleine thought he'd called her, to ask for money. She didn't know how much to give him, if she was decided to help him. I help Madeleine finish her wine and then we say goodbye and I thank her for showing me around. I say sorry for leaving so abruptly earlier in the trip and if she's ever in Australia, I'll return the favour and show her around.

'I already know Australia,' she says.

'It was just a common expression,' I say.

'Well, I'd like that anyway.'

When I check into the hotel near the airport there are a lot of people up watching the football. I go to my room, watch a movie and at midnight I go down to get two bottles of Coke Zero and some food from a raw bar which isn't bad. The light in the bathroom shines green and I close the blinds and go to sleep.

WANK

SIXTY MINUTES

Being in the bathroom makes me feel like I should do it. There's something about the tiles on the wall. The mirror above the basin. The sight of the toilet bowl. It feels like an invitation. It's a shrine for pleasure, a corner of the world that is mine to indulge in. The air inside my mouth changes. My heart beats faster. The rope pulls me in. I know I won't be able to stop thinking about it until I do it. I can usually fight it for five minutes but then it returns. I've got to do it now. It is that time of the week.

I walk out and tell Georgey-Boy and Pricey I have to head off. Without turning their heads from Coldplay's 2014 São Paolo performance of *Viva La Vida*, they say, 'That time of the week, Sixty?' and, 'Hardest working player at the club.'

I know they're taking the piss. But the rope is pulling me too hard.

The door closes behind me, and I get in my car and drive towards the club.

I was late to it. The first time I did it, I was sixteen years old.

Whenever the boys at school talked about it, I found myself on the outside.

I was ten years old when me, Jarrod and Mark were sun-baking on beach towels in the middle of Mark's street.

Jarrod asked what technique I used when masturbating. Having only ever seen videos of women masturbating in solo porn, I started to rub the area above my crouch.

'Like this,' I said.

Jarrod started laughing. 'That's not how you do it.'

I dug in. 'Yes it is, it works. Trust me.'

A year later Ryan Powell told me he had his first wet dream. I replied in turn saying I had them all the time. He asked what happened in them. I can still see his look of bewilderment at my reply, which was to describe a poorly detailed version of *The Persistence of Memory* by Salvador Dali, or at least, an appropriation of the artwork I had seen in an episode of *The Simpsons*. Dripping clocks hanging from street poles. A literal *wet* dream.

In Year 9, on a school excursion to the art gallery I had said to my friends that I could masturbate without even touching my cock. That's how often I did it. The following year the quote was attributed to a friend of mine who as a result was the recipient of sneers from the rest of us for months. The joke was to put your hands in the air and start moaning incredibly loudly like you were about to ejaculate. Cameron would defend himself and say that it wasn't him who had said it.

'Fuck off Cam,' I would say. Then I'd stick my hands in the air and scream out, 'I'm going to cum. I'm going to cum!'

The act of masturbation scared me because it involved rolling back the skin on my cock—something I had not done, which I blame my parents for. They had never told me; it only came up because they had seen me at football training scratching my crotch through my football shorts. When I was thirteen, my mother took me to the local GP after school. He asked me to lay down on the table and pulled the curtain so my mother couldn't see. He snapped his white gloves on and asked me to pull down my shorts. He examined my cock and slowly pulled the skin back for the first time, exposing the head of my penis. I remember seeing the purple head of my cock for the first time. It looked like a suffocated corpse. Or a new-born baby. Around it was a build-up of white matter, which the doctor said I had to clean away. The few times I had tried to roll it back to clean I felt faint. The skin was delicate and I feared I might pull back too far and tear it. So I would rarely do it.

I would watch porn under the covers of my bed at night without touching myself. I enjoyed the sight of naked women. I was aroused watching them get fucked and had my favourite positions to watch them get fucked in. I found pornstars to be the most attractive women, more so than movie stars and supermodels. There was, and is, something about the excess of a pornstar. Big tits that sit on the chest like balloons. Asses that you can really grab onto. Tight, hairless vaginas. Nowadays I would say I am more of an ass person, and I have a greater appreciation for hips and vaginas too. When I say that I am an ass person, what I mean is that I like the flesh of the ass. Not the asshole itself. I turn the screen away when I see a gaping asshole.

One day, when I was sixteen, I made a commitment to myself that I would masturbate until I came. I sat on the toilet in my family home pulling on my cock while watching a video starring a woman named Carmella Bing. The video was twenty-four minutes long and featured Carmella getting fucked on a green couch. She had dark brunette hair and olive skin, with large, spherical breasts and a pot belly. In other Carmella videos I've watched, her weight changes drastically. She's become a sort of fat fetish star—even fucking while pregnant, which is something I have masturbated to several times. I remember the sensation right before ejaculating the first time. A pleasurable pins-and-needles feeling took over my entire body. I slowed my stroking and held my cock in my hand. I felt very much like I was holding on to a rope at the top of a cliff. I knew that letting go would send me somewhere, and I didn't know if that would be pleasurable or not. I had never seen semen before, and in some way felt afraid of the substance that would come out of my body. What if, because I had left it so long, there was something wrong with it? What if there was too much of it and it drained me dry and caused me to pass out? What if it just kept coming out and didn't stop? I held still and stopped thinking. Then I remember when the valve was finally opened, and a rush of elation ran from my shoulders along my back. I closed my eyes and curled over, guiding the ejaculate onto the inner thigh of my left leg. I let out a shallow exhale as it continued to pump out. The next day I did it three times.

I think I might have a problem, but it's not that bad. The only person who knows is the club psychologist who says I shouldn't feel bad about it, that I'm doing the best I can with the tools I currently have. Once I start, I don't feel bad. It's only after that I do. It's exciting, it's natural. You hear about people who watch nine hours of porn a day. That's when it's a problem. They have kids and a family and they lock themselves in a room and watch porn all day. I'm nowhere near that. I do it once a week now. It relieves stress and it means all of my decisions aren't dictated by sex. It levels me out. In that way, it's healthy.

I park out the front of the club. The lights of the change-rooms turn on as I walk in and then the silence of the bathroom washes over me. I sit on the toilet and rest my phone on my right thigh as I scroll down the homepage looking for my usual type. A MILF with fake tits and a big ass. Someone whose body is made for sexual gratification. A woman like Sara Jay, Lisa Ann, Shyla Stylez or Priya Rai. I've masturbated to Sara Jay more than I have any other pornstar. She doesn't have a super pretty face. But her body is so hot that her face doesn't matter. That's all that matters. Her ass. Her tits. Her hips. Her pussy.

Another option is Gianna Michaels. Her tits are more natural-looking. They hang down and move freely around her chest when she's fucking on her back. She fucks very loud and with her eyes rolled back, like she's possessed. There's also Brandi Love. A blonde who looks great in lingerie, but her tits aren't as big and her hips aren't as wide. She's more fit-looking—she's got a sixpack and quite a masculine face. She's hot but sometimes I can't get off to her because when I watch porn I crave the exaggeration of bodies in a way that I don't usually see. The latest addition to my rotation is Nina Hartley. She's over sixty years old. You can tell in the close-ups on her face and by looking at her hands. But she has one of best asses I've ever seen. She wears lace lingerie and garters in all her videos and her entire mood changes when the dick goes inside her. There's only three good videos of her because she never gets fucked that hard. It's like the guys are scared of hurting her. I like to think that she's seen as a deity in the industry. So when a young guy gets told he is fucking Nina he sees it as his chance to fuck an idol. There's a different look in his eyes then. He's living out a fantasy. It's real.

301

As I scroll, thumbnail previews flick past. *Busty Satomi Suzuki fucks five of her coworkers . . . Naïve charity girl seduced by grandpa . . . Family Swap XXX—Swap mom: Get over here, I have some breast meat for you . . . My best friend's dad came to fuck me and leaves my pussy full of cum . . . Cuck watched his wife take a BBC in the ass . . . BLACKED: Anal-hungry Gabbie Carter craves Anton's huge BBC . . .*

I think about watching the last one, but I want to find something better. I go to the second page and scroll.

I don't want to watch a girl fuck another girl with a strap on. I don't want to watch an interracial gang bang. Sometimes I'll watch two guys fucking the same girl. I watch to see who she wants to fuck more. Whose cock she really wants.

There's nothing here. I tap the top of the screen and go to the search bar then I remember a girl from a video I watched last week. A woman with huge fake tits and black hair. I think she had a real Jewish-sounding name, or at least the name of the video had the word 'Jewish' in it. I begin to type 'big tit jewish'. The videos load and I can't see her face. Fuck, what's her name? It started with D. Denise? Danielle? It was definitely D, and there's an f sound there as well . . . *Daphne.* Daphne Rosen.

I search the name and her channel appears at the top, then her videos in order of upload date from newest to oldest. The first video goes for three minutes, which means there will be forty seconds of actual fucking. That's not enough to make me cum. Plus, I have to time it right, so that I get the kick. I'd have to loop it over and over and the repeat watch softens my libido. The second video is shot 360p which means the quality is super low. The third video must be a re-upload of an older video because she looks so different in it; her hair is blonde and she doesn't have fake tits. She looks pretty. But I don't want pretty. I stop scrolling and let the thumbnail play out to see anyway. The guy isn't really fucking her in it. I don't want something timid. I want something hard.

There's nothing jumping out at me. She's fucking on a boat. She's fucking in a house. She's fucking on a boat again. So I go to her profile page and order the videos by most viewed. I decide to click on the top video and go through the related videos. Towards the bottom of the page I find the video I watched last week. She's auditioning to be the drummer in a band. She fucks the guy in cowboy for five minutes straight. That's what I want to watch. I click on it and an ad begins to play. A twelve-foot high monster is fucking a small Asian girl. Her hands are tied behind her back and her mouth is gagged. She looks like she is in pain. But I can't tell. It could just as easily be pleasure. I skip the ad. The video goes for twelve minutes. I watch the intro to see how she looks. She's wearing a tight-fitting black dress that barely covers her underwear. It's like a second skin. Her breasts are bulging out. She has blue eyeliner on. Her skin looks flawless. It feels like I'm in the room with her. She begins to talk to the camera and I fast forward to three minutes in. In a twelve-minute video this is usually where the top comes off. I'm right. But I go back a little bit; I want to see the moment where they decide to have sex. That moment where they can't hold back the primal urge to fuck each other. Where her act is dropped and she decides his cock is all she needs. The video plays and I begin to stroke my cock. I use both hands. I used to do it with one hand. But now I can only get the force I need with two. It's like I'm controlling the joystick to a jet fighter. My elbows jutt out to the side and I hold on tight.

I skip to seven minutes so I'm past the oral sex. I'm waiting for the moment where it goes in. I want to see her face react.

She's looking at the camera. She closes her eyes. She lets out a moan. They show a close-up of his cock going inside her. His cock looks like it's twice the size of mine. I look at my cock in my hands and continue to pull.

I'm breathing faster. Pulling harder. My cock is hard but I don't feel close to cumming. I know that the kick is imminent, though. It's the only thing that gets me there now. I begin to talk to myself. *Yeah . . . all for me . . . all for me, right. Yeah . . . it is . . . it is . . . you only want my cock . . . all for me . . . all for me . . . fuck you like that . . . You like that . . . yeah . . . yeah . . . yeah . . . fuck . . . you have such a big cock . . . fuck me with that cock . . .*

Suddenly I lose it. I feel like I'm on the other side of ejaculation, but I haven't finished. A thought went through my head that it wasn't going to happen. Now it won't. I lost it. This happens a lot now. More often than not. That's why I come here. For the kick that I need. It was two years ago that I left breakfast the day of an underage rep game and pumped one out before our morning walk. The urge came over me and I couldn't resist. The hotel bathroom beckoned me towards it. I was rooming with Patty Rourke, who was still down at breakfast, and the thought of him coming back helped me reach climax. The ticking clock aspect of it gave me something to work towards. That became my kick. Waiting for someone to arrive. Waiting for a phone call. For approaching footsteps.

I sit with my cock slowly going limp in my lap. It's still a little bit hard. I can get it hard again. I start pumping it. It feels good going from semi to fully hard.

I try another video.

There's one that I really feel like watching now. There's a tanned woman wearing a yellow swimsuit, a one-piece that goes from her pussy in a large V over her tits. She's showering by the pool when two guys come and ask her if she wants to come back to their room. Her hair is pulled back and she has fake tits with a gutter gap between them. She looks like a girl I went to school with named Laura. I can't remember the name of the pornstar, but I remember the video had 'fuzzy peach' in the title. I search it and the video appears. I close the browser and open up Instagram. I go to Laura's profile to find a photo of her to screenshot so that I can have the video playing in the corner while the image of her fills my screen. She doesn't post hot photos of her onto her grid, but I know she has uploaded some thirst trap stories before. Her highlights are pinned to the page under categories. Her at the gym. Her out partying. Her travelling around Europe. The last one is of her dressed up nicely. It is labelled with a moon emoji. I'm looking for two specific photos. One is of her in a nurse's outfit with dyed blonde hair. The other is of her lying on the couch wearing a grey top cut so you can see her tits. I screenshot them both, crop them so I only have the image and not the Instagram background, and then I delete the photos so they sit in my deleted photos folder.

I go back to the video, refresh the screen, and play it in full screen. I make sure my phone is locked on portrait mode. I minimise the video it so it takes up the bottom third of my screen. Then I go to photos and select the image of Laura in the nurse's outfit. My gaze alternates between Laura's face and the video of Lexi Luna getting fucked. I imagine that the video is me and Laura. I start to say her name. *Laura. Laura. Fuck me, Laura. Do you like that? Do you like my cock?* I play out the time Laura and I talked at the school canteen. I play out Lincoln's house party where she was wearing a short skirt and had her top tied up under her tits. I close my eyes and feel like I'm about to cum. I speed up so that it doesn't get away. I've caught it. I'm going to cum. But I need the kick. It should be happening at any moment now. I look at the time above the video. The lights should turn on. The cleaners should be coming, like they always do. I can hear them wheeling in their trolleys now. My legs stiffen and I push back. In the moments before I cum it is like I am free. I am comforted by a blackness that only I know. I am an animal free to be as dark as I want to be. There is a second of relaxation. I feel exhausted. Then the guilt. I close the tab. Clear the history. Delete the photos of Laura. I tell myself that I'm fucking sick. I've got a problem. I'm a fucking sicko. I've got to clean myself up. I'm never wanking again.

MR ROGERS

Stick

Little smoke bomb number out the back door and none of these cunts will be any the wiser. Especially not Squidman in the corner playing fucking Freezemaster for the last four hours. Shit, he's in la-la land. Must be on the brown Special K horse tranks. Pisser of a sight though. Sunnies on, fully frozen with a full schooner next to him. Reckon we'll come back in a few days' time and he'll still be nursing that same beer. Mother's fucking milk, Squid. Drinky drinky.

Ah, well, who am I to point the finger? He's not the only one getting some pilly-pills. Mr Rogers' medicine cabinet awaits and I've got a hankering for a load of bullets. And yes, I am aware that I'm dressed like a sausage dog, the tomato sauce is a gratuitous effect, but how else am I meant to get these cunts to understand that I'm a dead sausage dog? Some of them need to be hit over the head with it. No rocket scientists in there, that's for sure.

I may have timed this perfectly. Proceedings are dying off. I reckon there's a few cunts about to have some honest conversations with each other that will lead to sooky socks.

Christ, I got a fair whack on the back of the head as well from the impromptu Jake King. Was just standing there, minding my own fucking business and some cunt's come in from the side with a schooner and clocked me. I reckon it was Fangs, dirty dog. He'll always throw the first one then run off when the repercussions come. Should cut the cunt some slack though. He's a dead man walking with that meeting he's got on Wednesday. No contract on the table, no prospect of playing here next year. No chance he can pull a Steven Bradbury and make this one work. Poor old Fangsy boy.

Hey, stop the cab! This is it. I have business to tend to. The pharmaceutical conglomerate that is Mr Rogers' Bathroom Cabinet has opened. In exchange? How about two tickets to Round 1's game next year, Mr R? Fingers crossed you'll still be kicking then. If not, it has been nice.

Knockity knock knock knock. It's your old pal Sticky Stick, Mr Rogers. Open up. Oh, you're going to play hard to get and make me wait are you? Well then, little piggy, how about I blow this fucking house down, eh? Wouldn't take much. Barely standing as it is. Knockity fucking knock knock knock. The little jokey-joke is over. Mr R, let me in, I've got the sweats and am in need of some bullets so I'd sincerely appreciate it if you'd open the fucking door.

Well, then, if you're going to be a stubborn prick, I guess Old Stick will just have to make his own way in. Can't say I didn't give you fair warning . . .

Shit, that was a decent knock, eh? I can feel the door starting to give. But never fear, piggy piggy, I'm not after your bacon. No no no, I'm after the little capsules of chemically compounded pain relief that you keep next to the dental floss above the shitter. That's all. And if you're too spaced out to have a chat, then that's all fine with me. Efficiency Kills, after all. Get in. Get out. Then back to the pub for the tail end of the day, assuming we haven't been kicked out by then, and if so, then off to get a succulent Chinese meal.

Shit, these hallways really are tragic. If you put your eyeballs close enough, the annual team photo can pinpoint the moment in everyone's career where it went to shit. Look at the smile on Fangs' face in year one. He's still got a glint of it in year two, then by year three the cunt is properly done. Even more fucking morbid is Squidman having a shaved head in year three because of the hair-testing, eh. Full fucking skinhead. Said it'd help with wind resistance and improve his running times. No wind resistance when you've got a seven-foot frame running around acting like a big fuck-off flesh-sail. Points for trying though, Squiddy. Ah, and looky here. There's old Coddy boy front and centre, that perpetually defeated look in his eye. Currently traversing the European continent by all reports on social media. Our crossover was brief, but there's never a cunt I've felt more for. Cod. C-O-D. Cock of Death. No wonder the bloke's been off the radar since he left. There would be some serious head noise as a result of that situation. He probably needs the little blue pills to get it hard. Might fucking trigger him though, when the blood flows to his cock and he goes full PTSD. Christ. Enough of that, Stick. Where the fuck are *my* little pilly-pills?

Jesus. You reckon that someone would pay for a cleaner for the poor prick. There's dog shit everywhere. Normally the old bloke at least picks it up, but he's been a bit slack of late, hasn't he? Naughty boy, Mr Rogers. And that stench. Fuck me dead.

Ah, we have arrived at our destination. And not a moment too soon. I am in the optimal territory for these to take full effect. Blood thinned by the alcohol. Stomach empty of food, except for the burger consumed at 4 am after the club decided to kick us all out, one by one. Who the fuck are those bastards to tell me that I'm not allowed to swim in the water, eh? Fucking cannonballlllll cunts. That showed them. And all those fucking virgins, sipping on their bottles of water. Every cunt is gacked off their face, and they single me out? At least I'm keeping it above board. You know what I'm consuming: straight piss. Legal.

Hmm, you're running a bit low, Mr R. When's the last time you got this prescription filled? We need to have a little talky-talk to make sure that you keep providing the goods. A gentle reminder of our arrangement is in store; I'll be fucked if the supply stops. Little chance I'm going back to those marketplace trade groups. That place is absolute maresville. Amityville Horrorshow. Creeps galore.

One downside to this costume, it now appears. Apparently sausage dog outfits don't have pockets, not even a pouch. I can't shelve all these now. I'll just do one or two for the road and then keep the rest warm in my jocks.

Here we go, the moment we've been waiting for.

. . . One . . .

. . . Two . . .

Great placement! Oh yeah, they're sitting nicely. Hmm. Very nicely. Now to go pay my dues to the old cunt, unless he's fast asleep. If he is then I'll leave him a little notey-note thanking him dearly for his continued service to the Bank of Stick's Oxycodone Addiction.

Ugh. Christ, that smell really is something else. Guess I had the blinders on, tunnel vision blocking out all my sensory perceptions. My god, it smells worse than just the shit that's on the floor. Smells like fucking, god, smells like . . . death. Mr R, how can you put up with this? These living conditions are appalling. Shit. We really do need to get you a cleaner or something, because I can't deal with this stench.

Jesus, Mr Rogers, you must be deaf as a bat now too. I'm making some noise—it's a bit bloody hard to walk in this costume and, admittedly being discreet is not Sticky Stick's forte.

'Mr Rogers, it's your old pal Stick, how's it fucking going?'

Deaf as a bat, the grimy cunt.

'Mr Rogers, I said it's your old pal Stick, how's it—'

Oh, fuck. Not just deaf as a bat. He's fucking done for. Christ. That explains the stench. God. Fuck, that's disgusting. How long has the poor prick been here for, congealing in his own filth? You never were a looker, Mr R, but this is a face that not even a mother could love. My eyes are starting to water at the stench. My god. Ah, I guess, that a moment's silence may be in order, let me get a decent look at you for old time's sake and . . . oh fuck, why . . . why does he look like me old man? No, he doesn't . . . he doesn't . . . he looks like . . . fuck . . . he does . . . he looks like me old man . . . fuck . . . for fuck's sake . . . pull it together, Stick . . . Pull it to-fucken-gether . . . he's not . . . Daddy . . . Daddy . . . No . . . no . . . Sticky, pull it together . . . No . . . I'm sorry . . . Fuck . . . Daddy . . . I'll be better, I'm sorry . . . *Don't resist there boy, don't resist* . . . Ok Daddy, ok . . . Why do you smell like that? . . . *Don't resist, you'll only make it worse for yourself* . . . Ok, Daddy . . . I love you, Daddy . . . I love you . . . Please Daddy, just . . . Just . . . leave Tommy boy alone . . . He's only a little boy, Daddy . . . *Don't resist* . . . I won't Daddy. I won't. Please . . . just leave Tommy alone . . . Daddy . . . where are you going now? . . . Daddy . . . I love you . . . don't leave me . . . Daddy . . . Please . . . don't shut the door . . . Daddy . . . please . . .

Elliott

It's late and Tammy calls me saying, 'You have to come out. You just have to.'

There's a lot of noise in the background. I can only just make out what she's saying.

'We're at Club Sanction. Me and Lewis. Lewis is with some guy. They're going home together soon. You have to come. You just have to come. Ok?'

I pour myself another glass of straight Cointreau. I'm all out of ice so I just take a sip of water after each nip.

I'm not drunk enough to meet Tammy. So, I keep drinking. I have four glasses then I order an Uber and tell her I'll be there in twenty minutes.

When I arrive, Tammy is cornered by some guy. I wave at her and she walks over towards me then grabs me by the arm.

'Elliott,' she says, 'Elliott, this is Chris, Chris this is Elliott.'

We shake hands and then I ask if anyone wants a drink. Chris just sort of looks at me like he wants me to leave, so

I ask if he's sure he doesn't want another drink and he shakes his head. Tammy holds up her glass which is still half-full and says she'll come with me to get another one. She grabs my arm hard. 'Let's go,' she says.

At the bar we make small talk. I ask how her day was and she says it's been good and that she's glad to finally meet me in person.

'That guy was a real asshole. He kept saying I should go home with him.'

The bartender interrupts us and I order a vodka soda and a prosecco for Tammy.

'No, no, no,' she says, 'don't you pay.' But it's too late because I've already tapped my card and she says thanks and we walk towards the dancefloor.

Tammy has a red dress on and some guy with his top few buttons undone says she looks like the red dancing girl emoji. She strikes a pose. The guy then leans in to talk to her and she looks at me and grabs my arm again. The guy shakes my hand and leaves her alone.

I tell her that this isn't my kind of crowd. Everyone here is wearing a suit and the shirt I'm wearing is from a Hong Kong flea market and missing a few buttons.

'You look good,' she says. 'Very cultured, Paris boy.'

We make eye contact for a while and I can see her thinking about something but she doesn't say anything.

Another guy comes over and he's a head taller than us both and he says that Tammy can go on his boat for the weekend. He leans in real close and tells her that he'll pay her $100,000 just to go on the boat with him. Then he says that the dress looks good on her. This happens a few more times, guys coming up to Tammy, and then she grabs my face and says, 'Look at you, you're so cute. You're too nice.'

It's 11 pm but I don't feel tired. My body is still adjusting to the time difference.

I go to the bar to get another drink and Tammy follows me and she says she wants to kiss me but it's too public here. Then she drags me back to the dancefloor where I use the three moves I have on repeat and sway my body in time with the music. While I'm dancing I see some guys standing over at the bar who look familiar. A couple of the guys from the footy club. I can make one of them out clearly: Fangs. Poor kid rocked up day one with a couple of extra shark teeth in his gums. What else were we supposed to name him? Once things stick there, they stick.

I go to the bathroom and do some coke and when I come back Tammy says we should go back to hers. When we get out the front we sit on a step and more people walk past and recognise her. When they leave, she reaches for my hand and puts my thumb in her mouth and starts sucking on it. She says, 'Sorry am I not supposed to do that?' and then we start kissing.

After we kiss she says her ex-husband sucks and I say that the Uber isn't coming so we get a cab as it drives past.

When we get in the cab Tammy rolls up into a ball and puts her head between her knees. The cab driver asks if she's going to be sick and I open her door and she starts making sounds like she's going to throw up. I ask, 'Are you ok?' and she says no but then she shuts her door and goes back into the airline safety position. The cab driver says he will go slow so she doesn't throw up but a few times he turns corners at speed and she rolls around. Eventually she puts her head on my lap and I start running my fingers through her hair and rubbing her back.

'You give good back rubs,' she says, 'that's nice, keep going.'

When we get out of the cab I don't know where her hotel is and she says she needs to sit down on the side of the road and then she starts throwing up. Like really throwing up. I sit down next to her and keep rubbing her back.

'I'm so sorry,' she says, 'this is so unattractive.'

'It's fine,' I say.

She just keeps saying, 'I'm so sorry, I'm so sorry,' and then she says she hates her ex-husband again. After about ten minutes I stand up and say that we should get her into bed and get her some water.

We find the hotel and take the elevator, which has floral pink wallpaper. Her room is the one next to the elevator on the third floor and when we get inside she goes to the bathroom and brushes her teeth and then I hear the shower turn on. I go and sit on the balcony and have a cigarette and count the windows of the offices across the road. She comes out and she's very talkative and she smells like lavender. She gets under the covers and says, 'Are you going to join me?'

I tell her that I'm happy to sleep on the couch if she wants.

'Don't be silly,' she says. 'Come in.'

'Are you sure?'

'Yes, I'm sure.'

I take off my shoes and get under the covers next to her and we press our noses against each other and then she starts kissing me. She's chewing gum and tastes strongly of mint.

I move my hand down along her leg and then start touching her and she moves her head back and breathes out and shudders.

'That's nice,' she says. 'Don't stop. Don't stop, Elliott.'

I start touching her breasts then gently biting her nipples.

'Do you want to fuck me?' she says.

315

'I do,' I say. 'I want to fuck you.'

'Well, fuck me,' she says.

I take off my pants and underpants and I start fingering her and when I get hard I rub my cock along her clit.

'Are you teasing me?' she says.

'Is it working?'

'Yes. I want you inside me. Now.'

I get on top and put my cock inside her and she says *Oh my god* and then she digs her nails into my back.

While we fuck the mattress starts moving around and I put my hands on either side of her head, and we kiss.

'I wasn't expecting this,' she says. 'I really wasn't expecting this.'

We change positions a few times and she says, *you can have me any way you want me.* Then she says, *come on me. I want you to come on me*, and eventually I do, on her stomach. She holds my hand and says I have nice hands and then she says, 'Elliott, I really like you. You're amazing, I'm so glad we did that.'

'I'm glad we did that too.'

I shut my eyes and when I open them it's sunny outside. Her friend Lewis is sitting on the edge of the bed saying, 'Tammy we need to message them about the kayaking, what do we say, what do we say?' And Tammy tells him what to say and then he sends the message and starts telling us about the guy he fucked last night who gave him head for two hours. Only after the story he turns to me and says, 'Who are you?'

'Elliott,' I say. The bed sheet is covering only a small part of my body and I'm completely naked.

He says to Tammy, 'Is this the guy you were waiting for?' and she giggles.

Then he looks at the mattress and says, 'Well, go Elliott.'

Lewis leaves and says that he'll wait for Tammy downstairs. We lie there and Tammy asks me to spoon her.

'Just ten more minutes,' she says, and I do.

I ask, 'So what happened with your husband?'

'Oh, I hate him,' she says. 'He was an alcoholic. We went to Italy and went out with another couple and he was ordering margaritas and he kept ordering them for me too. If I left them there, then he'd drink them. So I started putting them on the floor. I didn't drink any. Then when we got back to the apartment we had a fight and he started filming me.'

'That's fucked up.'

'Yeah, in so many ways. He started filming me and he says, "I'm going to show everyone how much of a drunk you are." I'd only had two drinks. I hid the rest on the ground. So he wouldn't drink them. Then he starts filming me and then he grabbed me and threw me on the ground.'

'Fuck.'

'Yeah.'

She rolls over in the bed and I get up and say I have to go to work soon. I have a call at 8:30 am. In truth it's at 9:30 but I say 8:30. I feel bad leaving like this, but I don't know how to help her.

'Stay a bit longer, Elliott, would you? At least shower.'

'Ok,' I say, and I stand and walk over to the bathroom. I see Tammy roll over and start using her phone and I slide the door shut, turn the taps on and steam fills the room. I stand there for a while, not really washing myself, just letting the water run over me. There's a song from last night that is stuck in my head that I sing a little bit and then when I feel like I've been in the shower long enough I turn the taps off and stand on the bamboo floor mat. My feet dry quickly and I look at my shaved face in the mirror. I have bags under my eyes and a small patch of dry skin under my bottom lip.

When I open the door, she's not in the room.

'Tammy?'

Her phone is lying in the middle of the bed, vibrating, and I go to grab it. It's Lewis.

I answer.

'Tammy,' he says, 'get your ass down here. We have to go now!'

'It's Elliott. I—'

'Where's Tammy?'

'I don't know, she was here but I just got out of the shower and—'

'Just tell her to come down when you see her, ok?'

I'm about to say *I don't know* when I turn around. There's these three guys standing there. Two of them are enormous.

'Here he is,' says the one in the middle, slightly smaller than those on either side.

I hear Lewis saying something on the other end of the phone, but the sound drops away when I drop my arms to my side.

'So, I see you're not using any protection this time, eh?'

I don't know what's going on. I'm trying to figure out if they were there last night and something happened. But I know it didn't.

The smaller guy talking has a ponytail. His hair is pulled back so tight his face looks like a mask.

'They said she suffered, that the air slowly went out of her lungs. Her windpipe blocked up.'

The two bigger men take a step towards me while the middle one keeps talking.

'They said she would've been fighting, choking, struggling to breathe, and you just kept going, didn't ya? You disgusting prick.'

The two men grab me by the arms and legs and pin me down on the bed. They've got a tight grip and it feels like my muscles are slowly being crushed. The guy with the ponytail pulls out a small orange packet from his pocket. He rips it open and stands over me.

'I want you to suffer like she did. I'm going to watch the life leave your eyes.'

He turns to the corner of the room and says, 'You, come here.'

Another figure stands over me now. He looks familiar, like I've seen him somewhere before, in this life, or one gone by.

He is told to hold my mouth open. Which he does. His hands shaking. I can feel the sweat on them.

'What is it they call you?' he says, moving his fingers towards my open mouth. 'COD? *Cause of Fucking Death?*'

A CHOICE

Fangs

I haven't slept for seventy-two hours. Sunday, Monday and Tuesday have merged into one catastrophic bender. Worse than the pain between the ears are the slashes on my arse, making it extremely uncomfortable to sit for longer than thirty seconds. My dim recollection is being convinced that an echidna was talking to me, saying it needed to be saved. My chemically demented brain told me to put the thing in my pants and run. Don't do drugs, kids. Or at least, don't do a lot of them.

Fuck knows how Squid and I wound up in a wannabe-Joe Exotic's house. A Burmese python and a Capuchin monkey should not co-inhabit the same dwelling. And that fucking echidna giving me the sad eyes. Prick. How either of Squidman and myself were in the state to communicate with any other living being after the amount of caps we'd consumed remains a mystery. Squid's jaw would still have been swinging—no, unhinged—at the meeting he had to go to this morning. But even then, his meeting would've been far cruiser than mine. Cunt's got two more years to figure it out. Whereas I've got all of fifteen minutes to plead my case here.

Big Fella (one of the numerous Big Fellas I'm seeing, due to my state): So, how would you rate your season?

Christ. Pull it together.

Me: Well, to be honest with you, up and down.

The Big Fella, the one in the middle of the three who I'm hoping is the real one, raises his eyebrows and his minions off to the side write on their clipboards. You should never play the victim card in these situations; the Big Fella hates it when players make excuses. Don't say, 'You didn't give me a chance, you prick.' Say . . .

Me: Well, I feel like I made progress in a lot of areas of my game. All the hard work I was doing in the off season started to pay off. It was frustrating not cracking into the team this year, but I think I'm ready to take that step. I just have to keep grinding away and take the next opportunity I get.

The fact that he hasn't thrown that clipboard at my head means that he's happy with that response.

Minion 1: We just have a few questions regarding your off-field behaviour.

Me (fuck you): Oh, sure thing.

Minion 1: Do you think you have a problem with drugs and alcohol?

Me: Ah, no. I don't really. Not at all. I mean, I don't consider myself an alcoholic. Like everyone else here, I enjoy a few drinks. But I know when to call it a night. And as for drugs? No, I've never touched them (*except for cocaine, MDMA, ketamine, brown ketamine, ecstasy, dexamphetamine, pseudoephedrine, methoxetamine, a particular glassy bag of white powder on one occasion and not to mention all of the substances I've pushed into my orifices when too fuck-eyed to otherwise remember). We're professional athletes, at the end of the day. We have to look for every edge over our competition, and I want my body to be in the best shape it can be at all times. So no, no problem there.

Minion 1: Good to hear. We've just had to ask that question in light of what happened with, ah . . . with the other night.

They can't even bring themselves to say his name. Ah, Stick. I hope you do get the help you need in that rehabilitation clinic. Apparently, the police found him sobbing over Mr Rogers' decomposing body. They'd been called by the neighbours, who thought that there was a demonic spirit in the house. Only Stick could sob that loudly. The club's angle is that he's taking time away from footy to deal with a 'personal issue' and now they're clearly going into damage control about the rest of our lives. Interestingly, there's been no mention here of Coddy. The poor cunt got caught up in some horrorshow situation and is in a coma. The club hasn't said a word to any of us about him, but intel from our own sources confirms that he's in a vegetative state and unlikely to walk on his own again.

I give it a week before Stick breaks out of rehab. Squid says four days. Shaggers gives him two and Mud reckons he's already back out, finding some new proxy for his insatiable addiction.

While Minion 1 utters more drivel, I can see the contents of the whiteboard behind him. On the left side of the board are the names of every cunt who's played this year, or who has a contract in place. On the right, two lonely islands: me and Big Sexy. That's it. The two offcuts it looks like they're choosing between.

I feel like they might be dangling a carrot in front of me. Nothing happens by accident around here. Especially with regards to the whiteboards and other various surfaces. This is by design. Message sent; message received.

Big Fella: Now I just want to ask a personal question . . .

Here we go, let's get personal. Soften the lighting. Light a candle. Put some throw pillows out. I'm ready.

Big Fella: Fangs, do you want to be here?

Me: Here, now, or here in general?

Big Fella: Here. At this footy club. Do you want to play football for this club?

Suddenly I feel like I've taken three ecstasy pills. Well, three more than I have over the last few days. The flight or fight response is triggered. Still caught in the debauchery of the bender, my mind can't reconcile it, but my body recognises the sensation of being the prey in the wild with the predators circling, licking their lips. The table between us provides meagre protection from the feeding frenzy about to take place. They've cornered me and have closed in. To the question posed, honestly, fuck knows. But what races through my head is the prospect of not being here anymore. Of waking up tomorrow and having to put together a resume for a job. What the fuck do you put on a resume? *My experiences in the high pressure environments of elite football have given me the skills necessary to thrive in any workplace culture.* What the fuck does that mean? Who the fuck would even give me a job? And if they did, I'd walk out the minute some cunt started telling me how to put together a spreadsheet. Then how would I pay rent? I'd have to move back home. Move in with the folks. Listen to them discussing the ABC over dinner every night and whatever shit they've been fed by the radio on their drive to work. Christ, full time uni? Sitting in the first lesson hearing a 'fun fact' about twenty pricks I don't know and who are all five years younger than me? The mature-age student? Nah, I'd rather be on the actual *Titanic* than deal with those icebreakers. Do I want to play football here? No. But do I want to be out there? Fuck that . . .

Me: I do. I really do. I believe in this footy club. I want to live by the standards of this club. I want to be a part of this club's long-term success. I will work my arse off and I will drag others along with me. That's for sure. Not just as a player, but as a leader. I know that I have the desire and will to do it. I fucking promise you that.

Shit, I've laid it on a bit thick there, but it looks like they're buying it. They're buying the fake meat on the shit sandwich. The feeding frenzy has been momentarily stayed and, astonishingly, I may have actually persuaded them to throw me a bone. The Big Fella almost smiles, that's how good it was.

Minion 1: Well, I think that's all we really wanted to hear.

Me: I mean it, with full sincerity.

Minion 1: We do notice the things you do here. And you're always writing in that notebook of yours. It's clear you pay attention and want to get better.

Me: I do. I really do.

Minion 1: Great. Now, just one more thing, we're just doing some internal drug tests for our own records. Again, we care about the welfare of our playing group and want to help anyone who needs it. So, there's a cup on your way out and a tester waiting down the hall.

Me (arse completely dropping out of my pants): Of course. Not a problem. Completely understand.

I am completely, utterly fucked.

If they see what's in my piss after that bender it's all fucking Linden Dunn. They'll burn that name magnet of mine in sulfuric acid. Shit, they might even use the sample I provide to dissolve it. A full fucking corrosive substance inhabits my bladder.

Walking down the hall, I am a wild animal clawing for a ledge. My brain has finally joined the party, well and truly.

Gatorade as fake piss? No. Take piss out of the toilet bowl? No. Wait it out until everything's out of my system? That'll take days. Fuck. What did those Russians do again? Condom filled with piss. I could pay off the tester? Or beat him senseless and make a run for it? Get some clean piss. Come back. Provide that. How? Sleeper hold from behind, tell him that someone stormed in and did it to him. Is that really the option here? Assaulting this poor bloke who's just trying to earn a buck . . . Hang on a second. Where's the tester going? Who's up there looking after me? He's going to the bathroom. Are you kidding? He's taken his eyes off the prize. The samples are already here. Black marker on the side with the playing numbers. That's it. None of this official shit. Just do a number change. Lick your thumb. Rub off a number and write yours down then fuck up some other poor prick with your sample. They'll be sent to the nearest rehab clinic for sure. Ok, who have we got . . . fuck. Not Squidman. Not Mud. Shit. Who else have we got? Whose life am I going to tarnish with the substance pooling inside my bladder? Ah . . . there's the obvious choice. The only other cunt that was on my side of the board. We've been stranded on an island together, Big Sexy, and I'm sorry, but there's only enough food for one of us. This is survival of the fittest. You'll be fine out there in the world. You're still young. If anything, I'm doing you a favour. You haven't been fully indoctrinated yet. There is hope for you. You can find a life outside. I swear, Big Sexy, this is the best thing for you.

Ok, wet your thumb and wipe it off. Mouth's as dry as the fucking Sahara. Come on. Come on . . . Shit, they've used permanent marker not whiteboard. It's not rubbing off. Think, cunt. Think! Old mate's prostate must really have him backed up, but you don't have forever.

Fuck it. Plan B. Let's do some basic chemistry. Fucking Walter White this situation. Move substance A from Beaker 1 to Beaker 2. Then, with the utmost care, refill Beaker 1 with substance B, which I will provide. Steady hands. Steady flow. Stop shaking. Waterfalls. Fountains. Drip. Drip. Drip. Uncork the bottle. Yes, I have made the choice. I am sorry, Big Sexy. But it's every cunt for themselves sometimes. One day you'll understand.

ACKNOWLEDGEMENTS

Thanks to the following for their roles in creating this book: my fearless/formidable/un-fuckwithable publisher Jane Palfreyman and Swiss Army knife of an editor Lizzie Levot, without whom this book would be nothing.

My literary agent, Jane Novak, who was willing to strap on the boots and stomp when need be.

Kelly Jenkins, Neysha Santos, Anna O'Grady and Dan Ruffino from Simon & Schuster—it takes a village.

Terri and Claire from Pitch Project for the PR campaign. Audiobook editor Reilly Keir, voice actor James O'Connell, and Bill Dowling, Karly Joyce and Ben Crabbe at Sound Kitchen. Jenny Hedges for typesetting and catering to the whims of my folly, and Katherine Ring for proofreading every 'fuck', 'shit', 'cunt' and 'piss' uttered by the crew.

Peter Long for designing a cover that embodies the heart and soul of this book and its connection to the game that I said I would never write about again but have found myself coming back to for more . . . *audible fucking sigh.*

In unofficial roles, thanks to the following people who have been taste-testers for various ideas, either knowingly or not: Dom x 2, Lloyd, Lech, Ronan, Vic, Jenna, random patrons/staff of the establishment with the finest happy hour in Sydney—the Shakespeare Hotel—and to the whole host of 'industry' people who responded to emails and calls and the ones who did not.

I deem you all honorary pissants.

ABOUT THE AUTHOR

Brandon Jack is a Sydney-based writer who played for the Sydney Swans for five years. He is the author of the acclaimed memoir *28*.